# ABERDEEN

# ABERDEEN

## JOSEPH JOHN SZYMANSKI

iUniverse, Inc.
Bloomington

# ABERDEEN

*iUniverse books may be ordered through booksellers or by contacting:*

*iUniverse*
*1663 Liberty Drive*
*Bloomington, IN 47403*
*www.iuniverse.com*
*1-800-Authors (1-800-288-4677)*

*ISBN: 978-1-4620-2413-1 (sc)*
*ISBN: 978-1-4620-2414-8 (e)*
*ISBN: 978-1-4620-2412-4 (dj)*

*Printed in the United States of America*

*iUniverse rev. date: 7/22/2011*

**NR**

This book has not been rated. It contains harsh language and brief nudity. Read it at the risk of improving your mind.

# Dedication

This regional novel is dedicated to the following people, none of whom I've met, except for the last entry:

First and foremost is Dr. Frederick Jelinek, who devised ways for computers to interpret human speech. His achievements in applying the mathematics of probability to the problems of processing speech and language have made it easier for storytellers like me to concentrate on the creative aspects of written words. Today, experts consider Dr. Jelinek's model for speech recognition the paradigm.

Second is David Warren, the Australian scientist who invented the 'black box' flight recorder in 1953 and never made dollar one from his invention. His invention saved thousands of lives after recordings were analyzed and improvements made in aircraft design to prevent accidents from reoccurring.

Third are the military men and women who have served in the defense of our country and risked their life without recognition and appreciation. They are unsung heroes and will remain so until someone comes forth to tell the story of their military life. Hopefully, family members and friends will begin to write their story for others to read and include in future publications.

Fourth is Mel Brooks, a genius whose dialogue from his films kept creeping into my psyche. No one could get away with murdering the English language, its rules of grammar and etiquette, or transforming a murder into a comedy by poking fun at life, better than Mel Brooks.

Finally, this book is dedicated to my parents, Joseph and Lola Szymanski, and their use of his policeman's belt, three inches wide and made of heavy leather. They used it to keep me in line and stop my talking back to them. Although they loved me, they were set in their ways and wanted things done their way or else. The 'or else' usually meant tanning my rear end with that policeman's belt.

Before a beating, they always told me 'shape up or ship out' and 'this will hurt me as much as it will hurt you.' I never believed this last part because the beatings were so severe, I couldn't sit down for a day or two without great discomfort; hence, the origin of the expression: *pain in the ass*!

# Acknowledgements

My appreciation is extended to Michael McGrath of Windham, CT for his critique of the storyline and characters in previously-published *BETTERTON* and *ROCK HALL,* and contributions to *ABERDEEN,* the finale of the trilogy of three towns on the Chesapeake Bay. My gratitude is extended also to Jeanie Woods of Mercersburg, PA., for her final review and regenerative feedback. None of the three books would have been written without their support and guidance, always accompanied with praise and encouragement.

Also, I want to acknowledge an unknown element called the *Beast.* It is a figment of my imagination that has a spiritual power all its own, waltzing around in my brain and groaning constantly in my ear with the words, 'Feed me and your story will grow stronger.' It has a mind but no conscience because it wakes me during the night, with new ideas for the storyline. I hate to admit it, but the *Beast* deserves some recognition, too.

Finally, I want to say *Dziekuje,* pronounced Jenn-Koo-Yeh, which means "*Thank You*" in Polish, to others who contributed their opinions and ideas to this contemporary trilogy.

# Preface

While this novel is the fictional finale about three towns on the upper eastern shore of the beautiful and bountiful Chesapeake Bay, the episodes in this story were inspired by actual events, taken from my forty-year experience as an art dealer and appraiser. However, any resemblance of characters in this finale to actual persons living or dead is entirely coincidental.

Before the reader proceeds further, a word of advice may be warranted: Take the time to read *BETTERTON*, published in 2009, and *ROCK HALL,* published in 2010, to learn about these towns and gain some insight into the continuation of the storyline and characters in *ABERDEEN.*

"I can see no reason why some TV producer would not jump at the possibilities projected in *BETTERTON* and *ROCK HALL*," Paul Gregory, legendary agent and producer, told me recently. "The frame work is certainly there. Your material would be a catch!"

So, if the first two previously-published novels are a sufficient endorsement from Paul Gregory, the finale should certainly entertain anyone willing to take the time to read it. The words contain no hydrogenated fat. It's Gluten-free food for thought. Also, no person appearing in *ABERDEEN* is puffing on a cigarette, cigar or pipe, which means I'm doing my part to keep the ozone layer free of smoke.

It's regrettable that I won't have a chance to write a scene with two people smoking a cigarette and blowing smoke out of their ears. This image always tickles my funny bone. Perhaps I'll file it way for a future book.

A final thought: Writing this book was hazardous to my health, with two falls out of my swivel chair. Reading it may be hazardous to your mentality since it might inspire you to "Be Better than You Are."

# Chapter 1

It's the first Monday in April, around six in the morning at Ridgefield Farm, five miles outside the town of Rock Hall on the upper eastern shore of the Chesapeake Bay of Maryland. An eerie silence pervades the recently plowed Kent County fields where last fall corn and soybean grew in abundance. Warblers and other songbirds begin chirping and flitting; their actions announce the beginning of spring.

At this first hour of dawn, a gentle breeze blows northeasterly along the eastern seaboard. It's not strong enough to stir any leaves of the maple, hickory, ash and oak trees growing along the Eastern Neck Road which connects Rock Hall to the Eastern Neck Wildlife Refuge next door to Ridgefield Farm. As the sun rises from the east, its rays manage to filter through the high trees and angle down to the shoreline of the 50-acre farm. Below its twenty-foot high cliff face is a narrow beach, where even the incoming waves of the Chesapeake Bay seem to tiptoe into shore.

About 200 yards from the shoreline, a mystical figure suddenly rises out of the Bay and stands motionless against the blue sky. It resembles a white bearded Rabbi, dressed in a long iridescent-gold robe, in an erect stance with his arms outstretched.

"Moses? Can you hear me?" he asks, moving his head from side to side and speaking in a bass that booms over the waves.

After getting no response, he begins to expel some water from his mouth with a loud gurgling sound. "Moses, are you on shore or fishing for converts?" he asks in a louder voice. "I was told you'd be working your way up the eastern shore of Maryland by now."

The spirit turns in a full circle to take a good look at the Bay. "As Spirit of the Chesapeake Bay, America's largest estuary, …" he says, sneezing and pronouncing estuary with an accent on the second syllable, i.e. 'es-CHOO-air-ree.'

"God bless me. Now where was I? I have a lot of ground, *ah* water, to cover; almost 4,500 square miles to be exact. Moses? Are you listening?" he asks, wiping his nose with his sleeve and disappearing into the water with only a white contrail to mark its descent into the Bay.

Suddenly particles of sand on the beach seem to come alive and glisten from the first rays of the sun; the reflections are all the colors of a rainbow. But that's not the only thing coming to life at this early hour.

Mark Hopkins, a trim six-foot four-inch, 27-year-old former Navy SEAL Lieutenant and owner of Ridgefield Farm has his back braced against a half-ton boulder, one of thousands piled into a six-foot high barrier (called *rip-rap*) along the 800-foot shoreline of his farm. Two similar barriers are installed perpendicular to the *rip-rap* barrier at each end of Ridgefield's property line (called *breakwaters*) to prevent erosion from waves generated by hurricanes and tornadoes.

In Mark's arms is Ruth Wayne, a gorgeous and unpretentious five-foot ten-inch, 26-year old flight attendant with long brown hair. She's using his chest as a pillow and wearing a pullover with *American Airlines* woven across the front. She grips a cup of hot coffee with both hands.

"Did you hear something?" he asks and waits for a response from her. "Someone must be playing tricks with my ears this morning."

Ruth squirms closer into his chest and rests her head near his shoulder.

"I smell *Obsession*," he says, leaning over to kiss her neck then raising his head to gaze at the blue sky. "No Canada geese flying anywhere this morning. They're probably *necking* at the Wildlife Refuge."

Ruth turns her head and kisses his neck.

"Guess someone's playing tricks with my eyes, too," he continues. "I thought I saw an image of a rabbi swirling about a thousand feet off shore, right where *Eisenwein Raceway* used to be before it was washed away into the Bay."

"My grandfather's eyes always lit up when he talked about attending sulky harness races out there when he was a boy," she says, pointing in the direction of the bay. "He claimed that over the past 100 years, landowners have surrendered more than 2,500 feet of earth to the bay. Even the Eisenwein home collapsed into the Bay many years ago."

"Well, at last, she speaks! You haven't said a word to me all morning."

"Until a minute ago, neither have you," she says with a tease. "You were tossing and turning all night long."

"Neither of us could get comfortable. We both seemed a little restless and edgy."

"More than a little, I'd say."

"For breakfast, you should have put some paprika on your sausage link left over from last night," says Mark.

"Why?"

"It's spicy and matches your disposition."

"Sorry. That wasn't my intention," she quickly answers. "Guess I was looking forward to seeing the Bay and you holding me close in your arms."

"It's good to be alive and enjoy the dawn of a new day on the Chesapeake. Is something on your mind?" he asks, squeezing her waist.

"That's just what I was about to ask you."

"Well, I might as well tell you that *I'm* going to have a baby," he whispers.

"Have you been talking to Dr. Rolf?" asks Ruth, turning her head around to face him directly.

"No. I've been talking to Judge Wohlfort."

"Judge Wohlfort?" she asks, with a puzzled look on her face. "Who's Judge Wohlfort?"

"Doctor Rolf?" asks Mark, tilting his head and widening his eyes. "Who's Dr. Rolf?"

"I think we better start over," she exclaims. "You, first."

"No, ladies first."

"I asked Dr. Rolf not to mention it to anyone until I could talk to you."

"Talk to me about what?" asks Mark.

"I'm going to have a baby," says Ruth, pulling him tighter. "And I think it's safe to assume that you're the father."

"Yippee-kai-yea!"

"What was that?"

"An old war-hoop used by the Ozinie Indians who inhabited this area hundreds of years ago and handed down to warriors like me."

"Is that all you're going say?" asks Ruth.

"I'm at a loss for words," says Mark, digesting the news. "Give me a minute to catch my breath and get down on one knee to pop the question."

"I'm listening," Ruth quickly responds.

"Will you marry me?"

"You *betcha*," says Ruth, giving him a passionate kiss.

Seconds later, he looks down at the sand to his right and notices an old soup spoon reflecting sunlight into his eyes. He picks it up, cleans off some particles to give it a clean surface and holds it up, as if it's a mirror, to see first, the reflection of Ruth and secondly, his own face. The images remind him of 3-inch oval miniatures painted by artists on ivory or porcelain. Pretending the spoon is a microphone, he brings it in front of his mouth.

"Ladies and gentlemen," he bellows out, "let me have your attention, please. We interrupt this program to bring you a news flash from Associated Press. Ruth Wayne of Rock Hall and American Airlines has agreed to become the wife of Mark Hopkins of Baltimore and Rock Hall. When we get more news on the particulars, you'll be the first to know. Until then, stay tuned to see how this story unfolds. This is *Strontium-Ninety*, your kinetic newscaster, reporting from the shoreline of Ridgefield Farm, on the upper eastern shore of the Chesapeake Bay. How about that!"

"You sound like Chuck Thompson giving a news brief on the radio," Ruth says, gushing a little and giving him another kiss.

"I can't think of anything better than spending the rest of my life with you."

"We'll have a stork paying us a visit around Christmas."

"That's just eight months away," says Mark, counting the numbers with the fingers on both hands.

"According to Dr. Rolf, we're going to have a girl," says Ruth, turning her eyes upward and thanking God. "Now, if you were related to the founders of Johns Hopkins Hospital, which you're not, we might get a discount on the delivery."

"Telepathy; that's what it is. I've been thinking all night what it would be like to spend the rest of my life with you."

"Deep down, I wanted you ever since we met on the deck of Java Rock Cafe when you said that you'd like to see me in a swim suit," says Ruth lovingly. "I felt something come into my heart that has always stayed with me."

"For me, it was seeing you on that American Airlines flight back from LAX to BWI. You crept into my heart that night."

"Lately, I've been tossing around the notion of settling down and raising a family," she says, "but little did I know it would be five miles away from the marina where I was born and raised. Now, what's all this news from a judge?"

"My application to adopt Jaime has been approved," says Mark. "But there's something else you should know about Jaime and me. According to DNA tests, our blood matches. I got the news yesterday and wanted to figure out how that was possible before telling you. I knew there was something about the way he grabbed and held onto my finger the first time I saw him in his cradle at Swan Haven Marina over a year ago. But how his mother, Vera, and I made love is a mystery to me."

"That means you slept with my sister-in-law," says Ruth with alarm in her voice. "You never mentioned it before. Were you ashamed to mention it? Furthermore, wasn't it Vera's promiscuity that turned my brother into the murderer who sent her to an early grave and got himself locked up for 22 years? How could you have sex with a married woman?"

"You've asked the same questions that I've asked myself over the last 24 hours. Of course I'm ashamed; Of course I remember that Bud tried to implicate me as a murder suspect. I've forgotten nothing, but it's hard to figure out much less explain."

"Give it a try," she says as an odd feeling stirs inside her stomach.

"It's difficult to put into words."

"You can do it if you put your mind to it," she says.

"It's hard to remember everything."

"Sometimes it's good when it's hard; the harder the better."

"Are you expecting a confession?" he asks, with beads of perspiration forming on his forehead.

"I'll settle first for an explanation, although a confession can be therapeutic. I'm more than curious to see how you intend to wrangle your way out of sleeping with Vera."

"It's all confusing, believe me, because I didn't sleep with that woman," says Mark, gathering the courage to continue. "It must have been an encounter two years ago when we completed a special training course at the Naval Academy in Annapolis. The last night we celebrated and consumed way too much alcohol. Our instructor asked us to test a new diving helmet, with a lens that worked on the same principles as those on night vision goggles. In the water we could see perfectly through the lens. Out of the water the lens turned opaque unless you flipped a switch on the side of the helmet, which also rejected all sounds. The helmet was intended to be used solely for underwater demolition purposes."

Ruth tries to rise and take a step toward the incoming tide as tears form in her eyes.

"Without any time to think it over," he continues, pulling her tightly into his grasp, "we were taken into a room somewhere in the building and ordered to have a *quickie in the sack*. Our instructor made it clear that everything would be anonymous; the female would not be identified. The whole episode was over in less than five minutes."

"So you had sex without any protection?"

"I admit I had too much to drink. It was so unexpected and reckless on my part, and it's no excuse to say that we were following orders without realizing the implications. It was a dumb idea, especially for me as a lieutenant who should have known better."

"It sounds as though you had a SEAL course that turned into intercourse."

"I can assure you that the encounter meant nothing to me," says Mark, wiping some perspiration from his forehead. I couldn't see or hear anything. For all I know it could have been with my sister if I had a sister. It was over and forgotten before I even realized what had happened. It meant nothing to me."

"Maybe risk-taking runs in your family."

"Never thought about it before, but now that you've mentioned it, we're all like that on my father's side of the family; my grandfather and father fighting accidental fires at the mill during the week and jumping over hurdles at fox hunts on the weekends. With me as a SEAL, one wrong move when a mine is being detonated and someone would be looking for my body to send home in a coffin. In the military, we don't have time to think about the risk. We're given an order and we carry it out."

"No need to go on any further. Only God is perfect. Your indiscrete act is forgiven and swept into the Bay. I love you and always will," she tells him slowly and surely, ending with a heavy kiss on his lips.

"You're too good to be true," says Mark.

"Over the past year everyone said the same thing about you. Now, you've come clean. So, you're not *perfect*. I'll take you the way you are and make a fresh start from this time forward."

Mark turns her body in order to give her a long kiss.

"Yippee-kai-yea!" says Ruth, catching her breath and turning her head to catch a glimpse of the sun over the Bay. "It is the dawn of a new day and a new life together."

"Before heading back to the house for breakfast and a staff briefing," he says, "I'd like to ask another question. What would you say about an elopement to Carmel and wedding in the old mission there? Actually, it wouldn't be an elopement per se because key personnel must be informed of certain responsibilities turned over to them."

"Can you manage to take a week off for a flight to San Francisco and drive to the coast of Monterey?" Ruth asks.

"Can I manage? Are you kidding me?" he bellows out. "I'm the boss and I'll follow Mel Brooks' axiom: 'Matters of love take precedence over… other matters and disorders of the heart!' "

"Now you're being silly."

"Perhaps, but I am incredibly happy. Moments ago my stomach was filled with butterflies and my mind was looking for answers and reasons why things happened the way they did with Vera and how to explain them to you. Now I'm floating on a cushion of air and feeling a little *flighty*."

"Me too," says Ruth. "The thought of getting married in Carmel never entered my mind."

"A wedding in six days has my heart beating like the pistons in a *Maserati* engine," says Mark.

"Did you ever own a *Maserati*? If not, how do you know about its pistons?"

"It's just an expression, darling," answers Mark. "Anyway I've been thinking of cutting back my hours at the mill and spending more time at Ridgefield."

"And I've been thinking about resigning from American for over a year, ever since I met you on that flight from LAX to BWI," Ruth says with a sparkle in her eyes.

"We can get all the blood work done and apply for a marriage license in the next few days before flying to the west coast," he says assuredly. "I'll telephone the mission after breakfast and try to arrange our wedding for Saturday afternoon."

"Perhaps you should break the news to everyone *after* breakfast," Ruth advises, "otherwise you'll be spending a lot of time with explanations and never complete your briefing this morning."

"I'm getting a kink in my neck from leaning against this boulder," says Mark. "York advised me install this barrier to prevent further erosion of our farm. But they weren't meant to be used as a backrest."

As Ruth rises and turns to climb a rope-and-wooden ladder constructed over the rip-rap, Mark looks up and sees a gaggle of Canada geese, flying in a V-formation overhead; they begin to honk as they break formation and swoop down in a westerly direction, to a height of about 100 feet. "They're probably a gaggle whose nesting grounds are the 2,300-acre Wildlife Refuge next door," says Mark.

Seconds later, a solitary goose leaves the formation, having lost control of its right wing. It honks at the top of its lungs in a high squeaky pitch as it glides downward with the aid of a gentle tail wind and lands safely on its two webbed feet. The crippled bird could not have selected a better runway since it's right in the middle of a 20-foot wide sandy beach. After landing, the goose looks around to survey the surroundings, takes a few steps until it spots Mark and Ruth only 20 feet away, then stops abruptly in its tracks. Its eyes reflect the brilliance of the sun and look as if they are cut crystal.

Suddenly, all Hell seems to break loose overhead when the

entire gaggle makes a U-turn and dives down to 30 feet, beating their wings and sounding like twenty washerwomen shaking out their wet laundry before hanging it on a clothes line to dry. Every goose in the gaggle begins to honk and cluck in two overlapping musical notes, releasing a low base discord. Obviously they're sending a message to the wounded goose that they have noted its location and telling it, "You're on your own, kid."

The wounded goose pulls back its long neck, thrusts out its chest and opens its beak, but no sounds are heard. It waddles forward until it's within Mark's out-stretched arm. He can see its black head and long neck, with white patches on its face and brownish gray feathers encircling its body.

"Hold it, Ruth. This bird is wounded. Wait a minute and I'll give you a hand up and over the *rip-rap*."

"Hey buddy, can you lend me a hand, too?" asks the wounded goose, gazing up at him.

Mark picks up the bird, folds the broken wing into its body and cradles it in one arm, like a halfback carrying a football. The goose looks up at him, rubs its face against his chest and allows him to do whatever he intends to do with it. He glances down at the bird and is especially careful not to cause further injury as he walks away from the beach. "Maybe a quick fix with wooden matches and glue will do the trick," says Mark. "It seemed to work when I was building model planes as a kid in Baltimore."

As he approaches the wraparound porch of his home, situated about 200 feet from the shoreline, a golden lab comes running through a doggie door and barking at the top of her lungs.

"I hear you, Jen. I'm not deaf," he tells her.

Jen looks up, tilts her head with a puzzled look on her face and says, "If it looks like a goose, moves like a goose and honks like a goose, it must be a goose in your arm."

"It's a Canada goose, about ten pounds, with a broken wing," he tells her. "Where've you been? Overslept this morning and waiting for some of Gabby's homemade buns for breakfast?"

Jen runs ahead of Mark, leading the way to the tool shed behind the main house.

"Looks as if we'll have a guest from the Refuge staying here," he says to Ruth, "until it's healthy enough to fly."

Several minutes later, Mark washes his hands in the kitchen sink when Abigail Woods nudges his arm. "Now, before you scold me for washing my hands here," he says, smiling broadly, "you should know that Ruth is using the bathroom to freshen up before breakfast. I thought I'd get away with washing them in the kitchen *zink*, as they call it in *Balmer*!"

"You should know that nothing escapes my oversight here at Ridgefield," says Abigail, looking trim and much younger than her 55 years. " Isn't that why you appointed me co-CEO?"

"That's true, along with several other assets."

"Like what?"

"Your recognition of the importance of the jeweled dagger I brought back from Iraq, your involvement in tracking down the killer who used it to murder his wife, and your delicate negotiation when it was sold for an incredible price. Need I go on?"

"It's always reassuring to know that one is appreciated."

"By the way, I like your flannel crewneck sweatshirt," he says, smiling broadly.

"You should. You gave it to me a few days after hiring me two years ago. Don't you remember?"

"My mind is saturated at this moment. I've been thinking of what to say and how to say it when we have our breakfast briefing."

"You told me, 'Let it be said that I gave you the shirt off my back!' That was a nice gesture although it *kinda* drapes on my frame."

"It looks good on you," he says. "Casual attire; that's what retirees and pensioners are wearing nowadays."

"I enjoy the informality here at Ridgefield. I knew right away that it would be fun to work *for* and *with* you on your projects for Ridgefield LLC. No board of directors and trustees, each with their own special agenda, to contend with."

"Glad you came aboard," says Mark, wiping his hands with paper towels. "Has it really been two years?"

"Seems like yesterday, doesn't it? Plus I always wear the blue one on Mondays. It matches my slacks and leather shoes. The color navy suits me to a T."

"I'm going to ask you to take on more responsibilities while Ruth and I are away for the next week or so," he says, taking her arm and escorting her over to the breakfast table near the front bay window. "You'll hear some of the reasons after breakfast."

After Mark opens the venetian blinds to let complete daylight flow into the open dining area of the main house, he takes his seat at the head of the table as Abigail begins to give the morning blessing.

"Dear Lord, we, who are about to benefit from your generous blessings, ask that you continue to watch over our family here at Ridgefield," she says, moving her glasses from her nose to the top of her head, "and continue to light our way towards a loving and peaceful world. Amen."

"First time I ever saw a lady with a near-sighted head!" Womble tells her, unfolding a napkin and placing it on his chest. "Hope no one mind's my invoking 'executive privilege' here. After all, I still hold the title of 'executive at-large,' and I'm not referring to my waistline."

Also sitting at the table and laughing at Womble's early-morning witticism are Sandy Welles, Liz Carter, Kim Bozzetti, Greta Howe and York McGuffin, all members of the staff at Ridgefield.

Ruth smells the hot plate of pancakes and waffles, takes one of each and passes the plate around the table. Because Gabby's pancakes are as light and wafer-thin as crepes, everyone covers them with liberal dollops of fresh strawberries and whipped cream and smacks their lips in anticipation of an extraordinary treat. There's little thought about calories, since they will be standing on their feet most of the day and burning any fat from this deluxe continental breakfast.

"*Finger-lickin'* good," Ruth admits after swallowing her second crepe in less than a minute.

"Gabby's crepes are *too good to be true*," York says. "I never had anything so light and tasty, except for *Tastykakes*, during my architectural studies at Penn."

"Spoken like a true Philadelphian," Mark tells him. "They were always within an arm's reach when I was growing up at Cylburn."

"They're like an electrolyte that helps to charge your batteries for the work ahead," says Liz, thinking about her undergraduate studies in physics at Hopkins and her current research project involving an electronic buoy at Ridgefield.

"They are addictive," says Kim, "melting in your mouth with a slight taste of burnt butter and almonds. Never tasted anything like that in Rome."

Greta is too busy smearing her third crepe with another spoonful of strawberry jam to give her two-cents; finally she stretches her head upward like a turtle looking for some food and says, "Gabby's crepes are simply *guurrreat.*"

"If everyone feels so highly of her crepes," Womble says, "perhaps we should file a patent on her recipe and contact one of the major producers, say, Kraft Foods, to see if they would be interested in making a deal for the rights to produce it on a large scale."

"We'll take that under advisement," Mark tells him, pulling out several 3 by 5 cards from his shirt pocket and glancing quickly at them until he has everyone's attention "I think we better start today's briefing. Yesterday, I was exchanging emails with one of my former SEALS, Monty Montgomery. He was writing about our combat days in Iraq and exposure to mustard gas and pepper spray and said that we were both *seasoned* veterans!"

After everyone has another laugh, Mark downs a glass of orange juice and pauses a few seconds to gather his thoughts.

"Now," he continues, "I know each of you is anxious to give an update on your department's plans for the coming week, which is our customary procedure. But we'll dispense with an update on the R & R Refuge for Red Cross Vets and plans for a small budget film like *Marty*. This morning is special. I'd like to take a minute or two to explain a new management strategy that will be implemented immediately. It's designed to face the challenge looming ahead for Ridgefield LLC and the stormy economic climate of the nation. Henceforth, Ridgefield will be decentralized, and each department head is hereby appointed Department President, responsible for its own autonomy, budget and agenda. He or she and their staff will be allowed the freedom to execute their leadership skills and talents. The switch to a decentralized team of four presidents may seem complicated, but I expect everyone to rise and face every challenge."

Ruth opens her mouth, thinking Mark has ended his remarks, but is cut off as he quickly surveys the expressions on everyone's faces and continues speaking.

"I call it 'Participative Management,' where each president has the freedom to exchange ideas between other departments," he continues, " and still retain the flexibility needed to lead their personnel in creative directions. Don't expect any orders from me. I'll be a coach, walking along the sidelines. If you need my help, ask for it. You all know what's required for success. As one of my SEALS said to me a few years ago in Iraq, 'If I don't know what to do, I better ask questions, otherwise you'll give me a swift kick in the ass.' "

Again, Ruth opens her mouth and raises her hand, requesting a chance to speak, but Mark announces that he'll arrange to meet in a week or two with authorities at the Aberdeen Proving Ground to discuss the canister of mustard gas that Jen found on the beach of Ridgefield as well as cleanup efforts of the Chesapeake Bay.

Ruth shakes her head in frustration and realizes she'll have to be more forceful if she wants to get a word in edgewise. Meanwhile, Mark looks down to Jen who's sitting near him with her head nodding up and down. He knows it's his cue to give her the last morsel of food on his plate.

"It's tough to get the military brass at Aberdeen to meet with us," Mark continues, "since the reality of finding a canister of mustard gas is not something they want to face right now."

"Isn't there something else you'd like to tell everyone?" Ruth asks, standing up abruptly and facing Mark, who may appear to be on the verge of closing the briefing but is teasing Ruth a little.

"Oh, yes. Thank you, darling," Mark says, smiling and nodding his head in agreement. "I was simply getting some business out of the way. My mind and heart are still working in unison. For the next week -- and perhaps a bit longer -- Abigail will be the acting CEO in charge of Ridgefield, so coordinate everything through her. Ruth and I will be busy in Carmel, California."

"What's going on in Carmel?" Abigail asks with a puzzled expression on her face.

"An exchange of marriage vows," he says proudly. "In four days, on Friday morning, we'll be boarding a flight to San Francisco for our marriage at the historic Carmel mission."

York rises from his seat and is the first to offer his congratulations, with everyone following closely behind him. The news has certainly caught everyone by surprise.

"You wanted to talk to me privately?" York asks Mark and Ruth as others leave the breakfast table.

"While we're away, would you draw up plans for a two-bedroom home?" Ruth asks with a blush.

"Only two bedrooms?" he asks her with a smile. "I always start with three, my lucky number."

"And I would like to install some exercise and weight-training equipment somewhere in the research lab," says Mark. "It's about time we had a Fitness Center with two treadmills and ellipticals as a starter."

"Would you mind submitting your architectural plans for the house to the Kent County Planning Commission as soon as possible?" Ruth asks. "Hopefully, we can get them approved so that Jack Johnson can begin construction as soon as possible. We'd like to move in before the snow blankets our farm."

The next day, Mark walks Ruth down the hallway of Cylburn, his family's mansion situated in a gated park in the center of Baltimore, as his mother, Sara, rushes through the library doorway to embrace her future daughter-in-law. "You both look so happy and beautiful," admits Sara, giving them a kiss on their cheek. "You caught me off guard when you said you were getting married in Carmel. My ticker can only take so much excitement in one day."

"While Ruth brings you up to date, mom," Mark tells her, "I have some business to take care of with Miss Potts at the mill."

A minute later, Mark is on the phone with Miss Potts, his executive secretary at Bethlehem Steel, and asks her to arrange for a board meeting one day earlier than scheduled.

Meanwhile, Sara and Ruth are huddled in the library.

"I know you're anxious to hear more details of our wedding plans," Ruth says, "but you'll have to be patient since everything is happening so fast."

"In that case, let me tell you that I couldn't ask for a more perfect daughter," Sara says. "From the moment Mark brought you to Cylburn over a year ago, I pictured you walking down the aisle with my son. Now, isn't there something I can do for you while you're in Carmel? Perhaps a little pin money to tie you over?"

"Money is the least of our worries," Ruth answers. "Everything has been a little hectic, but I expect we'll manage. Excitement is building so fast my heart is almost jumping out of my body."

"That's the way I felt when I married my husband thirty years ago," Sara tells her as Mark rejoins them. "Seeing the joy on your faces reminds me of the days before I married him. Are you certain there's nothing I can do for you?"

"No, thank you," Ruth gushes and gives Sara a kiss on her

cheek. "We have to get our blood work done, file the marriage application and, oh yes, buy the wedding bands."

"Please can call me *mom*," Sara whispers into her ear as she gives her intended daughter a warm embrace. "Perhaps I can help you out with that last part."

"Mom, Lola's on the phone and wants to talk to you," Mark says, helping to lift his mother off a settee.

"If you don't mind my asking, who's Lola?" asks Ruth.

"Lola Albright's a good friend and junior partner in Mike Bloomburg's law firm on Mount Vernon Place," says Mark. "Mike's our family lawyer and Lola's been a doll in looking after mom since my father passed away. Stops by before and after work every day, sometimes even on weekends."

"How old is she?"

"In her middle 20's, I think."

"Should I be jealous or thankful?" she asks.

"Both, darling, if it suits you," he says, giving her a passionate kiss.

The following day, Mark is standing inside his office at Bethlehem Steel, anxious to address the seven-member Board of Directors seated somewhat uncomfortably around an oval conference table.

Rumors have been circulating about changes at the mill, with some speculation of a possible change in management. Instead of sitting upright in their chairs, they seem slightly agitated, leaning a half-foot off center and stretching to hear what their president has to say on such short notice.

"No more *hear-say*," John Szymanski, finance director, says to Dr. Joost de Wal, who's sitting next to him. "Now, we're about to hear it right from the horse's mouth. When I was director of finance for Rouse and Company who developed Harborplace, James Rouse insisted on accuracy and facts, not innuendo and rumors."

"This will be the shortest briefing you've ever attended here," Mark tells them with a wide smile. "Dr. Joost de Wal will be not only head of manufacturing but assistant to the President. He's earned the title after landing us that contract for structural steel to rebuild Iraq and Afghanistan. He'll have power of attorney to handle all matters until I return from California with my wife, Ruth."

By the astonished look on Dr. de Wal's face, it's the first time he's heard this news. However, after being congratulated by Mark and the other members of the board, Dr. de Wal is perfectly at ease and confident in his ability to take the handoff of power from Mark, even if it's only temporary.

"The mill will still be here when you return, in better order than when you left it," he vows. "I'll get the job done on schedule if not sooner. After all, you'll be away only a week."

After everyone leaves his office, Mark is on the phone with Lois Carnegie.

"Do you have another treasure for me to buy?" she asks.

"Not exactly," he answers, "but I'd like to ask you to consider joining our Board of Directors and possibly arranging your schedule to run things from an administrative standpoint at the mill for three days a week. You would be working side by side with Dr. de Wal, our chief engineer. If you haven't heard it through the grapevine, Ruth and I are flying to California and will be married in Carmel on Saturday afternoon."

"Well, you *are* full of news. Let me be among the first to congratulate you and wish you and Ruth a life full of love and happiness. I'll take your offer about the mill under advisement, as it concerns Clowie too. You'll have my answer after you return from California."

As Mark turns to leave his office, he passes a large photo of his father alongside a sign hanging on a wall that his father copied from John Wooden's office at UCLA. It reads: **'IT'S WHAT YOU DO AFTER YOU KNOW IT ALL THAT COUNTS.'**

"Dad," he confides, gazing back at his father's photo again, "how I wish you could be here to see how everyone is making Bethlehem Steel a good place to work and carrying on the Hopkins tradition of 'quality guaranteed.' You always told me, 'Do it the best you can the first time. There may not be a second time.' I'll talk to you again in Carmel."

On Friday morning Mark and Ruth board an American Airlines flight from Baltimore Washington International Airport (BWI) to San Francisco International (SFI). They settle into first-class seats, courtesy of the airlines where she worked for six years.

"It's nice to be pampered and spoiled a little," says Ruth, sipping orange juice and leaning back in her wide seat, inside one of the newest 747's to join the fleet. "If I wasn't pregnant, my choice would be champagne."

"I'd like to hear all about your time with American, all the places and people you've met during your six years with them. You might consider starting a scrapbook and writing a diary of your experiences for the benefit of our children."

"Have you given any thought to loosening your reins at Ridgefield?" she says. "After all, you're going to a husband and father very soon."

"I intend to change my grip on the reins and pass more responsibility to others, so I can give you and our children whatever you need."

He hands a small box, gift-wrapped with shiny white ribbon, to Ruth.

"What's this?" she asks.

"You'll see," he answers. "It took some doing to get it through security at the airport without their opening it and ruining the ribbon." When she opens the box, a pair of gold wedding bands are inside, each engraved with their name. "My mother overheard us talking about the wedding bands we selected at the jeweler downtown and arranged for the engraving."

"Don't you love the texture?" she asks.

"Reminds me of the waves of the Chesapeake Bay," he says, leaning over to give her a kiss.

Thirty minutes after touchdown at San Francisco International Airport, Ruth and Mark stand outside the foyer of a rental agency, waiting for an attendant to pick up the keys to their car.

"Sorry to keep you waiting," the 21-yar old attendant tells them, wiping away some perspiration from his forehead after a 30-yard zigzag run through the maze of cars.

"No problem," Mark tells him, handing him the keys and noticing the name 'Willy Mayo' on a badge attached to his lapel. "The receptionist said 'Spot 21.' We requested a white BMW convertible."

"We have ten available, sir," Willy tells him and disappears in a flash, leaving Mark and Ruth alone to admire the bright sunshine of the San Francisco Bay area.

About five minutes later, Willy suddenly appears behind them.

"You'd make a good SEAL," Mark tells him. "I never suspected you were sneaking up behind me."

"No sneaking, sir. I can't seem to find your car and don't believe it's in spot 21," he tells him, looking ruffled from the search. "I better go inside and speak to the receptionist who took your order."

Mark puts his arm around Willy, leads him away from the foyer and whispers in his ear, "Hold the Mayo, Willy. Here's what I want you to do."     Twenty seconds later, the attendant is behind the wheel of the BMW, beaming from ear to ear, as he brings the convertible to a screeching halt and hands the keys to Mark. He shakes Willy's hands and presses a twenty-dollar tip into the upper pocket of his jacket.

"I learned something today," Willy tells him, loading their luggage into the trunk of the BMW. "If you need anything else, don't hesitate to call me."

"I can always use people who want to better themselves," Mark tells him, driving slowly out of the car-rental depot and turning onto an access road that leads out of the airport complex.

"What was that all about?" Ruth asks, turning her body sideways to get a better look at him.

"If you're referring to how Willy found our car, I told him to go into the middle of the lot and press the panic button on the electronic key pad. Then, all he has to do is look for a car with blinking lights or listen for a loud alarm going off."

"Funny. I never heard an alarm go off, did you?"

"It's probably because of the noise of so many planes arriving and departing overhead."

"I'll have to keep that in mind whenever I forget where my car was parked," she says, taking her left hand and tapping his thigh gently. "I think I'm going to enjoy being your wife. You're full of surprises."

They drive westward along Route 101, through the picturesque hills of Monterey County, in the direction of the coast of Carmel. "That's something we don't have around Ridgefield," admits Ruth.

"What don't we have around Ridgefield?"

"Mountains and valleys and gentle curves that seem to take you inside the heart of Monterey," she says joyfully. "It's so *gurreen* with blue skies above."

"Everything here is so peaceful, too," utters Mark, tightening his grip on the steering wheel of his car to take the unexpected curves of the highway.

"I'd like to smother you with kisses right now," says Ruth, "but there's a time and place for such things."

# Chapter 2

By 3 in the afternoon they are standing on the deck of the 30-foot motor sailboat that Mark has rented for the next seven days. "We'll raise the sail," he tells her, "*tack* around Monterey Bay and let the wind take us wherever it wants to take us."

"Ay Ay, captain," Ruth gushes. "You hug the steering wheel and I'll hug you."

For the next five hours, they cruise leisurely along the coast of Monterey, stopping occasionally for walks along the beach, snorkeling and diving off the deck of their boat. Although they bask in the sun, they are too much in love for even a quick nap.

Eventually, they are moored offshore in Big Sur. People in love usually experience this part of the Monterey Coast differently. A person's senses are keener and the mind memorizes everything and stores it in their subconscious memory bank. The waters seem greener and bluer in spots. The particles of sand on its beach sparkle more in the sunlight with all colors of a rainbow. Even the sights and sounds of seagulls flying everywhere seem different. And there's a 1,000-foot high wall of granite, colored gray and sanguine that first attracted explorers hundreds of years ago.

"When Mother Earth was created," says Mark, "God made

Big Sur heavenly. If you have no objection, we'll drop anchor and spend the night here."

Mark motors his boat gently into shore and tosses the anchor onto the beach. "I'll use a mask and snorkel to skin-dive near the shore," says Ruth with alacrity, "as I did at our marina in Rock Hall when my father asked me to find a tool he accidentally dropped overboard. Now I've gone overboard for a SEAL."

"A girlfriend of one of my seals told me that she's gone *dippy* over him," he says. "Now I know what she meant."

Mark is right at home in his polyurethane skin-divers suit, scuba mask with regulator and air tank. Swimming at a depth of 25 to 35 feet in daytime and perfect visibility is playtime. Within a half hour he manages to pry-off some scallops adhered to a rock, snatch a nice sized lobster crawling in a crevice, and snare some dozing sand dab.

An hour later, Ruth is serving a delicious seafood platter of shellfish. Afterwards the deck is cleared of all traces of their dinner and Mark takes Ruth into his arms and kisses her tenderly. As they gaze at the approaching sunset and glance toward the shoreline, he takes a micro-tape recorder, about the size of a pack of cigarettes, out of a pocket of his windbreaker.

"Perfect," he says.

"What's perfect?"

"Everything is perfect; You, me, this area. Do you know where we are right now?"

"Off the coast of Big Sur, I think."

"It's almost the exact spot where they filmed *The Sandpiper,* with Liz Taylor and Richard Burton."

"Are you referring to that sandy beach with a giant granite rock that looks like an asteroid?"

"I'd like you to close your eyes and picture you and me playing the parts of Liz and Richard," he tells her, switching on the recorder. "It's the theme from their film, *The Sandpiper.*"

After the first chorus the melody is repeated without any

spoken words. This is Mark's cue and he begins to whisper the lyrics into her ear:

*"The shadow of your smile when you are gone, will color all my dreams and light the dawn, look into my eyes, my love, and see, all the lovely things you are to me, our wistful little star was far too high, a teardrop kissed your lips and so did I, now, when I remember spring, all the joy that love can bring, I will be remembering The Shadow of Your Smile."*

"I never realized until now the power of music," she says. "And that had to be Reggie on the guitar. How in the world did you get him to record it for you?"

"I asked him on Tuesday, after proposing to you. The next day he sent me the tape and told me, 'You're a perfect fit. Be good to each other.' "

"Would you mind playing it again?" Ruth asks quietly.

In the silence of Big Sur, without even a seagull flapping its wings or the hoot of an owl nearby, the music from the miniature speaker inside the recorder seems so real, almost as if Reggie is on board, too. After the song ends, Mark pulls Ruth closer and gives her another long passionate kiss.

"This night, this song, with you in my arms, is a picture of perfection. I don't believe I could love you more than I do at this moment," he whispers and sings, *"Look into my eyes, my love and see all the lovely things you are to me."*

"They are the most beautiful words ever set to music," says Ruth.

"What would you say to another quick spin around the Bay? I'm *wound-up* tighter than a mantle clock and not ready to *turn-in*."

"Whatever suits you, suits me," she answers quickly.

Mark takes his recorder out of his pocket again, presses the play button and begins to sing *Dream a Little Dream of Me*, with music by the team of Fabian Andre and Wilbur Schwandt.

However, he changes the original lyrics written by Gus Kahn to fit the occasion of holding Ruth one last time as a bachelor under the stars of Monterey Bay. His voice is soft and comforting and has a decided impact on Ruth, who surrenders to his embrace.

*"Say good night and kiss me, take hold and show me how you will miss me, while we're alone and falling in love, once more 'round the Bay with you."*

After he finishes the first verse, he carries Ruth to the stern of the boat and sings the second chorus.

*"Stars shining all above us, cool breezes whisper 'How much I love you,' waves singing as they move us along, once more 'round the Bay with you. Night's fading, but I can go on, dear, still craving your kiss, I'm longing to hold you forever, never to end, sweet dreams are all around you, light beams are coming somewhere within you, all wishes made will come true tonight, once more 'round the Bay with you."*

The following day, a sunny Saturday, they stand in the foyer of the old mission of Carmel. Mark adjusts the collar of his white Navy Reserve First Lieutenant's uniform, as Ruth removes a buttercup-colored yellow cloak that has concealed her wedding dress up until now.

He takes her arm and escorts her down the aisle of this historic mission, built in 1771 by Father Junipero Serra, as its nine bells toll for twenty seconds to indicate one o'clock. In less than a minute they are standing in front of the altar railing as sunlight filters gradually through the stained-glass windows and shines on them.

Mark studies the Valentino-original, a white on off-white brocade dress, with miniature 'forget-me-not' flowers that match her wedding bouquet held gently in her hands. He finds it difficult to concentrate on the young Franciscan monk who stands before them and is constantly turning to gaze at Ruth.

"Please call me *Padre Pablo* or simply *Padre*. Let us begin the mass by making the sign of the cross and declaring with me, 'In the name of the Father, the Son and the Holy Spirit. Amen.' "

Padre opens his prayer book and begins to read the blessing: "The grace of our Lord Jesus Christ and the love of God and the fellowship of the Holy Spirit be with you all."

"And also with you," Mark and Ruth respond and then recite the *Gloria*: "*Glory to God in the highest and peace to his people on earth. Lord God and Father, we worship you, we give you thanks, we praise you for your glory...Lord Jesus Christ... you take away the sin of the world...have mercy on us...you are seated at the right hand of the Father...receive our prayer. For you alone are the Holy One... Jesus Christ...in the glory of God the Father, Amen.*"

Ruth and Mark take their seat as Padre begins to recite the First Reading, the Liturgy of the Word: "*Moses said to the people, 'ask now of the days of old, ever since God created man upon the earth: Did anything so great ever happen before?...This is why you must now know, and fix in your heart, that the Lord is God in the heavens above and on earth below...You must keep his statues and commandments that I enjoin on you today, that you and your children after you may prosper, and that you may have long life on the land which the Lord, your God, is giving you forever.' This is the* word of the Lord."

"Thanks be to God," Ruth and Mark answer in unison.

They rise from their seats as Padre reads a Gospel from Matthew: "*When Jesus saw the crowds, he went up the mountain... and his disciples came to him. He began to teach them, saying: 'Blessed are the poor in spirit, for theirs is the Kingdom of heaven...Blessed are the meek, for they will inherit the land...Blessed are the merciful, for they will be shown mercy...Blessed are the peacemakers, for they will be called children of God...Rejoice and be glad, for your reward will be great in heaven.'* This is the gospel of the Lord."

"Praise to you, Lord Jesus Christ," they answer in unison.

Now it's the Declaration of Consent, the exchange of wedding vows, the moment when their minds take over from their hearts.

"Mark Hopkins and Ruth Wayne," asks Padre, "have you come here freely and without reservation to give yourself to each other in marriage? Will you honor each other as man and wife for the rest of your lives? Will you accept children lovingly from God, and bring them up according to the law of Christ and his Church?"

"Yes," the bride and groom respond at the end of each question.

"Since it is your intention to enter into marriage," Padre tells them, "join your right hands, and declare your consent before God and his Church."

"I, Mark Hopkins," he vows, "take you, Ruth Wayne, to be my wife. I promise to be true to you in good times and in bad, in sickness and in health. I will love you and honor you all the days of my life."

"I, Ruth Wayne," she avows, "take you, Mark Hopkins, to be my husband. I promise to be true to you in good times and in bad, in sickness and in health. I will love you and honor you all the days of my life."

"What God has joined," says Padre, "men must not divide."

Mark and Ruth realize that this is the instant at which, sacramentally, they have become husband and wife. Padre blesses their wedding rings and nods as permission to place them on their ring finger.

"You may now exchange a kiss," Padre announces and waves his arms upward, in a semicircle, to offer a silent prayer and solemn blessing over the married couple.

When Mark lifts her veil to give her a kiss at the foot of the altar, he finds tears running down her cheeks.

"I've never been happier in my life," she says. "I pledge you my fidelity and all my love."

"I love you with all my heart," he says, moving some strands of her long brown hair farther back to expose a pearl earring, a wedding gift from his mother. "May God bless you and watch over you. I am yours and always will be."

They turn to Padre who closes his book and tells them, "The mass is ended. Go in Peace to love and serve the Lord."

"Thanks be to God," they answer in unison.

After thanking Padre, they raise their heads upward to study the six-foot high wooden crucifix, a carved replica of Jesus Christ nailed to the cross, which hangs behind the altar.

They slowly lower their heads and offer a silent prayer. As they turn to leave the railing, music from an organ in the small loft at the back of the mission reverberates off the walls of the mission.

A young organist, who has been waiting patiently, begins to sing the following refrain and verse chosen especially by them for this occasion:

*"On this day, O beautiful Mother, on this day we give thee our love, near thee, Madonna, fondly we hover, trusting thy gentle care to prove, Queen of angels, deign to hear, lisping children's humble prayer, young heart gain, O Virgin pure, sweetly to thyself allure."*

They walk slowly down the aisle, giving the organist enough time to play this song twice, first with single notes for the melody and refrain, and secondly with chords, foot pedals and all *pulls* of the pipe-organ console fully extended to create a symphonic sound. The music ends as they face each other, holding hands at the rear of the church.

"It seems as though the mission walls are coming to life and applauding," says Mark.

"The acoustics of the old pipe organ are astounding," she tells him. "I don't want the music to end."

They turn to have another look at the mission and its altar.

"Have you ever been in the presence of something so powerful, so overwhelming?" she asks as tears begin to swell in her eyes.

"This moment will live for eternity," he says, handing her a handkerchief.

By the time the sound of the last chord of the organ has dissipated, they are standing alone outside the front door of the mission as the nine historic bells in the tower begin to toll. The distinct tolling sends a tingling sensation up their spines.

"I'm at a loss for words," he declares, running his fingers through his hair. "Padre asked me how long I wanted the bells to toll."

"And you told him ...?"

"Two minutes, for the two of us," says Mark, taking a small box from his pocket and handing it to her.

When she opens it, inside is a gold-braided chain with a Saint Christopher medal.

"Would you fasten the clasp for me, please?" she asks, holding it in place. "It will always be around my neck to protect and remind me of this day."

He takes her again in his arms for one last kiss at the mission.

After the ceremony, they drive south from Carmel along Route 1 until they reach Big Sur, this time, by land. The highway is winding, so Mark watches the speedometer and rarely goes above 45 mph. At frequent intervals during the drive, Mark turns to Ruth to gaze quickly on her radiant face.

"You're still glowing from the wedding. Would you mind telling me about your dress?"

"After seeing it in a window in Rome," she admits, "I knew I had to buy it. That was a week after meeting you on the flight from LAX to BWI. When I tried it on, it fit perfectly. No alterations needed. It's a Valentino original that I hate to admit cost me a whole week's pay. I've been saving it with the hope of wearing it one day as we walked down the aisle together. The purse and shoes: Valentino red, his patented color."

"The car seems to have a mind all its own and knows where we're going before I do," he tells her, reducing his speed to make a left turn at a sign that reads, "Cabin in the Sky."

After a short climb up a windy hill, they pull into the last of four driveways, on a plateau with cottages that overlooks Big Sur. "The view from here is spectacular," he tells her admiringly. "So far, everything about this place exceeds the photos I saw while researching it over the Internet."

A minute later two attendants are eagerly carrying their suitcases into their private cottage.

It's exactly seven in the evening. After changing into more casual clothes, they walk into a small verandah directly above the driveway, where a candlelight dinner awaits them.

An appetizer of shrimp hanging inside the lip of a glass full of crushed ice begins their wedding dinner, followed by a small tossed Cobb salad with bacon, avocado and spinach. Their main course, prepared by Rico, the gourmet chef, is a small crab shell, stuffed with salmon and Dungeness crab, brushed with a buttery coat and broiled to a crispy finish.

"I trust that everything will meet with your approval and provide all the vitamins you'll need for your honeymoon in Monterey," Tico, their waiter and Rico's twin brother, tells them.

Two hours later, sipping a cordial of cognac, they listen to the voices of a tenor and baritone, singing a medley of romantic Mexican ballads and strumming acoustic guitars below their verandah.

"I can't make out their faces because of their wide sombreros," Ruth declares.

"It's the twins, Rico and Tico, our waiter and chef, I think," utters Mark with a chuckle.

As the sun begins to fall into the Pacific Ocean, its last rays shine on a wall of Bougainvillea that encircles the small driveway below them. They have only a few minutes to see the colors of their petals, ranging from pink, magenta, purple, red, orange, white and yellow, a bouquet of flora vibrant and alive in nature as God intended them to blossom for newlyweds.

"Let's play *Romeo and Juliet*," suggests Ruth.

"And which part do you want me to play?" he asks teasingly.

"Why, *Juliet*, of course."

"Me in drag? I never thought I'd see the day when…; perhaps it may be fun to reverse roles; might give a new twist and meaning to Shakespeare's tragic love story. Or we could play *Beauty and the Beast*."

"And what part do you want me to play?" she asks.

"Why, the Beast, of course!" he responds with a burst of laughter.

"Let's walk around the grounds of the cottage," suggests Ruth. "Perhaps get some creative ideas about how to make our first night as husband and wife *mav-el-ous*."

"You're just too marvelous, too marvelous for words," Mark begins to sing, "like glorious, glamorous, and that old standby amorous. It's all too wonderful, I'll never find the words that say enough, tell enough and mean they just aren't swell enough."

The following morning, after a continental breakfast, they begin to pack their suitcases when Mark notices three books on the mantelpiece. The titles are:

"What to Do on the First Night of Your Honeymoon?"

"What Comes First on Your Honeymoon Night?"

"How to Make Your Honeymoon Night Memorable?"

Mark opens each book and all the pages are blank. When he turns to the back cover, there's a large photo of the author with an unlit cigar in his mouth and the caption, "Artie *'B'* publishes all his books with invisible ink. Don't worry about making mistakes on your honeymoon. If you send him $100 for the printed text, then *you* will be making a big mistake!"

"While our honeymoon night may not have been memorable, we had a great time, without the benefit of your invisible words, Artie!" says Mark, laughing and returning the books to their shelf.

A few minutes later, Ruth removes a digital camera from her purse. "We can't leave without taking some pictures of the Bougainvillea in the morning sun," she tells him. "This scene reminds me of the film *Enchanted April,* when Josie Lawrence opened the shutters of her rented villa, *San Salvatore,* and saw, for the first time, wisteria in bloom everywhere. How I wish we could grow Bougainvillea at Ridgefield, but it needs a Mediterranean-seaside-type climate all year round which, unfortunately, is not possible around the Chesapeake Bay."

"We'll have to come back another time, if only to see if everything is as beautiful as it is this morning," he says. "Perhaps bring our children so they can see what God has created here."

Fifteen minutes later, Ruth is behind the wheel of their rental car as they drive north on Route 1. "The views are spectacular but the curves can be treacherous if you don't pay attention," she tells him. "I remember driving in a little fog, too, which can be daunting."

After less than thirty minutes, they're checking into the Monterey Country Club and one of their luxury lodges for honeymooners. It's Ruth's wedding gift to Mark, courtesy of a close friend and pilot for American Airlines who's a member of the private country club.

"Don't think I'll have time for golf, like those guys teeing off on the fairway," he answers.

"Did you ever feel inclined to join a country club and play with a foursome?" Ruth asks with some curiosity in her voice.

"The notion never seriously entered my mind. Perhaps if the right foursome develops, I might take up the sport."

"You should never say 'never.' You might find it relaxing from your workload at the mill and at Ridgefield."

"I'll take that under advisement," he tells her jokingly.

"Actually, I won't be disappointed if you shy away from the links. Anyway, most wives would prefer to do things together with their husbands."

Around 8 in the evening, Mark drives his car into a small

parking lot beside the roadway leading into Nepenthe, one of the most beautiful and famous restaurants in the world, and only a 20-minute drive from the country club. Positioned about 1,000 feet above sea level, its steel beams are embedded into a hillside of granite and volcanic rock to support the 7,000 square-foot restaurant, with one of the most spectacular views of Big Sur.

"Nepenthe," Ruth pronounces in three syllables and whistles. "I don't know another place that has its beauty and charm."

"Are you surprised?" asks Mark.

"Somewhat. If I had to choose a second home, it would be a cabin in Big Sur. It's also home of the Condor. But don't expect to see one when you're looking for it. They seem to drift out of nowhere when you least expect it."

"Look around at the expressions on the faces of customers," says Mark, taking Ruth's arm as they walk through the back patio of the restaurant. "Most likely, they're all enjoying fresh seafood from Monterey Bay."

"As much as I love the sunset over the Chesapeake Bay, I think the view over the Pacific tonight is magnificent. Of course, a lot depends on who I'm with."

"Isn't it 'whom?' " he asks. "And you're ending the sentence with a preposition, just like me. Why don't they change the rules of grammar? Then I wouldn't always feel so guilty. Of course, Winston Churchill easily solved the problem by declaring the preposition rule: 'one rule up with which I will not put!' "

Within a few minutes they are standing before the receptionist.

"Do you have a reservation?" asks a young girl, who looks like a starlet waiting to break into show business.

"No, we don't," answers Mark.

"Are you here for an affair?" the receptionist asks quickly and nonchalantly.

"What did you have in mind?" asks Mark, smiling in anticipation of unexpected news.

"Not likely," answers Ruth with a chuckle, tugging his arm. "Everything is legitimate and on the up and up."

"Then, you must be newlyweds."

"Is it that obvious?" asks Mark, with a wide smile and slight nod of his head.

"You could say that we're good at guessing. I didn't see any rice in your hair, otherwise that would have been my first question. Our maître d' will show you to a nice table."

Moments later the maître d' hands them a menu and asks, "Newlyweds?"

"How can you tell?" asks Ruth. "It can't be our clothes."

"When you're in the business as long as I am, I have a way of knowing. Call it a feeling."

They both skim the menu and begin to anticipate the fresh seafood selections.

"That's what a honeymoon will do to you," she tells him.

"What will a honeymoon do to you?"

"Increase your appetite."

"In that case," he suggests, "how about sharing another platter of Pacific Ocean scallops, sand dabs and lobster tails?"

"I love 'em so much, I could have 'em for breakfast," she admits.

"I've had them for breakfast when we flew into San Diego on the midnight express from BWI. It was a SEAL training course, which ended with dinner at *Anthony's On The Beach.*"

After dinner, they pass on dessert and Mark orders a cordial of cognac for himself and a glass of V8 vegetable juice for his wife.

After the waiter brings them their order, a slim, six-foot, gray-haired man in his 70's saunters by and stops when he notices the emblem of a SEAL on Mark's windbreaker and the SEAL Trident medal on his lapel. It's Clint Eastwood, who strides along as if he's on top of the world.

Clint is curious, asks for permission to join them and begins a conversation about SEALS and the risks they take on every mission.

"I've heard that a SEAL can't disclose anything about his assignment, which must make it very hard on his wife and family. I mean, not knowing where he's going and for how long," he says, starring directly into their faces with that Eastwood squint in his eyes.

"When I was a First Lieutenant," Mark replies, " I was single and living at home in Baltimore. Luckily, those days are behind me. My SEAL days are over, although I'm still an officer in the naval reserve."

"What about you?" Clint asks Ruth. "I assume you're hoping his reserve unit won't be called back into action."

'You've got that right, sir," she answers. "That's the first I've ever heard about the secrecy of his SEAL missions. We'll just have to put our faith in God to watch over us, and you too."

"Would you mind if I asked how you two met?" Clint asks curiously.

"We met the second time, when it meant something, on a flight from Los Angeles to Baltimore. Mark was anxious to buy a painting by Winslow Homer and I was eager to serve him in the first class section of my 747. Can't you tell that I was a flight attendant for American Airlines?" she asks kiddingly.

"Somehow I get the feeling that you're newlyweds," Clint asks slowly. "Are you?"

"You're the third person to ask us that same question within the hour of being here!" Mark tells him, bursting out in laughter.

Eventually the conversation leads to their life on the Chesapeake Bay, including the R&R Refuge for Red Cross Vets.

"If you don't mind us taking up a little of your time, we'd like to tell you about Ridgefield and our goals there," says Mark.

"You're not in the crab business, are you?" asks Clint. "I love those soft crabs from the Chesapeake Bay."

"Not likely. We're in the people business. We help Vets who served as medics in the Red Cross and came back home with mental or physical disabilities. When the government drops the ball and they're forced to look elsewhere for support, we're ready to help out, one family at a time, since our funds are limited."

"We're always looking for a sponsor if you know anyone who has some loose change in their pockets," adds Ruth.

After a few more minutes, Clint rises from his seat and extends his best wishes for a happy marriage. He takes a few steps away from their table, then unexpectedly returns to face them again.

"You can count me in," Clint tells them, "I'd be honored to sponsor anyone your people select. You can always contact me at Nepenthe."

"Thank you! I hope one day soon you can pay a visit to Ridgefield," Mark tells him. "And, as an afterthought, you might find it amusing to meet some of the characters, such as a retired tug-boat captain with his squawking parrot, a middle-aged lady who can read your horoscope and predict marital encounters, and a financial guru who made a fortune on Wall Street and lost it twice as fast. Need I go on? Would you be interested in hearing about two members of our technical staff who have ambitions on developing a small budget film similar to *Marty.*"

"Must be something in the Chesapeake Bay that's leading your people into unchartered territory," says Clint. "I applaud their ambitions, but hope they're prepared for lots of rejections. Even with my track record, I've never produced a film without facing a number of obstacles that requires teamwork and sufficient financing. The odds are against you, especially in these troubled financial times, but who knows? Give it a try. What do you have to lose?"

The following morning, after breakfast at the Monterey Country Club, they drive back to their sailboat. They will spend the next three days letting God and the Pacific Coast winds blow them along the coast of Monterey. During their final days here, they sing *I'm Just Sailing Along With the Breeze* as Mark steers his yacht, with Ruth clinging to his waist.

# Chapter 3

Abigail Woods, enjoying her role as acting CEO of Ridgefield, conducts an informal briefing after breakfast and pauses to take a good look at Mark's golden lab. "Mark left word not to forget you while he's away on his honeymoon," she tells Jen, who's sitting beside Mark's empty chair. "Here's a sausage biscuit from Gabby's kitchen."

She watches Jen give it a few bites and swallow it with a nod of appreciation. "Where do we stand on our film project?" Abigail asks, turning her attention to Kim.

"We've opened a file and are collecting ideas if anyone has something to contribute," says Kim. "At this time it's not the highest priority because we're turning most of our efforts to designing and testing solar-power electronic buoys to test for pollutants in the Bay. Our buoy, when installed closer to shore, will provide important data to the environmental protection and natural resources management agencies of the government."

"On the subject of the film," Liz interjects, "I might have something for your consideration; our first Vet at the R&R Refuge is Ben Bender, an amputee and recently widowed, who minored in screenwriting at USC until he was drafted and served as a medic in Vietnam."

Liz then mentions that Sandy has taken over day-to-day

management of the refuge so that she can assist Kim in developing the electronic buoy. "I can put my studies in metallurgy at Hopkins to good use, finally."

"About Ben Bender," Sandy says, "he's a terrific candidate for our R&R refuge since he's had a string of bad experiences. He lost a leg in Vietnam when a mortar-shell exploded as he was trying to save another soldier's life. Then his wife had a fatal heart attack after hearing about his injury in combat."

"I can't wait to meet him," says Womble. "Those Red Cross medics are unsung heroes, which is why Mark came up with the idea for the R&R refuge in the first place. But we have to remember that there's no quick fix to relieve all the flashbacks of blood and guts he's seen in combat."

"We have to do whatever it takes to make his life worthwhile; we owe it to him," says Abigail. "Does he have children?"

"Ben brought along his son, Little Ben, known as *Chubby*," says Sandy. He's nineteen with muscles bulging out of his *bod* and a *gas*; cocky as *all get out* and only thinks about playing baseball one day for the Orioles. He believes that someday he'll win a pennant for them as a knuckleball pitcher."

"Nothing wrong with his aspirations there," says Womble. "When can we meet them?"

"He's waiting in Mark's office and anxious to meet everyone," says Sandy.

"Pardon me for busting in here," Ben tells them, "but, I heard my name mentioned *dadgummit*."

"*Dadgummit*?" Is that your real name?" asks Greta. "I thought it was Bender."

"It is Bender, but you can call me 'Little Ben'."

"Good to have you with us," says Greta. "I think you'll soon find out that Ridgefield is a special place for lost souls. Look at me. A few weeks ago I was on the verge of putting my head under the hairdryer and turning the dial to microwave cooking. That would've been the *Mother of a blow-dry!*"

"Good grief. What brought you to that crisis?" asks Ben.

"An inspector in the Kent County labor office knocked on my door," says Greta, "and was investigating whether or not I was paying a worker a proper wage. I explained that she was paid $150 a week for doing 20 percent of the haircuts plus free room and board, whereas a slightly mentally-deficient worker got $10 a week, did 80 percent of the work and paid for her own room and board; I also mentioned that she occasionally slept with a man who brought her a bottle of rum and stayed overnight. He said that the slightly mentally-deficient one is underpaid and wanted to talk to her right away."

"So what happened next?" asks Bender, eager to hear more.

"I told him 'you're talking to her,' watched him tip his hat and fly out the back door, mumbling something about another *wild goose chase* in Rock Hall!"

"Those inspectors are just doing their job, probably responding to a complaint or maybe they heard how sexy you are," says Bender, winking his right eye.

"Thank you. Compliments are always welcomed," says Greta. "So I closed up my hair salon, gave myself a good scolding for trying to do business in Rock Hall and asked Mark for a job. He ordered me to report for work the next day and here I am, now a member of the Ridgefield family."

"Actually, I'm not looking for anything special except to prove that I can still be of value to my son," Ben answers with a slight twitch in one eye. "He's definitely not interested in helping me to run a small farm in Easton. His mind is on baseball. He is on the verge of something big because he really has talent; he just needs the right people bring it out of him."

"We've talked to his coach, Frank Szymanski, at Chesapeake College in Wye," says Sandy, "who rates Chubby as an up and coming pro prospect with a nasty knuckleball. Frank suggested that we buy a batting cage with a pitching mound so he can train all year round."

"That would represent an investment of almost $25,000, but may bring benefits to others," Liz explains. "If he develops into a professional baseball player, the publicity for Ridgefield would be tremendous."

"With your permission," says Womble, "I could contact Cal and Billy Ripken of Aberdeen and see if their Ripken Foundation will provide some funds and initiate a one-week baseball camp, perhaps on the campus of Washington College in Chestertown. They might be interested in using our batting cage to promote their camp."

"Weren't you a coach in one of the schools in Philly?" asks Abigail. "Would you take over all responsibilities pertaining to sports?"

"With pleasure; I might try to get some sports celebrities to meet our Vets and their families," says Womble, "anything that will give them a lift in their lives. If the baseball camp is successful, perhaps Michael Phelps and his swimming coach might be persuaded to conduct a swimming camp. Who knows what can develop here? Do you see what I'm saying?"

They burst out in laughter, mostly because of Womble's enthusiasm and excited gestures with his hands and arms flinging all over the place.

"OK, have your laugh, but I'll have the last laugh when I ask Dave Montgomery, an old colleague from Wharton School of Business and current President of the Philadelphia Baseball Club, to arrange for us to see a game at Citizens Bank Park. With a little arm-wrestling, he might even give permission for some Vets and their families to meet a few of the ballplayers on the Phillies roster."

"Don't get your feathers ruffled too much," Abigail teases him slightly. "We're interested in doing what's best for our Vets."

"I'm basically a counselor," Womble continues, "that Mark hired over a cup of coffee at Java Rock to make your work easier and happier. I'm a detail man and believe it's not enough to get *most* of the details; it's important to get *all* of them."

"You'll have your work cut out for you, trying to keep everyone in line," Kim declares with a chuckle.

"I admire someone like you who can laugh in the face of adversity and give it a good kick in the rear end," Womble admits. "Mark told me about the secretive research you're conducting. Let me know if I can be of any help. By the way, if you haven't heard it through the grapevine, I'll be engineering Greta's radio broadcast on Friday at noon."

Abigail asks York for an update about his design plans and building permits for installation of wind turbines at Ridgefield.

"It's a losing battle," declares York, shaking his head with disappointment on his face. "They'll give us a permit for only one wind turbine. The idea of constructing turbines, I'm afraid, is tabled until there's a change in the mindset inside the Kent County planning office."

"Reminds me of the feuds in the old west," answers Abigail, "where the settlers and ranchers battled each other about expansion and potential for development."

"Ordinarily, we might try to talk to the local people and get an ordinance passed, except they don't want those wind turbines blocking their view of the bay or disturbing the geese." says Liz angrily.

"Let's get back to reality," says Greta. "Before Mark left for his honeymoon, he gave me approval for a one-hour broadcast from inside the soundstage of Ridgefield. The first show with Womble as engineer-producer will air over the Kent County Radio Network this Friday at noon. Hope you'll tune in during your lunch hour."

"That should be a barrel of fun," says Womble. "No one can predict what someone will say over the air, and that means Greta and phone-callers. We'll have to be on our toes all the time."

"In case anyone is interested in our financial picture," Abigail acknowledges, "everyone seems to have a good grip on the reins and is staying within their budget. Also, I would like to advise you about a show at the Washington County Museum of Fine Arts (WCMFA) in Hagerstown, in which Sandy's life-size clay model of Liz as Pompeia is on exhibition and drawing rave reviews. Perhaps you can give her a publicity plug on your broadcast."

Everyone applauds Sandy for her success as a sculptor until Abigail resumes her briefing.

"There is one correction that should be noted here for the record," Abigail advises them. "Pompeia was the second wife of Julius Caesar and the embodiment of beauty and brains, just like our own Liz Carter, who posed for Sandy's sculpture. Furthermore, if enough of you want to see the exhibit, we'll rent a vehicle on Saturday and pay all expenses, including lunch."

Manny is poised like a jockey in the starting gate at Pimlico Racetrack, waiting to give his two-cents worth to close the briefing. "Listen up, everyone," he boasts. "Get 'em while their hot. No, I'm not referring to the crab cakes from Gabby's kitchen. I'm talking about photos on exhibit inside the R&R Refuge building. You'll see images taken when you weren't looking, plus a new display of the decoy collection donated by Judy Ridgefield, in a gallery bearing her name."

"Fabulous photos," Abigail admits. "If I'd known you were shooting me, I'd have applied some make-up to look a little younger. The photo exhibition will change weekly, so if you miss seeing it one week, not to worry. Manny has lots of photos to show us at work."

"You mean *goofing off,* don't you?" asks Manny facetiously.

"Don't tell Mark," Liz declares with a laugh. "Otherwise, he'll want a rebate from our salary."

Greta begins her first broadcast on Friday at noon from a make-shift studio inside the research lab. "Ladies," says Greta, overflowing with great expectations, "the show is *Love and Other Disorders of the Heart* and if you can hear the melodic tones of my voice coming to you over the Kent Broadcast Network, grab a cup of fresh coffee, find an easy chair, loosen up your bra to let everything hang out and give me your thoughts for the next hour. The same applies to men listening in. I want to put everyone completely at ease so you can tell me what's going on in your life. If you have any marital problems, spousal problems, man-woman, man-man or woman-woman problems, toss them my way. But be honest because I'll tell you where you're headed, based on your horoscope and the alignment of the planets and stars."

Greta pauses to look at the monitor and quickly gauge the information Womble has gathered about the first incoming caller.

"You're on the air with Greta 'Bow-Wow' Howe," she clamors, officially taking her first caller of her first show. "If you're married, tell me if you're giving more or less than 50% and why."

But before the caller's voice is switched to the 'live' position, Womble interjects, "For all you listeners calling in, we want to hear everything you have to say right from the horse's mouth. We don't want *hear-say*. We want *horse-say*. Don't be shy. Tell us who you are, what's going on in your life, and what you'd like to ask Greta."

"I don't know how to measure any percentages," the first caller tells Greta. "All I know is that I try to make the best of each day and leave it at that. My birthday is December 10th and I'd like to think that I'm a woman who can think for herself. Independent up to a point, but still need my husband for moral and financial support."

"You're a *Sagittarius* and, as you say, independent and very smart," answers Greta confidently. "My advice is to you is stay independent and close your pocket book. Don't spend a dime on anything you don't need. This isn't the time even to think of investments or purchases. Continue to be smart and vigilant and on guard. If you're shopping for something special, bargains will soon unfold before your very eyes."

Greta turns away from her monitor to motion a handsome and dapper man in his 50's to have a seat beside her.

"I see that my next guest is here for an *in-person in-studio* interview," says Greta, "so, without further ado, welcome to our *really big shoe*, Henny Youngster."

"Good to be on your show and talk about *Love and Other Disorders of the Heart*," he says, smiling and using both hands to push the hair on the sides of his head back in place.

"As a marriage counselor for Kent County, Henny, first tell us something we should know about *your* marriage," says Greta.

"Generally speaking, it's good," Henny begins. "For example, take my wife…please. We go out to restaurants twice a week for a good dinner and companionship; she goes on Mondays and I go on Tuesdays. The other day she suggested we try something different in our marriage, so I asked her to check out the kitchen. We don't speak to each other much; I hate to interrupt her. Last night she asked me if there was something on the television that made me upset and I said, 'yes, dust.' "

"How long did you say you are married?" asks Greta.

"Tomorrow will make it 20 years of marital bliss or martial art, take your choice," he says, moving the microphone closer to his mouth. "The other afternoon she called me on her cell and said there was water in the carburetor of the car. I asked her where she was and she said, 'in a lake.' "

"Lately, I've seen you at odd hours around town, flying a kite," says Greta curiously.

"I often get the urge to ask my wife for a little sex and she always says 'Go fly a kite!' "

"Any suggestions about how to strengthen a marriage?" asks Greta.

"When you go to a mall, always hold hands; if you let go, your wife will go shopping," he answers, "and sleep in different beds; the husband on the eastern shore and the wife on the western shore of the Bay."

Womble signals with his right hand at his throat, meaning it's time for a one-minute commercial break.

"Good timing. I have to take a *pee* anyway. Watch the console for me, please," she says, dashing out the door of the broadcast booth.

On the walk to the woman's restroom, she passes a large sign:

**"NO DOMANI.**
**Do what you planned to do tomorrow, today.**
Kim Bozzetti."

After flushing, Greta washes her hands in a sink, sprinkles some water on her face and rushes to the door, only to realize that she's accidentally locked herself inside.

"These new damn security locks," she shouts in desperation. "What'll my listeners think if I can't *pee* without a crisis. There goes my show down the drain, before I even got started. Maybe information can be relayed through the keyhole to Womble's cell phone, which should be connected to the 'live' microphone on his console."

"For our listeners in radio-land," Womble interjects over the airwaves, "we're experiencing some technical problems with Greta's microphone and transmission. Until everything is resolved, I'll try to relay your questions to Greta and she'll answer them in her own words with me as a sort of temporary interlocutor."

He kneels down on one knee and presses his mouth to the keyhole.

"Hold on, Greta," he yells through the keyhole, covering the microphone in his cell phone with his cheek, "until the next commercial break and we'll get you *outta* there."

"Interior lock 'n door? Is that what Womble said?" she mumbles through the key hole.

"No. I said that I'll be an interlocutor," he shouts. "And these floors are linoleum over concrete, very painful to kneel on. As for our listeners waiting to hear Greta's voice, let me give you a little news from farmers in Kent County. Did you hear about the race between four silkworms that ended up in a tie? And this police report just in: two officers from the Tobacco and Alcohol Squad arrested a woman for making home-made whiskey, but nevertheless, loved her still!"

Kim and Liz stand outside the broadcast booth, watching Greta and Womble rush from their console and begin talking to each other through the keyhole in the women's restroom door.

"Womble, I have a pass key to the women's restroom in my office," Kim tells him. "Greta should be back at her console in a minute or less."

"One more story like these and I think I'll have to use the john, too," Liz says, still laughing at the hectic way things are developing in Greta's first broadcast.

"What's an interlocutor? Something connected to the lock?" Greta mutters through the keyhole.

Because her words don't seem to make much sense to Womble, he rushes quickly back to his broadcast console.

"Greta will be with you momentarily," says Womble as rapidly as possible. "We think the problem with the feed from her microphone is resolved and she'll be back on the air in a minute or two. In the meantime perhaps you'd like to know that yesterday, I shot a goose in my pajamas!"

Realizing this is Greta's show, he switches back to his normal voice and cadence to take the next caller.

"We have an incoming call from a middle-aged woman with feelings of desperation. She confesses to being battered by her live-in boyfriend. And what is your question for Greta?" he asks the caller.

"Should a woman be permitted to bear arms?" she asks slowly and nervously.

"A woman should be permitted the right to bear arms and ...legs...or any other part of her anatomy that she wants to *bare*," he says facetiously. "Seriously, if you feel threatened, call 911 or, at a minimum, talk to the people at the Battered Women's Group of Kent County as soon as possible. Their number is listed in the telephone directory."

After another commercial break, Womble presses the 'on-the-air' button on his console with one hand and wipes some perspiration from his brow with the other.

"During our commercial break," he continues, "I found a quote from Thomas Jefferson, who said 'The strongest reason for people to retain the right to keep and bear arms is, as a last resort, to protect themselves against tyranny in government.' While that may not be helpful to our last caller, it's something to keep in mind."

Eventually, Kim finds the key and opens the door for Greta, who looks like a peacock with ruffled feathers. Her hair is standing straight up, as if she's had an electric shock. It's a cartoonish picture, hardly the image of a cool and collected radio-show hostess. Her looks, however, are deceiving, as she takes her place at her console, combs her hair with one hand, gives herself a slap across one cheek and begins to chuckle.

"I'm back, folks, and energized to take your calls again. I thought I saw my career going down the drain, but it was only an optical illusion. Here's another report, hot off the press of the AP wire service. While I was away, a golden retriever gave birth to puppies in a gully of Ridgefield farm along Eastern Neck Island Road and was cited for littering! That birth and today's broadcast are now hysterical – correction -- historical."

"Greta, I've been informed by the network engineer that we have five additional minutes," says Womble, using both hands as if he's stretching an imaginary girdle.

"Five extra minutes; wonderful. Let's take our next caller. You say you're a waterman?" asks Greta, leaning closer to the microphone.

"Retired after 50 years of crabbing on the Chesapeake Bay and still living in the same house in Betterton," he answers.

"What's on your mind today? And please don't start talking about *peelers*?"

"I won't talk about 'peelers.' But like a 'peeler,' I feel reborn at 70 and fit as a fiddle. Is it too late to start a serious romance?"

"Are you kidding me?" she asks. "You're still a young *whipper-snapper*, as George 'Gabby' Hayes used to say in those old western movies. Who's the lucky girl?"

"She's a farmer's daughter; inhibited, lived a very sheltered life and unwilling to make a commitment."

"How old is she?"

"She's 42 and never been married," he answers quickly.

"How fast can you run?"

"Why do you ask?"

"Aren't you afraid of her father coming after you with a shotgun?"

"Never gave it much thought," he says. "I was thinking more about how hard it is to get it up if you give me the green light to proceed in this romance."

"Have you tried any of those sexual enhancement drugs? Of course, you should consult your doctor before taking them. Do you smoke?"

"You mean cigarettes?"

"Yes. Cigarettes, cigars, a pipe?" asks Greta in a louder voice.

"I do."

"In that case, have you given any thought to a possible heart attack during liaison with a much younger woman?"

"By liaison do you mean sex?"

"That's precisely what I mean," says Greta. "A heart attack can often be fatal."

"Yes, I've thought about it a lot."

"And do you know what to do?" Greta asks curiously.

"Sure, I know exactly what to do. If she goes into cardiac arrest, I call 911 and give her CPR."

"I think you're missed the boat."

"Did I say something wrong?"

"According to my engineer, it's time to break away for a brief commercial," Greta says hurriedly, switching off the 'live' control knob and falling backward into her swivel chair. She pauses to release a big sigh, turns her head from side to side and grins at Womble.

"These are unexpected moments," she tells him, wobbling her

head like a bobble doll, "when we haven't a clue what the caller will talk about."

After a one-minute commercial to publicize the poultry specials on fresh chicken, turkey and goose at Bayside Market in Rock Hall, Womble signals with an index finger that she's back on the air and should take the next caller.

"I've inherited an upright piano and I'm afraid to touch it," the next caller, nicknamed *Moushy*, begins nervously.

"How old are you?"

"Just turned 25."

"In that case, you have a mature body and mind. If you won't touch it with your hands, sit on it with your rear end, just to see if it plays and it's in tune," Greta answers, laughing at herself. "You might produce a sound no one's ever heard before and never wants to hear again."

"I was also given a computer for my birthday, but I'm afraid to turn it on."

"Why?"

"Because I might short-circuit the electricity and blow a fuse in my house."

"Your house has fuses?" asks Greta. "The first thing you should do is talk to an electrical contractor about installing a panel box with circuit-breakers."

"I'll do that right away."

"Let me ask you another question, honey. Do you feel the walls of your home closing in on you?"

"Yes, I do."

"You have too many inhibitions. I call them *hang-ups*. You definitely have a *hang-up* syndrome and must get hold of yourself before it's too late."

"Too late for what?" asks *Moushy*.

"Too late to begin living, to enjoy life as God intended you to enjoy it," says Greta. "You don't want to be a caterpillar all your life, do you? Wouldn't you like to become a Monarch butterfly?"

"What should I do?"

"Because you're a Pisces, my advice is: Take some piano lessons with a private teacher and enroll in an introductory course in Information Technology. As Larry King says, 'You can do it. It *ain't* brain surgery!' I assure you, after one lesson with your teacher, you'll have the confidence to play the piano and turn on the computer and begin to learn how to put them to good use. These are baby steps. All you need is a little shove. And that's all the time I can give you today. Please call back in a couple weeks and let me know how you're progressing."

During the final commercial break, Greta swallows a half-liter of spring water, squishes the plastic bottle and gazes back again at the monitor of her computer.

"It might be wise to rehash the problem facing that last caller," she says. "It's a lesson we all can learn something from. Call it: 'The Shackles of Life.' We've got to be our own surgeon and cut those shackles off our hands and feet, off our backs and *outta* our minds. We'll feel free again, lighter and stronger, after those inhibitions are gone. Nothing to hold us back from doing the things we want to do in life. Great things lie ahead for us. We can begin to live each day like there's no tomorrow and do things in a way we never dreamed was possible. I guarantee that happiness is right around the corner. It's up to you and me to find that corner."

Womble holds up two fingers, indicating two minutes remaining.

"If you missed anything that Henny Youngster said earlier in the show," says Greta, "you didn't miss much because he'll be a regular on our show, so tune in for an update on his tips about how to make your life better. I've been informed by my line producer, Womble Weinstein, that we have two minutes left in this show, time enough to give you all my forecast, based on the alignment of the stars and planets and inspired by the Baltimore Sun's horoscope column. So sit back and enjoy the best last two minutes in broadcasting. It's our big closing."

"For *Aries,* March 21 to April 19: Don't lose your footing and climb *outta* your predicament. Know when enough is enough, and come in out of the rain.

"For *Taurus,* April 20 to May 20: It's all right to feel eager to help those around you, but they might be intimidated and threatened if you back-slap when you shouldn't.

"For Gemini, May 21 to June 20: Be on guard. The people you were looking forward to meeting could be fleas waiting to have a free ride at your expense.

"For *Cancer,* June 21 to July 22: Turn off your fears and turn on the charm. This is your time to walk-the-walk and talk-the-talk. If people put hurdles in your life, stride over them.

"For *Leo*, July 23 to August 22: It's a good time to face up to your misdemeanors and ask for forgiveness. It's also time for you to make new friends. It's no good to be alone or lonesome.

"For *Virgo*, August 23 to September 22: Put your time, talents and energy into something productive, like making love to someone you love but are afraid to get serious with.

"For *Libra*, September 23 to October 22: Stop stepping on someone's toes. It's time to find someone in step with you.

"For *Scorpio*, October 23 to November 21: When everything looks dark and hopeless, switch on the auxiliary power inside your brain that will command you to stop looking for the light at the end of the tunnel. The light is already inside you.

"For *Sagittarius*, November 22 to December 21, don't let anyone tell you it can't be done. Remember always, 'You Can Be Better than You Are.'

"For *Capricorn*, December 22 to January 19: Stop feeling that you're the center of everything and the world revolves around you.

"For *Aquarius*, January 20 to February 18: If you're thinking about a new job, have no fear and go for it. It can't be worse than the one you're in now.

"Finally, for *Pisces*, February 19 to March 20: If something inside you is urging you to try something new, hesitate no longer.

The change will be good for you and your family, too. I hope that one of our callers today is still listening since she's a Pisces."

"Time flies here at Ridgefield," Womble says, "but fruit flies like bananas. This fact comes courtesy of *Smiling Jakes*, the haberdashery at the corner of Sharp and Main Streets in the heart of that thriving one-block metropolis called Rock Hall. Sorry folks, but without sponsorship, this program would be merely a figment of our imagination."

"Yes, time flies, as Womble Weinstein said. We've had a ball today. And if you enjoyed our chat, tell your friends about us. As a waitress told me yesterday, she saw two hats hanging on a rack at Java Rock Coffee House. One said to the other, 'You stay here. I'll go on a head!' "

Greta and Womble giggle and wiggle in their swivel chairs like two kids served a chocolate sundae.

"See you next time on the radio," Womble signs off. "Hope you enjoyed it as much as we enjoyed bringing it to you. But I can't let Greta have the last word, so here's a quickie from Joe Szymanski, nuclear-physics grad of Washington College and the Oak Ridge School of Reactor Technology (ORSORT), who aspires to be a storyteller, along the lines of Preston Sturges. He told me the story of two atoms colliding inside the core of a nuclear reactor. One said to the other, 'I must have lost an electron,' and the other asked, 'Are you positive?' "

"Take your hand off that control knob, Womble," Greta says enthusiastically. "I must have the last word about *Love and Other Disorders of the Heart*. So, here's a news quickie about police who found a hole in the wall of a nudist camp outside Betterton. It says, 'Police are looking into it.' Hmmm, can't figure out if they will be cited or sighted. Guess it depends on their perspective of the situation. I wonder what kind of telescope they're using. And for all those on drugs, there's a drug rehab center in Chestertown ready to help you out. It's the one-story brick building near High and Lowe Streets, with a sign on the lawn that reads, 'Stay Off Grass.' And next broadcast, I'll spend some time not showing you how to be a Vanderbilt, but how to live like one. And always be good to your kids, so they'll be obligated to be good to you."

As Womble prepares to flip the switch to end the electronic feed from their console to Kent Radio Central in Chestertown, he looks at Greta, who's beaming from ear and ear and eager to continue. "Folks," Womble suggests, "maybe we should think about doing an entire program on the life of Thomas Jefferson, since what he had to say over a hundred years ago is still relevant today. I'll leave you with one of his better quotations: 'I predict future happiness for Americans if they can prevent the government from wasting the labors of people under the pretense of taking care of them.' Until next time if there is a next time, always remember: You Can Be Better than You Are."

"Don't flip that switch just yet, Mr. Womble Weinstein. I've read about one-third of Roger Rosenblatt's recently-published book, "The Craft and Art of Writing" and would like to invite him to appear on one of our upcoming shows. Anyone who espouses that 'writing makes suffering endurable, evil intelligible, justice desirable and love possible' deserves a chance to be heard and explain why writers write."

After Womble flips the switch to end their broadcast, he and Greta erupt in laughter and jump out of their chairs to give each other a high five and bear hug.

"You were incredible, like you've been doing this all your life," he says.

"In a way, I have. It's like talking to the people who came to me for a haircut, shave and shampoo," she admits.

"Women came to you for a shave?"

"All included in Greta's low-budget package for $40," says Greta, laughing. "And you were marvelous, too. Never caught off-guard, an especially good listener with good instincts and intuition. I like the idea of us being a team that can think quickly on our feet."

"I wonder if all of that went out into the airways?" he asks her. "This was fun."

Within hours of the close of their initial broadcast, Kent Radio Central in Chestertown is deluged with listeners anxious to express their pleasure with their broadcast. Almost all empathize with Greta and her astrological forecast for people facing difficult times in their lives.

"She calls *'em* like she sees *'em*," said one caller to the station, "sincere and eager to give advice based on the alignment of the stars and their horoscope. I never believed in that stuff about your horoscope before, but she's made a believer *outta* me."

# Chapter 4

Mark sits at his desk, massaging Jen's neck with one hand and scrolling the in-box of his emails with the other as Ruth walks through the doorway with a cup of hot coffee for him. "Can't wait to jump on the computer, can you?" she asks. "I assume you're sorting out emails that piled up during our honeymoon."

"So far, nothing earth-shattering."

"Looks like you haven't lost a step, *hon*," she responds. "I assume Abigail is sleeping after picking us up at BWI last night."

"Wasn't that nice of her?" he says. "Maybe you wouldn't mind sorting out some of these emails, so I could grab the phone that's been ringing off the hook this morning."

"Glad to pitch in."

"Take a *go* at answering some if you can; shouldn't be many for me since most of the important ones go to the mill in Baltimore."

After Ruth and Mark exchange seats, he's about to grab the phone when Liz pokes her head through the doorway.

"Welcome home. Room for one more?" asks Liz, chewing on an apple. "I want to hear all about your honeymoon, but can't wait to tell you that Greta's show was a blast. Too bad you missed it. If she and Womble can keep up the repartee, they'll put Ridgefield on the radio map."

"Maybe I should have stayed away longer!" he says, grinning. "You all run things better than I can."

"Secondly, I wanted to tell you that Reggie intends to loan Red Cross Vets and their children a guitar and give them free lessons. He calls his program 'No Strings Attached,' designed to help all medics, starting with those from Maryland, who can drive to his studio outside Betterton. And it's not restricted to Vets staying at the R&R Refuge at Ridgefield. It's for all Red Cross medics. He wants to be an integral part of Ridgefield and told me he was mostly responsible for getting you to drop anchor in Betterton a few years ago."

After Liz leaves the office, Mark grabs the phone and takes the first of a succession of quick calls. "Slow down, please. Is there something in your mouth?" he asks. "I can barely figure out what you're talking about."

The first caller, like those that follow him, is a small home-improvement contractor, who's anxious to sign up for sponsorship of Greta's radio show. It's a good predicament for Mark, as executive producer, who squirms in his lounge chair and begins to bask in the success of Greta and Womble's first venture into broadcasting.

Womble pokes his head suddenly in the doorway.

"I can't believe it," Mark tells him. "The phone's ringing off the hook. Everyone's talking about Greta's performance. They all said she reacted to her callers with passion and wit."

"She walked the walk and talked the talk," says Womble, smiling widely.

"In that case, you can tell her, as executive producer of her broadcast," Mark continues, "that I always knew she had talent and only needed a way to showcase it. She merits a pay raise and step up to MTS."

Greta strolls into his office just in time to hear Mark mentioning her name.

"Did I miss anything here?" Greta asks, anxious to hear about the response to her first show.

"No more housework for you, young lady," says Mark. "You're moving up, promoted to MTS."

"What's that?" Greta asks.

"Member of the Technical Staff, with a bump in pay commensurate with your new responsibilities here at Ridgefield," says Mark proudly. "It's recognition and appreciation for a job well done. If the response continues for the next three shows, your broadcast may be expanded from once a week to Monday, Wednesday and Friday at noon."

Womble nods his head in agreement and escorts Greta out of his office as Mark opens his cell phone and speed dials Reggie Perdue in Betterton.

"What's all this about offering to loan a guitar and give free lessons for Red Cross Vets?" asks Mark.

"It's true. No one should be left behind if they want to better themselves. Isn't that what you always preached at Ridgefield? However, the guitars are a loan from Paul Reed Smith, who makes some of the best guitars in America at his factory in Queenstown. He gets the publicity and we get the satisfaction of helping out our service men and women."

"Thank you, *Regg*. Great to have you aboard," says Mark, ending his call.

It doesn't take long for Mark to resume his routine of working Wednesdays, Thursdays and Fridays at Bethlehem Steel (BS) in Baltimore. Two weeks after installing Dr. Joost de Wal as CEO in charge of all engineering aspects of the mill, Mark manages to track him down on his cell phone.

"Now I know why they call you the *Flying Dutchman*," he tells him. "Can you take a break from your schedule long enough to have lunch at noon? We'll meet at Gertrude's, a restaurant on the ground floor of the Baltimore Museum of Art (BMA). And bring along the Wew twins, Ying and Yang. It's time that I learn more about the computerized robotics that they single-handedly introduced to our production line of cold-rolled steel."

Two hours later, all four are sitting in a corner of Gertrude's.

"I love this place," Joost tells them. "I often bring my family here on the weekends to enjoy good food and fine art. They have a Rembrandt upstairs that is one of his best works."

"I love this place, too," Mark tells him. "After lunch, you have my permission to show the Wew twins around the galleries. I won't tell your boss that you're all delayed on company business."

After studying his menu, Dr. de Wal asks for permission to order something special that's not on the menu.

"It's something that we can all share, called *rijsttafel*; an assortment of small dishes of Indonesian delicacies, such as crispy chicken in a gooey peanut sauce, duck roasted in banana leaves, stir-fried chewy beef sautéed in burgundy wine, varieties of rice and velvety vegetables flavored with spices from the orient. All the ingredients are carefully selected and added to recipes handed down from generation to generation."

"I never knew that my chief engineer was also a gastronomical genius," Mark says to Dr. de Wal. "And in case our computer whiz kids haven't a clue what I'm talking about, *gastronomical* refers to the art or science of good eating. Now, Joost tell me more about the delicacies we're about to taste."

"I telephoned and spoke with the chef earlier this morning; he's a Dutch émigré. I asked him to make a special lunch for us. These delicacies are always exotic; some say they're erotic but that's a matter for discussion at another time and place. Nevertheless, all are popular dishes served in restaurants not only in Indonesia but to Dutch families all over the Netherlands, even in my adopted hometown of Utrecht. It's in keeping with what we would call in Holland a 'Dutch treat,' meaning Mark will be paying for it!"

"Wow. That's a mouthful," says Mark, handing the menu to the waiter. "I certainly didn't expect a lecture, but bring it on. I can't wait to try everything."

"It usually comes with rice rolls with spicy fillings, too," Ying acknowledges. "We're familiar with *rijsttafel* because we have Indonesian restaurants near our apartment in Berlin."

By the end of the lunch, it's clear that Dr. de Wal's choice of a *rijsttafel* was a winner, with not a kernel of rice or peapod left in any of the serving dishes. Mark shakes his hand and turns to the Wew twins. "My ingenious computer wizards," he says, glancing back and forth at their faces, "I'm as curious as a cat as to how to tell you apart?"

"You can't," boasts Ying.

"My brother's right," Yang interjects with a chuckle. "You can't tell us apart. Even the monks who rescued our mother and brought her from her village in China to Tibet, where we were born, couldn't tell us apart."

"There must be some difference. Which one of you was born first?" Mark asks with a suspicious grin.

"He was," they both respond and point their finger at one another, chuckling.

"Bet your mother could tell you apart, couldn't she?" asks Dr. de Wal.

"No. Not even our mother could spot a difference," confesses Ying. "I guess we are truly identical twins."

"She died one year after we were born," Yang admits, "according to the monks who raised us."

"I studied your file when we processed your application to immigrate to America," says Mark. "I am very pleased by your devotion to each other, how quickly you've adapted to America, and especially what you've accomplished in six months at BS. You both are a great addition to BS."

"But that's only the beginning," Joost tells Mark. "They're redesigning another production line and installing computerized robotics in our high-strength, corrosion-resistant-steel production line that should increase our annual profit by at least 30 percent."

"Reminds me of those girders and trusses in the stadiums around the world," Mark says, nodding his head. "Wouldn't it be nice if we could get our hands on a contract to produce them here instead of developers having to import them from Japan and China?"

"It's amazing what the addition of only 11 percent of chromium does to the strength of carbon steel," Dr. de Wal says, laughing and leaning backward in his seat.

At this point, Mark has something serious cross his mind, something that affects the Wew twins, but bites his tongue and decides this is not the time and place to discuss it.

Later that afternoon, Mark is speed-dialing Lois Carnegie at Heavenly Manor, her estate halfway between Betterton and Rock Hall. She's at her desk, trying to read a report of minutes from her last board meeting at Carnegie Steel (CS) in Pittsburgh, and answering his call at the same time.

"This better be good news, Mark, because I have a ton of work on my desk," she replies with a chuckle. "It's sad that the financial collapse of the housing market has crept into our sales at CS with a scary forecast. Our sales are down almost 50 percent from last year."

"Welcome to a new way of doing business," he answers. "Consolidation is the answer, and always remember, 'hope springs eternal.' "

"Oh, congratulations again on your marriage to Ruth," she says joyfully. "It's good to hear your voice. I trust you won't let your business at Sparrows Point slow you down too much and take time away from your family. Now, what's all this talk about consolidation?"

"It's time for you to join forces with Bethlehem Steel. As a first step, which I mentioned to you before leaving for California, I'd like you to join the board of directors. There are many reasons, but the main one would be to keep our mills up and running against foreign competitors and exchanging patents and computerized processes. Carnegie would benefit immediately from such a union as much as we would. At BS we have two remarkable computer whiz kids, the Wew twins, who emigrated from Germany and are installing computerized robotics and giving our plant a respectable profit for the first time in a long time. The results of all their efforts would be available to CS."

"Yes, you mentioned something about joining your board just before you left for your honeymoon," says Lois. "I've discussed it with Clowie, who believes it's a 'win-win' deal for both of us. She even mentioned how it reminded her of our buying the Philadelphia lowboy from you. You made a quick sale and profit, and we made a good investment in antique furniture."

A week later, at precisely five minutes after nine in the morning, Mark is addressing his board of directors when he hears over the intercom the voice of his secretary, Miss Virginia Potts.

"You told me to advise you when Miss Carnegie arrived," says Virginia.

"Please ask her to come in," Mark replies.

He walks over to the door and opens it just as Lois reaches for the door knob.

"Good to see you looking so well, Lois," he tells her with a gentle handshake, then motions her over to a seat beside him after all members of the board rise to greet her.

"Gentlemen, I trust you'll excuse me for taking the liberty of introducing into this somewhat stale but profitable board a new and remarkable person," says Mark. "Don't let your mind dwell too much on her charming physical attributes. Inside are the genes of the Carnegie clan. She was born and descended from Andrew Carnegie's younger brother, Tom, and is destined for greatness in the steel business after graduating from Northwestern University with honors. I take pride in introducing our newest member of the board and Administrative CEO, Lois Carnegie."

The board members circle around the conference table and introduce themselves one by one. John Szymanski, Director of Finance, removes the vase of flowers from a corner table and hands it to her. "Welcome to Bethlehem Steel, Lois," says John. "It's a pleasure to have you aboard our ship. Everyone in our finance department will be anxious to see if some of your Carnegie magic will rub off on us."

"I'm no magician," Lois tells them succinctly. "All good things happen from good old-fashioned hard work. Although I'm a great grandniece of Andrew, you can forget protocol and call me *Lois*."

"Gentlemen, you're all excused so Lois can get familiar with our operation here," says Mark.

A minute later, Mark and Lois are seated side by side at the conference table and peering into a manual.

"Here's a brief history of BS, starting with the days when our families worked side by side in Pittsburgh. Near the end of the manual is an organization chart. Notice your name already embossed in bold print," he explains with a chuckle. "We've included a section identifying our department heads, phone numbers, personnel records with photo; practically everything you might want to know about our board members."

"Wish our fathers could be here to see us working together," Lois says, skimming over each page.

"If my Dad were here he'd explain the history of BS with pride. The facts may not have been completely accurate, but the way he told them made it plausible. I know he's looking down on us and pleased that our families are working together again."

"What goes around comes around. Isn't that the cliché apropos for this situation?"

"Correct. And the last section includes a flow chart of our current production and operation," he says and hesitates a few seconds. "Would you like me to show you around the mill?"

"That's won't be necessary, but I would like to see my office," she suggests with a wide smile. "You've given me a lot to digest and I'd like to know if there's a recliner where I can collapse without anyone seeing me."

The following day, a bright Thursday, Mark has a noontime lunch with everyone at Ridgefield, after which he asks them to remain seated for a few announcements. "Jen, this doesn't concern you," Mark tells her, "so go to my office and have a seat on the lounge chair."

As Mark watches his golden lab walk to his office, he says, "Wish everyone was as obedient as you." He removes a pad from his shirt pocket, glances at the first page and pauses to take a deep breath before continuing.

"Abigail has handled everything in my absence better than expected," he tells them, "and will become CEO of Ridgefield. It's important for me to spend more time with Ruth during her pregnancy. Then there's the responsibility of taking care of my mother and running the steel mill at Sparrows Point. We have about 10 employees here, but Bethlehem Steel has over a thousand. Furthermore, Lois Carnegie has agreed to join the board of BS and will take over most of the administrative responsibilities. That should give me some time to discover another good painting at the auctions or inside dusty antique shops. My art business has been floundering."

The following Wednesday morning at 7:30, Ruth and Mark are walking the aisles inside Dixon's auction at Crumpton, where they're prepared to buy the furniture needed for their three-bedroom home under construction.

As he peruses the aisles in a far section of the hangar, she maneuvers herself into a position near the auctioneer, Albert Hobbs, and prepares to bid on a painting she spotted on one of the tables. It's approximately 48 x 44 inches, of a beautiful young lady in a long dress with a low-cut bodice and a red ribbon around her neck. The model has an alluring smile below a lovely wide-brimmed hat decorated with flowers that match her dress. Hanging on the wall in the background of the painting is an antique tapestry, woven with a scene of an ancient English castle.

"I love the pose and the light reddish-orange color of her costume," Ruth tells herself. "Reminds me of the color of my Valentino wedding purse and shoes."

As she examines it one more time, Hobbs leans back in his chair atop a mobile cart and says, "Ah, now here's a beauty and remember: *If you snooze, you lose.*"

The bidding opens at $1,000 and Ruth exclaims "Luck be a lady today."

A minute later, after some furious bidding between three competitors, Hobbs shouts, "Sold for $3,000 to ...?"

"Mark Hopkins. Number 233," says Ruth. "I'm his wife."

"I think you got a bargain, Mrs. Hopkins," says Hobbs. "Tell Mark it was worth the money and a little too late to change your mind. When I say 'sold,' I mean 'sold.' You now own it!"

When Mark hears his name and number over the loud speaker, he walks briskly over to her and she gives him a big embrace.

"I had to have it," she tells him, with a kiss on the cheek, and ushers him away from the auction area. "She looked at me and her eyes followed me as I studied her face from different angles. It was hypnotic."

"Let's get it into our van as soon as possible to avoid any damage," says Mark.

"Being close to you for the past year or more has taught me a few things about collecting art," she tells him, opening an exit door of the hangar. "I think that the lady in the painting said, 'Take me home.' "

"A great painting," says Mark, "should stand on its own, and when you look at it, you admire and enjoy the composition and seldom think about the reputation of the artist. For me, I'd rather own a great work by a little known artist than a mediocre work by a great artist, if that makes any sense."

"I'll buy that," she tells him, kissing both of his cheeks.

Ten minutes later, Ruth is positioned near a different auctioneer, Dylan Dixon, whose about to sell quality furniture in another section of the hangar. With Mark standing at her side and encouraging her, she buys a Mason and Hamlin baby grand piano, circa 1935, in a French walnut case.

"I've always wanted to play the piano," she tells Mark with

exuberance, "and let others, such as Annette's husband, Richard, play it for parties and special occasions."

"Our van is getting fuller by the hour," says Mark, laughing, "but you have a keen eye for quality so whatever you're doing, keep at it."

A few hours later, Ruth is at the computer to find out any information about the artist, Mary Clay, who painted the portrait she just bought at the Crumpton auction.

"Well, *whataya* know?" she says to herself. "According to *Who's Who*, she was born into a well-to-do Philadelphia family and named after her aunt and her grandfather, John Randolph Clay, a diplomat. On her mother's side, she descended from the Livingston family of New York. Ah, there's more. Like many women artists of the time, she studied at the Pennsylvania Academy of Fine Arts, the first art school to accept women in this country. How about that!"

Suddenly, Liz appears in the doorway.

"Heard your excited voice," Liz declares. "What's going on?"

"I'm interested to see if there's any information about the artist who painted the painting I bought this afternoon," she says. "I have no regrets or buyer's remorse. I'm just curious if my intuition was good."

"I heard you also bought a baby grand," Liz says, putting one hand on her forehead like a mind-reader. "Congratulations. News, especially when it's good news, travels at light speed around here. We heard it through the grapevine, which means I'll bring my books of exercises from Peabody Institute in Baltimore where I studied as a teenager. But you'll have to find a good teacher, one who'll give you guidance and encouragement."

"How nice of you. Whenever you want a break from work, you're always welcome to come and play it."

"Music should play a role in everyone's life," says Liz. "It'll take your mind off your pregnancy, especially when you have morning sickness. By the way, I've never seen you look more beautiful and glowing."

"Compliments are always welcomed," says Ruth quickly. "Thank you."

Champagne bottles are popping inside the main house at Ridgefield to celebrate Thanksgiving and toast the upcoming arrival of Ruth's baby around Christmas. Music is blaring in the background from CDs chosen by Liz and Reggie for this special occasion. Gabby and Manny have prepared everything imaginable that goes with their 23 pound turkey baked in a bag, so all the juices are contained and gravy-ready.

Following dessert, Sandy taps her glass with a spoon and asks everyone to settle down for a special presentation.

"With your permission and indulgence," Sandy begins, "I'd like it known to everyone that Ruth has been posing for me whenever she could fit me into her schedule. And so, without further ado, here is my painting of Ruth."

Sandy walks over to a corner of the room where a painting is resting on an easel. She turns it around so everyone can see the front of it. It's a portrait of Ruth from her waist up, with two faces in profile, each facing one another but not mirror images. The colors are bright and bizarre, reminiscent of cubism and Picasso's technique of painting an outline around his images.

Sandy's painting is not based on any particular painting from Picasso's *oeuvre*. It's not his Blue or Pink period, but slightly earlier. Perhaps his teal and purple period of 1907-11, which marked the beginning of abstract art. Sandy, however, chose to paint Ruth's mouth, chin and cheeks white, forehead yellow, long hair black, with a blazing red hat angled downward.

"It's a painting that requires your attention and study," Sandy admits with a grin. "And I guarantee that you will change your mind each time you see it. It's like looking at a chameleon."

Ruth rushes over to give Sandy a kiss and a careful embrace since she's about four to five weeks away from full term.

"I like it. I really do," Ruth gushes. "And here's a surprise for you, for changing your schedule to accommodate me."

Sandy opens the beautifully wrapped box with a big iridescent blue ribbon and finds a bracelet inside.

"It's an original by Alexander Calder, in sterling silver," says Ruth. "The alternating letter 'U' reminded me of horseshoes and good luck. Best wishes from everyone here at Ridgefield, as you continue on your road to artistic success!"

Sandy is momentarily stunned but regains her senses, hugging both Ruth and Mark.

# Chapter 5

It's noon, Christmas Eve, inside the Birthing Center Ward of the Chester River Hospital. Beautiful ornaments are hung everywhere. In the waiting room two young men listen for their name to be called. Mark paces up and down, from a far window to the main corridor, as perspiration begins to form on his forehead. "Hope Jaime is not too much trouble for Abigail to look after," Mark says to himself. "Nice of her to assume the role of babysitter."

Sitting nearby, continuously combing his hair and giving all the nurses a wink, is Pretty Boy Floyd.

"Mark Hopkins?" the attending obstetrician, Dr. Bruce Rolf, calls out in a squeaky, timid voice.

Mark rushes over and looks down at his pink OBGYN surgeon's gown and smiling face.

"Your wife is almost ready to go into labor," says Dr. Rolf. "We'll try to make her as comfortable as possible."

Concurrently, an attractive nurse, about 23, walks into the waiting room and glances down at the clipboard in her hands.

"Maxwell Floyd?" she asks softly.

"That's me," Floyd answers, rising slowly out of his chair and combing his hair again. "I'm the only one left."

"You don't look eager to get the latest news," she acknowledges.

"It's complicated," he answers. "I have mixed feelings."

"Complicated? Your wife is the one having the baby."

Floyd drops his head to his chest and sighs at little. When she fails to get a more meaningful response from him, one way or the other, good or bad, she hesitates to get involved.

"I don't mean to probe," she blares out, "but is there anything I can do for you?"

"Not right now, Betty," he answers after glancing at her shapely figure and looking at the name on the badge pinned to the collar of her uniform. "She's not really my wife, and it may not be my baby she's having in there."

"Well, if I can be of any help, feel free to call me," she tells him in a low voice, taking a closer look at his handsome face. She notes his resemblance to Brad Pitt.

"Does that go for now or can I call you later?"

"Around noontime is best. I'm working the middle of the swing shift," she says with an enticing smile. "I'm in the phone book with a listing for my younger sister, Sally Youish. In the meantime, you better get comfortable. It might take a while."

She turns away and walks slowly toward the corridor and the main office of the ward.

"What in the world am I getting myself into, here?" she asks herself. "So he looks like Brad Pitt. Is sex so important? 'You bet it is,' says the devil in me."

"See you around," he bellows out, then does an about face and walks over to a window to watch the nurses parade in and out of the employee entrance.

"Hmmm, Betty Youish?" he asks himself. "I've heard of a pathologist named Dr. Youish, who did some DNA testing of my blood. I wonder if she could be his daughter. She certainly doesn't look like Youish. He was gaunt and five-foot five. She's gorgeous and five inches taller at least. Hmmm, I've always wanted to date a Youish girl."

Nurse Betty leaves the waiting room and walks down a long corridor when suddenly Dr. Footsie pops out of the doctor's lounge, with his stethoscope dangling around his neck.

"How's the handsome intern from *Down-Under*? " asks Nurse Betty, with frankness and familiarity.

"Not bad, really. I'm ready to throw another shrimp onto the *barbie*," he says, pronouncing the words with an Australian accent, "if you can fit me into your schedule."

"I'll raise the flag or fly a kite to let you know when it's safe to drop by," she tells him with a laugh. "By the way, your zipper is down again. You Aussie's are getting more absent-minded every day, I think."

The 23-year-old twin nurses, Betty, the oldest by three minutes, and Sally Youish, are daughters of the chief pathologist and graduates of Kent County High in Worton. They later studied nursing for two years at Chesapeake College in Wye, Maryland, and are renting a house in Chestertown, only minutes away from the Chester River Hospital.

The twins' ticking biological clock seems to grow stronger with each passing year. After working 40 hours a week in the birthing center and helping so many expectant mothers suffer through labor and give birth, they want to experience it, too. And each is independent enough to have their child out of wedlock, like so many of their classmates at Kent High. They are filled with both confidence and anxiety, and have no second thoughts or reservations about what it takes to raise a child. There's no rivalry between them. In fact, over the past year they've both dated the handsome young intern from Australia and enjoyed playing tricks on him as to who's who. Dr. Footsie really doesn't care which is which.

The conversation between Betty and Dr. Footsie is interrupted by the footsteps of Dr. Rolf coming out of the obstetrics operating room and walking across the waiting room to greet Pretty Boy Floyd.

"Mr. Floyd, it's a boy! One of my best deliveries," says Dr. Rolf with a smile. "Your wife has given birth to a baby boy, an ounce less than nine pounds, to be precise. Congratulations. Better sit down before you fall down."

"I always wanted a son," he tells Dr. Rolf. "Bonnie said that it would be a son and we'll name him 'Les Paul,' after the legendary guitarist."

Nurse Betty reverses her direction and walks back to the waiting room.

"Congratulations, Mr. Floyd," Betty tells him with a wide smile across her face. "Doctor Rolf will tell you when it's time to see Bonnie and your baby."

About an hour later, Dr. Rolf smiles as he approaches Mark, pacing the hallway.

"It's a girl, one of my best deliveries, an ounce under eight pounds to be exact," he tells him. "Mother and child are doing well. Give us twenty minutes, then you can go in and see them. Congratulations and best wishes."

Mark lets out an Ozinie war whoop, thrusts two fists upward then hugs Dr. Rolf and swings him around in a circle. "I can't believe it. Did you say that mother and child are safe and well?"

After being reassured by Dr. Rolf again, Mark raises his head upward and says, "Thanks be to God."

A half-hour later Mark is comforting Ruth in the recovery room. "This is the best day of my life," she says, smiling and clutching his hand.

"This *is* the best day our life," Mark says lovingly. "Now Jaime will have a younger sister to play with. We'll call her 'Baby Ruth,' if that's O.K. with you."

About an hour later, Dr. Rolf appears again in the waiting room, looks around to find Floyd, who's still combing his hair and staring at the nurses through the second-story window.

"You can go in to see Bonnie and your baby, Mr. Floyd," he tells him. "How does it feel to be a father of a baby boy?"

"I'm at a loss for words," he tells him.

"Well, words are not important now," Dr. Rolf tells him. "Just go in and comfort your wife. That was a big baby for a little lady. Congratulations again and best wishes."

Pretty Boy Floyd enters Bonnie's room in the maternity ward and finds her wide awake and energized. "I think I've been touched by God just as I reached for the door knob and walked in here. Something has clicked in my mind; images of you and a baby. It would be the right thing for the baby to have a legitimate father and for you to have a husband to care for you. I never thought of saying it before but it's time for me to settle down and take some responsibility; otherwise one day I'm going to wake up and find myself alone, with no money in the bank or even a soft-crab business to run."

"And so what have you decided?" asks Bonnie.

"To marry you. There I've said it, my first proposal, and if you want me to get down on one knee, I will."

"Oh, that's not necessary. Are you sure that's what you really want for yourself?"

"Yeah, and it doesn't make any difference if the baby you're holding in your arms is mine or Bud's. As far as I'm concerned, it's my baby."

"Blood tests are required as part of the marriage application," admits Bonnie, "so sooner or later, we'll know who his father is."

Two weeks later, while nursing her baby at home, she receives a call from the lab that ran the tests to compare her baby's DNA with that of Bud and Pretty Boy. It comes as no surprise when she's told that it matches Bud Wayne, now behind bars in prison for 22 years. Everyone in town knew that she was sleeping with Bud and Pretty Boy whenever it was convenient.

"Sooner or later, he'll ask me about the results of blood tests," she tells herself reluctantly, "so I might as well get the truth out now, in case he changes his mind about marrying me."

"As far as I'm concerned," says Pretty Boy, after hearing the news, "that doesn't change a damn thing. I'm ready to settle down."

Meanwhile at Ridgefield, Mark and Ruth are in heaven on earth, as proud as can be, bragging to anyone willing to listen to their plans for their children.

"Did you see the way Jaime is playing with his toy? Looks like a right-hander to me, and you know how valuable pitchers are as big leaguers," he boasts. "I wonder when Dr. Rolf will give me permission to begin exercises to build up his muscles. I can't wait to hear Rex Barney Jr. announce over the loud speakers at Oriole Park, 'Give that kid a contract.'"

"For God sake, Mark, Jaime's only two years old," says Ruth. "Aren't you rushing things a bit?"

"I also noticed how strong Baby Ruth's fingers are when she gripped my hand," he says.

"All babies grab and hold on," says Ruth. "I love the way she giggles."

"All babies will giggle if you tickle them," says Mark, reaching over to tickle Ruth's waist. "Even big babies like you will giggle if touched in the right place."

"I'd like her to take piano lessons if she has an inclination for music. She'll be the first artist in our family."

"Do you think Jaime will be as tall as me?" he asks. "Wonder when I should start him on sports?"

"Why not arrange for Manny to photograph them?" she asks him. "Never too early to start a photo album with their finger and foot prints. I wonder when I can begin to teach them the letters of the alphabet."

On February 3, Mark is at the computer browsing the news of the day with Ruth peering over his shoulder. "Well, how about that?" he says.

"How about what?" asks Ruth with mild curiosity. "Did the Orioles sign a new Brooks Robinson to play third base?"

"How do you know about Brooks Robinson?"

"Everyone who was ever born on the eastern shore knows

about Brooks and considers him the greatest player to ever wear an Orioles uniform."

"I was referring to Punxsutawney Phil, the groundhog of Western Pennsylvania, who saw his shadow as he emerged from his burrow yesterday. It means winter will last six more weeks."

"Just how accurate is Punxsutawney Phil?"

"I'm guessing he's almost as good a prognosticator as Greta and her horoscope," he answers, laughing when he sees the video of this fat and colorful groundhog emerging from his burrow.

A week later, Womble pulls his chair up to Mark's desk and notices the way he's massaging Jen's neck with one hand and scrolling through emails in his in-box with the other. "Ambidextrous, aren't you?" asks Womble with a grin. "But I think you can put both of your hands to better use."

"How?"

"By probing into a probate in Philadelphia."

"Go on," Mark answers, logging off the computer but continuing to massage Jen's neck.

"A probate attorney and former classmate from Wharton called me because he knew I was out of work and might want to get into the business of cleaning out vacant properties in and around Philadelphia. He said that several antique dealers and auction houses have already combed this former dealer's business, Windsor Gallery, on Chestnut Street. But no one would venture into the cellar, where rats and spiders have run freely for 40 years.

"I recognized the dealer's name, Bernard 'Bernie' Feuerstein, who resided in a high rise overlooking Rittenhouse Square, lived to be 95, and made a good living, primarily with Philadelphia Main Line clients of the Hebrew faith. I met him a few times and felt his life would make a good Disney film; even walked with him through the gardens in the Square, where he called out the names of squirrels and fed them nuts."

Mark has a hunch, similar to the one he had two years ago that led him to a dusty antiques shop on Howard Street in

Baltimore and the discovery of an impressionistic painting by the nineteenth-century Finnish artist, Albert Edelfelt.

"If I can arrange to get a couple of my *Betterton Breeze* boys to help out," Mark tells him with a cunning grin on his face, "I'll rent a box truck and drive to *Philly*. From what you've told me so far, it looks like an opportunity that I shouldn't pass up. Tell the probate attorney we have a deal, then get back to me with a specific time to meet him there and start the clean-out."

Two days later, Mark parks his box truck in an alley behind Windsor Gallery on Chestnut Street. Within ten minutes, he and two of his *Betterton Breeze* track stars look like spacemen in their protective HAZMAT gear, with masks and a bright flashlight mounted on their helmets.

"There's never a good time to be scrounging around and cleaning out a cellar," he tells them, "but now's as good a time as ever, since it's cold and the rats and spiders won't be moving around too much. Get everything you can into the boxes as carefully as possible, just as I explained on the way here from Rock Hall. Try not to drop anything and if you do, don't walk on top of it. OK, let's get cracking!"

Within three hours they've managed to clean out the basement full of old furniture, dusty picture frames, moldy art works and dilapidated boxes of records.

Mac Speedie, the tallest of the *Breeze* team, sneezes twice as he emerges out of the cellar and into daylight. After raising his hand to wipe his nose, he begins to laugh at himself.

"I plum forgot about the mask," Speedie tells Mark. "Guess I'll simply have to wait to blow my nose after you give the O.K. to remove it."

"It's a good thing that you explained what to do during our drive up from Rock Hall," admits Jesse James, the smallest but fastest runner of the *Breeze* team. "Everything went exactly as you planned it, didn't it?"

"Now, you see why planning is important, even on little jobs like this one," Mark says. "Remember what I told you long ago about 'Plan your work before you work your plan?' In that cleanout, I also saw some asbestos falling off those rusty pipes, but we were protected and took the necessary precautions."

After Mark gives the cellar one final inspection to make certain everything is transferred into their box truck, he gives the signal that it's safe to remove their HAZMAT gear and place it in individual heavy-duty contractor bags with their own name written on an adhesive label applied to it.

Mark sees the probate attorney in the rear doorway with a smile on his face and rubbing his thumb and two fingers together, a sign to come forward with the money for the cleanout.

"You wanted $250, so that's what you're getting in cash," Mark tells the attorney. "Give me a signed receipt, please. You should be paying me $250 for hauling all this junk out of the cellar so that you can show the building properly when it's auctioned next week. By the way, there's still a lot of rodents living down there. Might be a good idea to call in the pest-control people. You certainly don't want them climbing the stairs to see the auction, too. Plus it looks like asbestos covering some of the pipes."

When everything is transported to Ridgefield, Mark invites all his employees to wear protective masks and gloves and help him sort out anything that looks worthwhile from the junk. In the middle of all this clutter, Mark discovers a painting on plywood, about 30 x 40 inches that Abigail and Sandy both grab out of his hands before he can open his mouth.

"Looks like someone splattered paint all over it," exclaims Sandy.

"Or dripped paint all over it," acknowledges Abigail.

"You're right on the money," answers Mark as he watches the expressions on their faces. "My intuition tells me it could be an original by Jackson Pollock, which means a lot of research is required for confirmation. If it's a Pollock, it could be worth millions."

"I'll be happy to volunteer for this investigation," says Abigail.

"Something is urging me to take on this project. It's the same feeling I experienced when looking through your files at photos of the jeweled dagger you brought back from Iraq. Who would have suspected that it would be an historical treasure which I eventually sold for $500,000?"

"Only you, my dear," says Mark with a chuckle. "By the look on your face, your intuition is shifting again into overdrive. Thanks for volunteering. When you're hot to trot, you're very hot to trot. It's all yours."

Around the first week of March Mark is conferring with Abigail inside his office as Womble hesitates near the doorway. He's talking excitedly on his cell phone with Dave Montgomery, his classmate from Wharton and current president of the Philadelphia Phillies. "I have a pretty good prospect for your club," he explains. "Not ready for the big leagues, but in a few years, who knows what can happen?"

"We can't afford to look at anyone that our scouts haven't already seen and documented," Montgomery yells back. "Since the kid's from Maryland, try Jack Dunn Jr., owner of the Baltimore Orioles. He's always looking for home-grown talent. Our finances are already strained and you know it takes thousands of dollars to invest in a 'walk-on' in the Class A Rookie League. You've caught me at a bad time with spring training about to begin in Florida."

A few days later, Chubby Bender is standing inside the office of Jack Dunn Jr., the 70-year old owner and president of the Baltimore Orioles. It's located on the top floor of an eight-story brick building, which was converted from a grain warehouse into a block-long commercial high-rise along the right field line of Oriole Park at Camden Yards, near the Inner Harbor of Baltimore.

As Mr. Dunn appears on the verge of ending his phone call, he motions Chubby to come closer to his desk. Somewhat nervous, Chubby picks up a 4-inch high porcelain figure off the owner's desk and notices the resemblance to Mr. Dunn. The bald, heavy-set man is carrying an advertising billboard strapped over his shoulders: the front sign, angling out over his beer belly reads 'If at first you don't succeed;' the back sign, protruding over his large rear end, reads 'Sue the Bastards.'

Chubby puts it back carefully in the exact same spot. Since Mr. Dunn is still talking over the telephone, he wanders over to a window with a view of the baseball diamond from right field and tries to imagine what it would be like to play professional baseball in Oriole Park at Camden Yards.

"Womble tells me that you want to be a catcher. Why a catcher?" asks Mr. Dunn, hanging up the phone with a thud.

Before Chubby can answer his question, Dunn looks at the calendar on his desk, tears off a page so that the calendar now reads March 1 and pulls the suspenders away from his chest, letting them snap back. It's a habit he picked up from his father who ran the club in the 50's.

Chubby has some difficulty finding the best way to begin his interview and hesitates a few seconds more. Dunn leaves his seat, walks over and spins him around to measure his height from his backside. As Dunn stretches out his tape measure, Chubby begins bouncing a baseball off a wall and glancing at some photos of personnel who played a prominent role in the history of the Orioles.

"Tomorrow," he continues before Chubby can answer his question, "I'll be heading south to Fort Lauderdale where the *Oryuls* will open spring training at our newly renovated complex."

Dunn grabs the ball in midair before it can strike the wall a third time.

"Careful, kid. You don't want to knock any of those framed photos off their hooks. *Wanta* know something about the history of the *Oryuls?*"

"They all look serious," says Chubby.

"The top row: our managers starting in 1954 with Jimmy Dykes, Paul Richards, Earl Weaver, all the way up to Buck Showalter," he says, pointing at each photo along the row.

"And the bottom row?"

"General Managers, starting with Art Ehlers, Harry Dalton, and others leading up to Andy MacPhail."

Mr. Dunn senses that Chubby's anxious to talk about his chances of getting a tryout with the Baltimore Orioles, not discussing history. "What makes you think you can be a catcher?" he continues. "Look at yourself in the mirror over there. Stocky catchers like Jimmy Foxx, Yogi Berra and Roy Campanella are out. Today it's 'lean and mean,' a build like Buster Cody of the San Francisco Giants. Just because you hit .320 down at *Chesspeak College* on the eastern shore of *Murlin,* doesn't mean that you have the talent for a career in baseball."

"My coach at *Chesspeake* used me as a catcher and reliever. Good arm and a pretty good knuckleball, too," boasts Chubby, who smiles for the first time inside Dunn's office.

"Don't remember any of our scouts mentioning your name. Did you tell me you played in Easton? Who'd you play for there? What's the name of your ball club?" Dunn asks a succession of quick questions.

"The *Clams.*" replies Chubby, smiling and pulling his ear like a third-base coach giving the signal to bunt.

"*Clams?* Never heard of them either. That's a *helluva* name for a ball club."

"That's probably because they changed the name recently," says Chubby.

"What was it before?"

"*Ursters.* But that name never really stuck with anyone, except the people who love those salty, slimy Chincoteague Island *ursters,* loaded with iron and slurped down raw on the half shell."

"My intuition tells me you should go back home and find another line of work," he declares, putting his oversize hands on the kid's shoulders.

"When Womble arranged for you to see me, I thought you'd at least hear me out before tossing me out," Chubby answers. "Ever since I can remember pitching a baseball to my Dad on the

Eastern Shore of *Murlin*, long before he lost a leg in combat, all I ever wanted to do was play baseball for the *Oryuls*. I don't know what other kind of work I can do."

Mr. Dunn ignores the telephone ringing on his desk as Chubby wipes some perspiration from his brow and takes a step backward.

"You're not God Almighty, Mr. Dunn," he continues, "You could be wrong about me. You know nothing about my will power and my knuckleball. All I'm asking for is a tryout."

"I'm doing you a favor, son, trying to spare you some pain and suffering," he says, pulling down a screen that shows the entire roster of the Baltimore Orioles Class A, double-A, triple-A, and big-league personnel. "You remind me a little of Don Zimmer, who came to my father 50 years ago looking for a job as a catcher. My father told him, and I'm telling you, there's no way in hell for you to crash into our farm system as a catcher. We've got 23-year old Matt Wieters behind the plate right now in the majors, with bonus babies at Triple A, Double A and….you want me to go on?"

He pauses and releases the screen that rolls up faster than a window blind and gives a loud noise while spinning and coming eventually to an abrupt stop.

"Just where in the hell do you think I can put your name?" he declares, biting his tongue. "Now, look what you've made me do, bite my tongue. Give it up, kid. It can't be done."

"It's in my blood, sir, I can't give it up. It's something I've dreamed about all my life."

"Then go back home and forget about being a catcher. Trade in your catcher's mitt for a pitcher's glove. Pitching is the fastest way to the big leagues. Managers need at least 10 pitchers on a team. That way you might have a better chance. Try to stretch your frame. How tall are you anyway?"

"Five feet nine inches."

"*Whataya* weigh?"

"About 215 pounds."

"How old did you say you are?" asks Dunn, scratching the few remaining hairs on his almost bald head.

"Nineteen."

"Stretch your frame another two inches and transform twenty pounds of fat into muscle. When you're close to six feet tall and can throw your fast ball at least 92 on the radar gun, maybe even knock over the catcher, send me a video so I can see your mechanics. I don't care if you can't throw it over the plate. Neither could Sandy Koufax when the scouts first saw him. If I like what I see, we'll give you a tryout with the Daytona Beach *Islanders*, our affiliate in the Class-A Rookie League. You have my word on it."

A tear begins to form in the kid's eyes, clearly visible to Mr. Dunn.

"That's all the time I can give you. Now get *outta* here," he says, pushing the kid out of his office with a pat on the back.

An hour later, Chubby is driving his jalopy over the Chesapeake Bay Bridge, about 40 miles away from Easton, a town of 15,000, where they measure progress with a sundial. The good part about living in this town is that almost everyone loves baseball and strives to know all the players on the local team. Ballplayers like Chubby never have to buy a meal at a restaurant because someone always wants to help a kid out and brag that they knew him on his way up to the big leagues.

It doesn't take long for Chubby to begin a backyard routine of wind sprints, sit-ups, push-ups, and stretches outlined in a manual of basic training his father gave him. He's determined to prove to Mr. Dunn that he has what it takes to be a pro for the *Oryuls,* looking for their next 20-game winner.

During his workouts he recalls stories about another 'good ole farm boy' from the Eastern Shore of Maryland, William Beck Nicholson, nicknamed *Billy Nick* by friends and *Swish* by teammates because of the sound his bat made when he swung at a pitch. Nicholson was lucky when a Philadelphia Athletics scout Ira Thomas gave a talk at Washington College and hung around to watch him play centerfield and knock the cover off the ball for the *Shoremen* in 1935.

The following year, 1936, Nicholson signed to play for Cornelius McGillicuddy, better known as "Connie Mack." When he initially failed to live up to Mack's expectations, the Athletics traded him to the Chicago Cubs, where he developed into a fearsome hitter. Near the end of his career, he played for the Philadelphia Phillies, his last game being in September of 1953. But people from the eastern shore of Maryland, particularly those who love baseball, always gave *Swish* the status of a legend in his own time. After he died, friends from Chestertown installed a bronze statue of him outside the Visitor Center.

But Chubby knows that no scout ever watched him pitch, so he'll have to be patient, prepared to undergo six-months of aggressive training and act as his own agent to promote himself.

"First things first," he tells himself, and begins a strict regimen of calisthenics and diet to reshape his body and become the kind of pitcher Mr. Dunn is looking for.

Two weeks after his interview with Mr. Dunn Jr., Chubby is brought to Ridgefield by his father and introduced to Mark. They hit it off immediately because Chubby's resolve and tenacity remind Mark of his *Betterton Breeze* runners. Even Jen has found a new friend as she sneaks between them and jumps uncharacteristically to put her paws on Chubby's chest.

"That's a good sign, Chubby," Mark tells him. "If Jen likes you, it's good enough for me. You have permission to use the indoor pitching mound behind the laboratory. Womble will be your contact man if you need anything. He's arranged for you to practice under the guidance of two instructors. Everything we're doing for you is in recognition and appreciation of your father and the risks he took as a medic in Vietnam."

After running his usual sprints and stretching exercises in tattered sweat pants and shirt, Chubby walks into the indoor batting cage and pitching mound for his first meeting with instructors that Womble has hired.

"Pay attention to what Jim tells you," says Hoyt Wilhelm, a lean, five-foot eight-inch, 65-year old former Orioles reliever. "Jim Honochick was one of the best umpires in the majors for almost 25 years and probably has seen more pitchers than any coach in the big leagues. He'll analyze your mechanics to make sure you have a fluid motion, with minimum stress on your shoulder and elbow."

"And listen to what Hoyt tells you, too," says Honochick, a smiling five-foot, ten-inch, 65-year-old with a kid still bouncing around inside his overweight body. "He was one of the best relievers in the big leagues and is in the Hall of Fame, all because of his knuckleball."

"When it comes to throwing it," Hoyt advises, "remember at least two things. First is the grip of the ball. Let your fingernails grow and keep them filed so you can dig into the cowhide and stitches of the ball. Second is your arm speed and angle. Try to throw your ball with the same arm speed as a fast ball, but vary your arm angle and release point. Don't rush it and, *heavens to Betsy,* don't look for quick results. It'll take about eight to twelve months for your fingers to get comfortable and, with that comfort, comes the confidence you can throw it over and around the plate. The ball will become alive and move in unexpected directions. It takes on a life of its own."

"You'll know if you're making progress," Honochick interjects, "when those hitters begin to fume and curse you on the way back to the dugout."

Chubby can't wait any longer to take the mound and begins throwing his knuckleball toward an old mattress wired to the wall about three feet behind home plate. After he throws about a dozen balls, he races Jen to see who can get to the mattress first, so both get a good workout in running short sprints. This exercise will also help Chubby when it comes to fielding bunts.

"One final thing, kid," Hoyt tells Chubby after a solid hour of work, "raw talent will take you only so far. Then it's what you have inside your heart and mind that counts. Always remember, when you come to the ballpark, come ready to play and give everything you have until the last out of the game."

A few days after the first of April, Liz taps her glass of water with a spoon to quiet down everyone at the conclusion of breakfast inside the main house at Ridgefield.

"We've been waiting for the right time to unload some news," Liz tells them. "In short, I've always wanted to be a June bride, and Reggie is making my dream come true. We're going to be married on the first Saturday in June."

"Didn't know you were even engaged!" exclaims Kim. "Talk about secrecy. I've been working at your side for over a year and never knew it."

"Neither did I until last night when Reggie proposed," Liz admits joyfully.

"And where's the blessed event to take place?" asks Sandy.

"Not far from where you're sitting now. With Mark's approval, we'll have the wedding ceremony and reception next door on the small sound stage. That will make it easy for everyone to attend and share this special day with us. And after the reception, we'll honeymoon aboard Reggie's yacht and explore the coast of Virginia."

"It seems as if you borrowed a page out of Mark and Ruth's playbook," Abigail says with a chuckle.

"You're right, as usual," says Liz, then turns to address the entire group. "Better dust off your western wardrobe because we'd like to have everyone wear outfits from the film *The Misfits*. Now, if any of you feel inspired enough to imitate Clark Gable and Marilyn Monroe, we'll keep you in mind when it comes time to cast actors for our film project. Dress in casual clothes unless you want to show off your *bod* and wear tight-fitting denim jeans and blouses."

"I doubt if anyone can ever look like Marilyn, can they?" asks Sandy.

"You can, if you put your mind to it," Liz tells Sandy. "But one thing's for sure. We're going to have ourselves, as Reggie told me, 'a *hoot-hoot-hootenanny* of a wedding.' "

In no time, it's the first Saturday of June and everyone is gathered around the stage of Ridgefield's R&D Lab.

"It's Showtime for Liz and Reggie," Mark Mumford declares in a baritone voice. "Many of you know me as Clerk of the Circuit Court of Kent County. Today, however, I'm here as Justice of the Peace to administer the bonds of matrimony."

An organist begins playing the Wedding March as Liz Carter, dressed in an original Yves St. Laurent western blouse and skirt, is escorted by her father to the front of the stage where her fiancé, Reggie Perdue, adjusts his turquoise and silver squash blossom over an iridescent-gold shirt. Standing beside him is his famous father, the founder of Perdue Farms, who keeps gazing back and forth at the wedding rings in his hand and Liz coming down the aisle.

"Dearly Beloved," Mumford says, "we are gathered here today to witness the bonds of matrimony between this handsome man and this beautiful woman. If anyone can show 'just cause' why this union shall not occur, let them come forth now or forever bury their cause along the shores of the Chesapeake Bay."

Mumford pauses to survey the crowd. "Do you, Liz Carter," he asks, "take Reggie Perdue, to be your lawful wedded husband, to have and to hold from this day forward, for better, for worse, for richer, for poorer, in sickness and health, to love and to cherish, until death do you part?"

"I do," answers Liz.

"Do you, Reggie Perdue," asks Mumford, "take Liz Carter, to be your lawful wedded wife and consent to the same vows?"

"I do," answers Reggie, moving his right hand over his heart.

"And now, Reggie, you may place the wedding ring on your bride's finger," says Mumford.

"With this ring I thee wed," Reggie tells her.

"And now, Liz, you may place the wedding ring on Reggie's finger," says Mumford.

"With this ring I thee wed," Liz tells him, squeezing his hands tightly.

"You have declared your consent to be married," says Mumford, taking a short step forward. "May the Good Lord strengthen your consent and fill you both with his blessings. What God has joined, let no one divide. The bonds of matrimony are complete and official. You may now kiss each other."

"We've come a long way together in a very short time," says Reggie, "and it's just the start of a beautiful friendship."

"I feel the same way, "Liz tells him, "and I know it's going to last a lifetime."

After the ceremony, a section of about 2,000 square feet is ready for the reception and buffet that Manny has prepared for everyone. The bride and groom have made it clear that everything from this point forward will be 'informality personified.' That means no special toasts unless someone rings a cowbell on stage.

The buffet includes heated trays of broiled Maryland crab cakes, soft crabs sautéed in butter and chardonnay wine, baby shrimp in a light cream sauce rolled into fajitas, and chicken tenders provided by the groom's father, the biggest chicken farmer in Maryland.

When it comes time to cut the wedding cake, Liz and Reggie are asked to say a few words.

"Many of you wanted to know when I first realized that Reggie was the man for me," Liz tells them. "It was not instantaneous as you might suspect. I first fell in love with his music and the way he played the guitar. Before I knew it, he was pulling the strings of my heart and I was singing *Zing Went the Strings of My Heart*."

"As you know, I'm a man of few words and will let my music do the talking for me," says Reggie, tightening the grip around his wife's waist. "Oh boy, even my wife is in for a surprise here: A good friend, who is still winning admirers after almost 50 years in the music business, and with whom I've had the pleasure of recording his songs, has driven here from Nashville, where he's made another blockbuster album. He celebrated his 75th birthday recently, but doesn't look a day over 39. His name is John Royce, better known as Johnny Mathis."

Behind a curtain, Johnny Mathis walks out and quickly announces, "Country music. It's a first for me and my long time guitarist, Gil Reigers. But I'd like Reggie to join us on stage for a medley of country-western ballads, starting with *Crazy,* followed by *I Can't Stop Lovin' You,* and ending with *Love me Tender.* Reggie's father wanted me to change the name to 'Love My Chicken Tenders'!"

When Mark hears Johnny's rendition of *Crazy,* tears begin to roll down his cheeks.

"That was the song Reggie sang at my father's funeral two years ago," he tells Ruth.

For his encore and closing number, Mathis chooses to sing the chorus of *Time After Time,* written by Sammy Cahn and Jule Styne in 1947, which became one of Frank Sinatra's biggest hits.

*"Time after time I tell myself that I'm so lucky to be loving you, so lucky to be the one you run to see in the evening, when the day is through, I only know what I know, the passing years will show, you've kept my love so young, so new, and time after time, you'll hear me say that I'm so lucky to be loving you."*

After Johnny Mathis' performance ends, everyone walks the bride and groom to the *rip-rap* along the shoreline of Ridgefield Farm where a yacht awaits them and the beginning of their honeymoon. A few minutes later, Ruth and Mark are alone and gazing at the sunset over the Chesapeake Bay when a spirit, in the form of a white-bearded Rabbi in an iridescent gold robe, rises close to shore and stretches out his arms.

"Moses? Are you there, Moses? For heaven's sake, where in the hell, ah world, are you?" the spirit asks.

"As I told you before and I'll tell you again," Mark shouts

with his hands cupping his mouth like a megaphone, "there's no Moses here."

"You must be Mark and Ruth," he says in a baritone voice that reverberates over the waves. "Congratulations on your marriage and best wishes from the Spirit of the Chesapeake Bay. Actually, I'm here as protector to remind you about following up on that canister of mustard gas from Aberdeen."

In a flash of white light, the spirit plunges downward into the Bay and disappears with a gurgling sound.

Two weeks into the New Year, Sandy and York announce their engagement at breakfast inside the main house of Ridgefield.

"We haven't set a date for the marriage yet, but June would suit me just fine," Sandy boasts, tugging at York's arm. "We've decided on Rome as our honeymoon destination. It's called the *Eternal City,* and for a good reason. It's a place where architects, artists and sculptors, from Michelangelo to Rembrandt Bugatti, have studied and prospered."

"By the look on your faces," replies York, "our announcement doesn't seem to come as a big surprise. It must be something in the Chesapeake Bay that helps so many people find love here at Ridgefield."

# Chapter 6

The Tuesday following Labor Day is hot and humid with temperatures reaching 100 degrees and a humidity of 70 percent. After Mark, Kim and Liz arrive at Edgewood Arsenal of Aberdeen Proving Ground (APG), they are ushered into the office of Captain Ira Rook, a 26-year old West Point grad.

"You're in the Fifth District, Kent County, aren't you?," he asks. "Let me know if you need any help with your projects. I've got political clout to spare."

"Is that you standing beside Governor O'Malley and Senator Mikulski?" Mark asks him, taking a close look at one of the photographs on the walls of his office.

"Yes" answers Rook, stretching his head like a crowing rooster. "Influence peddlers. Doesn't hurt to have a few politicians in your back pocket, actually my father's back pocket. Amazing what doors can be opened when the right hands are greased. I didn't get to be Captain Rook on my good looks. We military men have to stick together, don't we?"

"Cozy relations," Mark says to himself, wiping his hands with his handkerchief because of oily sweat from Captain Rook's hand when he first greeted him. "Being promoted to the rank of Captain by the age of 26 is one thing, but responsible for inventory of all munitions stored at Edgewood Arsenal is hard to fathom, especially for a SEAL."

"Just call me Ira," Rook tells them as he takes a seat behind his desk. "I was named after Ira Gershovitz." When he sees the puzzled look on Kim's face, he continues, "He was a cashier in his father's Turkish bathhouse in New York, later dropped out of CCNY and started writing lyrics to his brother's music. You must've heard of Ira Gershwin?"

"You mean the older brother of George?" asks Liz.

"Yes," answers Rook, nodding his head proudly. "They changed their name from Gershovitz after immigrating from St. Petersburg and George's name looked better on the marquee when spelled *GERSHWIN.*"

Mark scratches his head and pulls his ear lobe as a strange look crosses his face. His intuition tells him that he may be in the presence of a rascal or a varmint. "He's good with the chatter," he whispers to Liz, "but doesn't give the impression of a military officer responsible for ammunition, including canisters of mustard gas, stored at APG."

"Or someone anxious to discuss the deployment of our electronic buoy off the shore of Edgewood Arsenal," whispers Kim, overhearing Mark's comment.

"If any of you want a picture of yourself posing with the president, just let me know," say Rook boastfully. "I know a graphic artist that can air-brush a cutout of the president and insert you into the computerized photo."

"Let's get right to the point, if you don't mind," Mark tells him, handing him the canister. "This was found on the beach of Ridgefield farm, a few miles outside the town of Rock Hall."

"Where in the hell is Rock Hall?" Rook asks nervously.

"On the upper eastern shore of the Chesapeake Bay. It's similar to the ones we used in Iraq to smoke out terrorists from their underground caves."

"Hmmm. Interesting," answers Rook, pronouncing

each syllable slowly. "We'll have to study the markings very carefully."

Unexpectedly, Rook's cell phone, attached to his waist, rings and he retreats to a corner of his office to take the call.

"I'll get right on it, sir," he declares in crisp words, then turns to face Mark. "I've been called away for another meeting."

"At least have a look at the code on the canister. It reads ECBC-APG-HN1. The first four digits mean it came from Edgewood Arsenal. We've driven two hours to meet with you, not only about the canister, but also to discuss our proposal for an electronic buoy to detect pollutants in the Bay. Aberdeen would be the perfect spot to install one of our buoys, since it's common knowledge that workers from Edgewood Arsenal deposited waste products from the manufacture of bombs, beginning in the 1930's."

"Any further talk will have to wait for another time," Rook says abruptly. "Orders are orders and I have to get cracking."

"In that case, I'd like a receipt," says Mark. "Isn't there someone else we can talk to?"

"I'll have my orderly prepare a receipt for you. And no, there's no one else available on such short notice. I'll get back here as soon as I can."

After 15 minutes cooped up inside Captain Rook's office, they look at each other with anger mounting inside them.

"We've waited long enough," Mark declares. "I've looked at all the photos lining the walls of his office twice. Let's check with his orderly."

"Receipt?" asks the orderly with a puzzled look and timid squeaky voice when confronted by Mark. "I'm sorry, but I don't know what you're talking about. Captain Rook never said anything to me before rushing away."

"Let's not waste any more time," says Liz to Mark and Sandy, then turns to the orderly with a look of exasperation. "Tell Captain Rook to call us at Ridgefield. Here's our business card. We'll expect a response within 24 hours."

The following day, Mark is on the phone with Captain Rook, who is surprised by his call.

"I seem to recollect," says Rook, "you wanted to discuss something about an electronic buoy to detect pollutants in the Bay. I never saw a canister. You must be imagining things."

Mark is shocked and hangs up the phone, arching his body as if someone just stabbed him in his back.

Liz pokes her head through the doorway of his office and notices the anger on his face.

"I was just about to summon you," Mark says and gives her a quick replay of his conversation with Rook. 'Something's gone haywire here."

"Let me look into this situation with my former superior, Colonel James Raymond Spencer, director of Crisis Management for Military Affairs (CMMA)," says Liz, still in shock by Rook's behavior. "He'll know how we should proceed in this matter."

Within the next 10 minutes, Liz is speaking on the telephone with Colonel Spencer inside his office at the Pentagon.

"I'm not passing the buck here, just following protocol," he tells her, making a notation of her call in his daily journal. "You should contact the Inspector General and Judge Advocate General's Offices immediately. You can use my name as a referral, too."

With Liz's efficiency and knowledge of government protocol, she is able to cut through a lot of red tape. Within the hour, she's on a conference call with officers representing the Attorney General and Judge Advocate at Aberdeen Proving Ground.

"Send us a written report outlining the facts in this case, in triplicate," says an assistant to the Inspector General.

"If what you say is true, and I'm not doubting for an instance your account of the canister," answers an aide to the Judge Advocate, "this appears to be a crisis in the making."

Realizing how documents get easily mishandled or misfiled, Liz asks each officer for a personal appointment, at which time she will hand them a written report.

Two days later, Liz, Kim and Mark are seated at an oval table inside a small conference room at Aberdeen Proving Ground and facing representatives of the Inspector General and Judge Advocate's office.

"It's not our intention to take down an officer in the military," Mark declares forcefully. "We want only to know how the canister of mustard gas, with the markings shown in this photo, left its storage facility at Edgewood Arsenal and made its way south to the opposite shore of the upper Chesapeake Bay."

"Based on what you've told me so far, an investigation is merited," says Major Al Widmar, representing the Inspector's General Office.

"Can you tell us who to contact about a new electronic buoy," asks Kim, "equipped with a sensor for monitoring pollutants in the Bay? We'd like to install a prototype along the shores of Edgewood Arsenal, in an area known to have deposits of pollutants from waste dumped there in the 1930's."

"Give us a day or two to get a handle on this case," says Widmar.

Two days later, Colonel Spencer conducts a briefing with two of his top aides, 30-year old Captain Daniel Ganz and his 26-year old colleague, First Lieutenant Gil Thomas, inside a basement bunker of the Pentagon.

"You all remember Major Liz Carter from her fine work here at the Pentagon," says Spencer. "When I spoke to her a few days ago she mentioned a problem with Captain Rook, who has inventory control of armaments at Aberdeen Proving Ground. Little did I realize the investigation would fall into our laps as a potential crisis. Open the file before you and read the scope of our work. You'll also find a photo of a mustard-gas canister found on the beach of Ridgefield Farm outside Rock Hall. Note the markings of Edgewood Arsenal."

Colonel Spencer removes his coat and slowly rolls up his

sleeves, giving them enough time to examine at least the first few pages of the file.

"Very interesting," says Ganz, chewing on each syllable. "Here's a notation from Liz Carter: 'Rook's deceptive and a scatterbrain. Not the type to control armaments.' "

"Ditto," Thomas says abruptly.

"I hate that word!" exclaims Colonel Spencer. "Shows me that you're a follower instead of a leader. I want everyone to have the freedom to think and act individually within the concept of a team."

"Sorry, sir," Thomas says and sneezes, ruffling some pages in his file. "It was murmured under my breath and not meant for your ears. Liz claims that Rook wastes his time lollygagging instead of getting to the point. He should be in politics instead of the military."

"Time is of the essence," says Spencer, "and every hour could mean the loss of American lives here and abroad. We'll start the investigation with Captain Rook who, according to Liz, is unethical and not acting in the best interests of the military. She claims he might have a few screws loose and some tricks up his sleeve. After you report to Aberdeen in the morning, you'll be working out of a make-shift office near Rook, under the guise of the Inspector General. Your first order of business is to compile a complete dossier of his activities for the past month, even when he took a break to go to the john. All phone calls, credit card receipts, his whereabouts every hour of the day for the past 30 days. This investigation is labeled 'top priority.' And be on guard. Only one canister of mustard gas was found so far. That could be only the tip of the iceberg."

"We'll get right on it, sir," says Ganz, closing the file and pounding the desk with his fist. "We'll be on top of Rook like two fleas on a hound dog without him knowing it."

"Lickety-split, sir," says Thomas, pounding the desk with both fists. "You bet we'll get right on it. I'm itching to get Rook itching without him knowing he's itching and under surveillance."

Two days later, Captain Ganz and Lieutenant Thomas are seated at a partner's desk inside an office at Aberdeen Proving Ground, plowing through records of everything transported in and out of Edgewood Arsenal over the past 30 days. Ganz suddenly leans back in his chair almost to the point of falling backward after spotting a memo from Captain Rook; Subject: Pallet of MRE's (Meal, Ready-to-Eat), trucked from Aberdeen Quartermaster Command to Dover Air Force Base (DAFB) for shipment to "Mess Officer, Yemen Air Force Base, Attention of Asharq Al Awsat."

"This doesn't make sense," says Ganz. "In all my 10 years in the military, this just doesn't make any sense."

"You said that twice," says Thomas, anxious to know more.

"What and why in the hell are we shipping a pallet of MRE's to a known arms dealer in Yemen?" ask Ganz, dialing DAFB and shaking his head in disbelief.

"MRE's," says Thomas assuredly, "are self-contained, individual rations for military personnel in the field."

"I know that. The question is why are we shipping them to Al Awsat? The authorization is signed by Captain Ira Rook. Damn it. Their lines are always busy."

"Be patient, Daniel. The Air Force moves an incredible amount of materials in and out of Dover. Their telephone lines are always humming."

A few minutes later, Ganz learns from his telephone conversation with Major Roger Smoot at Dover AFB that the pallet of MRE's is scheduled to be loaded later that afternoon for transport to Yemen.

"Countermand that order, Major," Ganz shouts at the top of his lungs and pounds the desk with his fist. "While I arrange for a copter to fly me to Dover, First Lt. Gil Thomas will fax over the paperwork by authority of my boss, Colonel J. R. Spencer. In the meantime, put a sentry on guard and don't let that pallet out of your sight. And don't touch a damn thing on the pallet."

After Ganz rises from of his chair and rushes to the door,

he pauses for an instant and looks back at lean and studious Lt. Thomas, shuffling through telephone records.

"While I'm heading to Dover, check out all long distance calls," he says. "Maybe we'll get lucky and find a record of Rook to Asharq Al Awsat, from Aberdeen to Yemen."

"I wonder if Rook ended his last call to Al Awsat, *with love*," Lt. Thomas says facetiously. "Based on what I've read so far, someone's going to be surprised."

"Maybe a surprise for whoever opens the crate," Ganz tells his colleague. "Arrange for a demolition expert to meet me at the hangar. Someone may have rigged the shipment with a booby trap."

"I'll get right on it."

"Thanks, pal. When you mentioned 'surprise,' you might have just saved my life," says Ganz, slamming the door as he rushes out of the office.

An hour later, Captain Ganz arrives at Dover AFB in his UH-1N Iroquois copter, a light-lift utility helicopter used for key government officials. He is met and driven by a corporal who must have been trained on the Indianapolis Speedway, considering how fast he powered his way from the helipad to a cargo terminal on the perimeter of the base. He covered the distance of about a mile in less than 40 seconds.

"Corporal, what did you say your name was?" asks Ganz, wiping some perspiration from his forehead.

"Corporal William Laddyluck, sir. Around here they call me, 'Wild Bill.' "

"Did you realize your jeep was airborne in some spots along the way? Now, I can certify that jeeps can fly with all four wheels off the ground."

They both are still laughing as Captain Ganz exits the jeep and exchanges a salute with Major Smoot.

"This is Captain James Hornblower, the demolition expert that Lt. Thomas arranged for while you were in the air," Smoot says. "If you'll follow me into the cargo terminal, I'll show you the pallet transported from Edgewood Arsenal by authority of Captain Rook. We've kept a sentry guarding the pallet, per your orders."

"Stand 50 feet away from the pallet and give me time to see if this pallet is rigged with a booby trap inside," Hornblower tells them. "I'll let you know when it's safe to inspect the crates."

After adding protective clothing and headgear, Hornblower drills several peepholes into one of the top crates on the pallet which is located in a far corner of the hanger. He attaches one end of a flex cable to a 5 by 7-inch monitor placed on top of the crate and inserts the other end which has a miniature camera to peer inside.

"Take your time," he tells himself to steady his nerves. "Defusing a bomb is not for the faint-hearted, but you have a job to do and people are counting on you to carry it out."

As he maneuvers the flex cable along the top layer, images of a network of wires crisscrossing appear on his monitor.

"Aha. Just as Ganz suspected," Hornblower says to himself "The crate is rigged."

Suddenly, a motor roars, sending a nearby 12-foot high overhead door downward. The ball bearings at the end of each high-tensile steel panel vibrate until the bottom panel strikes the concrete floor with a thunder that not only breaks the silence and echoes inside the hangar, but slightly jars Hornblower's flex cable.

"Good thing I'm not defusing one of those state-of-the-art, electro-magnetic, motion-activated bombs or whatever they're called nowadays," he tells himself.

A few minutes later, Hornblower smiles and nods his head as he faces Ganz and Smoot.

"I haven't seen this type of hand-made mechanical booby trap in a long time," he tells them. "Someone must have been reading an old magazine about "How to Make a Bomb"; they rigged up a system that when the crate is opened, wires attached to the lid tear open the seal of MRE's on the top layer. Breaking the seal activates the water, an exothermic reaction, which emits heat and hydrogen fumes that could ignite the mustard gas canisters below them."

"When the seal on each MRE is torn open," says Ganz, "a chemical reaction is supposed to heat up the meatloaf with gravy; never thought of a booby trap until Lt. Thomas mentioned the word, 'surprise.' "

"Doesn't Rook know that putting meatloaf with gravy over mustard can lead to one helluva case of heartburn and possibly diarrhea?" says Smoot, putting his fingers in his mouth as if he's about to vomit. "Not a good way for a soldier in the field to enjoy a hot meal."

"I wish I thought of that," Hornblower says. "I could use a shot of *boybin* right now but there's still a lot of work ahead; can't assume that the other crates are rigged the same as the one I opened."

"Don't rush yourself, Captain," says Ganz, signaling with both hands outstretched. "When you finish up, the drinks are on me."

He turns to Smoot and motions him to move another ten feet away from the pallet.

"Rook undoubtedly informed Al Awsat about his rigging the crates and how to open them safely," says Ganz, "otherwise he'd be in for a surprise."

Two hours later Hornblower waves to Ganz and gives him a thumbs-up sign that it's safe to begin his inspection of the crates.

"Just as I suspected," says Captain Ganz, emptying about one-third of the contents of the top crate. "Must be 50 canisters to a crate but never expected they'd be hidden under a layer of MRE's."

He reaches in a pocket and pulls out the photo taken from the file for comparison of the markings to those in the crate.

"Each canister bears the markings of Edgewood Arsenal, identical to the one found on the shore of Ridgefield Farm," he says out loud, pounding his fist into the palm of his left hand, like in the old days when he was a professional catcher on the Cincinnati Reds triple A club. "Assuming 50 canisters to a crate, let's see, one, two..."

Ganz bends over to count the number of wooden crates on the pallet.

"I counted twenty crates," says Major Smoot.

"That totals 1,000 canisters of mustard gas, mislabeled as MRE's," says Ganz, tightening the necktie around his collar. "Somebody should be hung for this conspiracy."

The next day, Ganz stands at attention inside Spencer's office as the Colonel signs an order authorizing the pallet of canisters to be transferred from Dover AFB back to Edgewood Arsenal at Aberdeen Proving Ground.

"Captain, what's the worst-tasting MRE's we have in the military?" he asks Ganz, scratching his signature hurriedly at the bottom of the order.

"Is that a trick question, sir?"

"On the level," answers Colonel Spencer, grinning.

"Actually, it's all good, ah palatable."

"If it all tastes good, you've been in the army too long. In a week or two, I'm cutting orders for you to take a breather in the sunshine of any base in Florida or California of your choosing," Spencer says with a wide smile. "I was thinking of sending Asharq Al Awsat a pallet of the worst-tasting MRE's we could find to replace the mustard-gas canisters."

"I'd send him a variety pack! But wouldn't it be wiser to wait and not disclose that we know what he was up to? That way, we might catch him in a bigger crime of collusion with Rook. He doesn't know what we know."

"Good thinking," says Colonel Spencer, shaking his hand. "I'm beginning to see why your star is on the rise at the Pentagon."

"Arthritis?," asks Ganz, noticing the unusual grip of the Colonel's hand.

"An old combat injury," says Spencer, smiling.

"In Vietnam?"

"No, not there. You probably don't remember me since I was a few years ahead of you at Patterson Park High in Baltimore. After I graduated, Boston signed me to a pro contract and converted me from a third baseman to a left fielder, eventually reaching their triple A club."

"And?" asks Ganz, anxious to hear more and watching him lower his head to his chest.

"Seems like it was yesterday. In a game against the *Yankees* of Scranton/Wilkes-Barre at PNC Field in Moosic, Pennsylvania, I was forced to slide into second base on a hit-and-run play. Their second baseman was in the air, trying to complete a double-play ball, and came down with the metal cleats on his shoe directly on top of my wrist. Nerves were cut so that I couldn't grip a bat or ball again, but the surgeon saved my right hand."

"What a bummer!" exclaims Ganz, dropping his head dejectedly.

"I've seen worse injuries on my comrades after graduating from Officers Candidate School and serving in Vietnam," says Spencer. "The toughest part of my baseball career was dealing with the fact that I was scheduled to report to Boston on the first of September, two days after the accident."

"If you're an optimist like me," says Ganz sympathetically, "things seem to work out for the best in the long run."

"Here at the Pentagon," says Spencer, patting him on his shoulder, "everyone's immensely proud of you. It appears you're still throwing out runners trying to steal a base, like you did when you signed a pro contract after graduating from Patterson Park High, too. In this case, it was Capt. Rook trying to steal a pallet of mustard-gas canisters from his base at Edgewood Arsenal."

Ganz arches his back, stiffens his shoulders and comes to attention.

"Relax, Daniel," says Colonel Spencer, motioning him to the door. "You put yourself in grave danger. You gambled with your life and the demolition expert's life when you inspected those crates of canisters. If that crate had been opened in Aberdeen, there's no telling what would have been the consequences to all the residents relocated there as part of the BRAC realignment."

"You call it a gamble," answers Ganz. "I call it a calculated risk."

"Based on your actions under considerable stress, you merit a raise," says Colonel Spencer, shaking his hand. "I'm going to file the paperwork to bump you up a grade to Major. How's that sound?"

" 'Major Ganz.' Has a nice ring to it," he replies, beaming from ear to ear and stroking his hair, trimmed close to the scalp in a wiffle cut. "But Lt. Thomas deserves some credit here, too."

"I intend to bump him up a grade, too. We won this battle against an infection like Rook, but the war goes on and we need good people like you. Over a year ago, we lost Major Liz Carter, who abruptly resigned to enter the private sector as a consultant. The army can't afford to lose you or Thomas. Picture yourself taking over when I retire."

About a week later, Liz receives an unexpected phone call from Colonel Spencer as she and Kim are making an adjustment to their electronic buoy inside the Research and Test Lab (R&TL) building.

"Your problem with the missing canister was handed over to me, probably because it involves a potential crisis and mismanagement of chemical munitions. A single canister of mustard gas is serious business, especially if it falls into the wrong hands. A missing pallet of canisters could be catastrophic."

"Get to the point, Colonel, please, as I'm in the middle of a vital final test of our electronic buoy," she blurts out in a rush of words, without fully realizing with whom she is speaking.

"You've always been a stickler for being concise, so here's the poop, plain and simple. It turns out that Captain Rook at Edgewood Arsenal was on the verge of a clandestine operation. During Hurricane Isabel, he seized the opportunity of discarding a few canisters into the Bay, and recording the loss of an entire pallet in the inventory under his command. Under the guise of falsifying inventory records, Captain Rook was about to transfer a pallet of those canisters, like the one you found on the beach of your property on the Chesapeake Bay, to Asharq Al Awsat, an arms dealer in Yemen. He, in turn, was operating on both sides of the fence, so to speak, and was negotiating to obtain all he could get from Rook and sell them to the highest bidder."

"Who would that be?"

"Al Qaeda and the Taliban on one side of the fence, and procurement officers of the Minister of Defense of Afghanistan, who would be spending American dollars sent to them to rebuild their country," he admits. "Fortunately, Captain Daniel Ganz uncovered their scheme before they could execute an arms deal. The surprising thing here is that this was such a small deal for Asharq Al Awsat. We can't quite figure out why he would get involved, unless it could lead to bigger and better weapons down the road."

"And what about Captain Rook? Can you tell me where he stands in all this mess?"

"Yes and a no."

"You're giving me *double-talk,* again."

"Yes, you can ask a question about Captain Rook, but no, I can't give you an answer, other than to tell you Rook will probably change his name to Ira von Schmuck. He was an arrogant and dumb *S-O-B* whose career as an officer in the military will soon end. His crime certainly deserves punishment and I suspect he'll face a court-martial, but that's up to the Commanding General of Aberdeen Proving Ground."

"And where does that leave us?"

"In a few days," says Spencer, "you'll be updated with the results of our investigation, and, furthermore, there are people at the Corps of Engineers who are excited to know more about your electronic buoy. In the meantime, you have our appreciation for a job well done, not just in cleaning up the Bay, but also heading off a major crisis in the military. Can you imagine the consequences if those canisters were used against our own troops? I hesitate to venture into that nightmare. I'm also recommending a promotion for you and Mark since you're still officers in the reserve."

Meanwhile, inside in the office of the Commanding General of Aberdeen Proving Ground Captain Rook stands at attention, with two MP's guarding him.

"Here's the court-martial charges against you, based on an investigation by the Offices of the Inspector General and Judge Advocate General," says General Maxim Powers, handing Rook the document. "First, you falsified records of inventory, specifically mustard-gas canisters, under your control. Secondly, you transferred this inventory without authorization. Thirdly, you rigged up a booby trap in that pallet that could have caused great harm to personnel. Fourth, you entered into an agreement with a foreign arms dealer without authorization. Fifth, you used military vehicles to transfer such inventory and military phones and fax machines to transmit information without authorization."

General Powers pauses to let his anger subside and looks at Rook, who is stunned by the sudden turn of events and unable to speak.

"The list goes on," says Powers, handing him a statement of charges that he will face in a court-martial. "You have the right to hire an attorney to represent you in your defense, or one will be appointed by the court. Your actions could have jeopardized the lives of military personnel, as well as civilians not only here at Aberdeen but also in the Middle East, where our brave soldiers are fighting and dying every day to preserve peace. You are hereby arrested and will be incarcerated until a trial date is set for your court-martial. The charges against you may change depending on continuing investigations by the Inspector General. You will have an opportunity to answer these charges during your court-martial, which will be convened as soon as possible."

After hearing the charges, Rook never looks up at the General and keeps his head buried in his chest as he is led away by MP's.

As Rook reaches the door, General Powers rises out of his

tight-fitting chair and lets it drop intentionally to punctuate his anger. "I don't think those politicians your father has in his back pocket will be of much help to you this time, you bastard," says Powers. "In the old days, I'd walk you to an isolated place on the post and beat the living shit *outta* you. I can't do that anymore. Too bad."

When Liz gets a chance to talk privately with Mark to update him on the Aberdeen situation, she is taken aback and somewhat shocked by his unemotional response.

"I can't help feeling sorry for him," he tells her. "When he faces that court martial, he'll wish he was never born. I never believed in exploiting a man's stupidity and greed. His criminal behavior has had its way with him. It brings me no joy, no personal satisfaction, to see his life go down the drain. He had no morals."

"What you say is true," answers Liz, "but his actions jeopardized the lives of innocent soldiers fighting to preserve peace around the world."

"In one of my psychology classes at Hopkins, we touched on the subject of signal detection theory (SDT), and how it affects people in making right and wrong decisions in their lives. The theory assumes that the decision maker is not a passive receiver of information, but an active decision-maker who makes difficult perceptual decisions under conditions of uncertainty. Rook should have read about it before his receptor saw greed and profit. His circuitry went haywire, and he sold his soul for a quick dollar."

"I wasn't impressed with Rook and doubt whether or not he could comprehend such a complex subject," says Liz.

"I suspect he'll have a lot of time to catch up on SDT in prison. But let's get back to Ridgefield. My objective, our objective, hasn't changed. It's still centered on Ridgefield and looking for an opportunity to show the world what American ingenuity can do if given the chance, and that means getting the military interested in our electronic buoy. Tell Colonel Spencer how much we appreciate all his work and recommendations to the Corps of Engineers."

A week before Thanksgiving, Mark is seated in an old barber's chair in the back room of Greta's house, secluded in a wooded wetland area of Rock Hall.

"Instead of looking like my boss, you resemble Jascha Heifetz without a Stradivarius in his hands," Greta tells him with a laugh. "You've let your hair grow so long I don't know how to shape it. How long has it been since your last haircut, a year? It won't be long before I'll be trimming the heads of your babies, too."

"With Thanksgiving coming up next week, I'd like only a trim. As for my babies, I intend to let their hair grow and see their curls."

"A trim it is," she answers with a chuckle. "Did I thank you for saving my life, too?"

"It's you that should be thanked. Everyone is thrilled to have you in the Ridgefield family, and our work is just beginning. There are rumors circulating around Ridgefield that a screenplay is being developed and you will play a big part."

"I guess it's safe to say that my horoscope is coming true. I'm getting good at predictions."

She hesitates after pronouncing the last word and has a quick flashback to a moment that she will always remember. It was two years ago when Vera was sitting in the same chair that Mark is now sitting in, when Greta told her that tonight she would have a collision with a military man at the saloon in Rock Hall.

"You're quiet all of a sudden," says Mark. "Are you thinking about Vera?"

"I will never forget her as long as I live. She was something special and I see her every time I look at Jaime."

"Jaime is very special to me too," says Mark. "I wish I could have known Vera under a different set of circumstances. She was a lost soul, floundering hopelessly. Her husband never took the time and energy to care for her properly. As Jaime's father, I intend to make sure that he has everything he needs to develop the way Vera would have wanted."

A few hours later, Mark and Ruth are standing on the beach

below the 10-foot bluff fronting Ridgefield Farm. They begin laughing as Jen licks Jaime's face. "Why do kids and dogs have the most fun playing in the sand," Marks asks her, "when they have 50 acres to roam around on the farm topside?"

"The sandy beach is their playground," says Ruth, sitting under a large beach umbrella and cradling nine-month old Baby Ruth in her arms. "Wish I had a camera handy to take a picture of them."

"Who would have expected," asks Mark, "that, a week before Thanksgiving, the temperature would be in the low 70's and we're enjoying the beach with our children?"

"Why is it that scenes like this one always happen when you don't have a camera?" she asks.

"As soon as Jaime is six months older," Mark tells her, "I'm going to take him into the shallow waters of the Bay and give him his first lesson in swimming. Come hell or high water, they will learn how to swim after they walk and talk, just like I did."

Mark unsnaps the dog's leash and finds a piece of old wood about the size of a rolled-up newspaper and throws it down the beach.

"Go fetch it, Jen, and bring back any canisters you might find along the beach," he says, grinning.

Later that night, Mark is seated inside his bathtub playing with Jaime and trying to get him to float on top of the water. The child giggles and slaps the water with both hands, his head bobbling one moment above then below the level of water in the tub.

"Go, baby go!" he says to Jaime, urging him to slap the water again and again. It's an expression that he discovered and one that both children seem to respond to.

"For goodness sake, don't let him drown before we find out what he can do with his life!" Ruth chuckles at all the commotion.

About an hour later, Ruth is inside the same bathtub with fresh water, of course, holding Baby Ruth in her arms, splashing the water around her little body.

Mark pokes his head into the doorway with a devilish smile across his face.

"I could hear your laughter bouncing off the tiles. Maybe you'd like some music to go with all that *splish-splash* in the tub," he shouts and turns on a speaker in the bathroom.

"Sounds like a recording of Bobby Darin's *Splish Splash*," Ruth tells her baby and begins singing:
*"Splish splash, I was taking a bath,*
*Long about a Saturday night,*
*A rub dub, just relaxing in the tub,*
*Thinking everything was alright."*

"Okay, laugh if you want to," she tells Mark. "So I can't sing like Bobby Darin. Nobody can. At least I'm giving it a try."

Ruth stops singing but continues to rock her baby in time with the music. Baby Ruth notices the St. Christopher medal hanging on a chain around her neck and puts it in her mouth.

"No, no, no. This is not meant to eat," she tells her lovingly. "Your father gave it to me on our wedding day. One day, it'll be yours."

After breakfast the next morning, Kim Bozzetti is sitting at the head of the dining room table with Liz, Sandy, Greta, York and Womble all licking their fingers after putting the last morsel of Gabby's muffins into their mouth. "For four weeks," Kim declares in her distinct Italian accent, "we've been meeting every Wednesday for what you call in your country, 'a barn-storming session,' to discuss ideas for a small budget film. Mark told me, 'It's time to take a crap or get off the pot.' Of course, he was speaking like a crude dude and not the executive producer of our film, but we know the meaning behind his poor choice of words."

She rises and walks around them as they scribble on the note pads in front of them. "Imagine me as a cameraman," continues Kim, angling her hands to form a box. "Picture this opening as if it's the beginning of a Fellini-directed production at Cinecitta outside Rome and shot in black and white film: A carnival on the grounds of Ridgefield, with people of all ages, walking, mingling, meandering around the grounds and having fun inside mechanical rides, like a revolving tea cup or a bumper car, perhaps even a carousel."

They all concentrate on Kim as she walks slowly around them. "I realize I'm talking off the top of my head as if I've directed films all my life," continues Kim with increasing enthusiasm, "but that's because a colleague, from my years at the University of Rome, has been hired as acting director. His name is Sergio Leone Jr., son of the international film director who made all those classic spaghetti westerns. Junior's a chip off the old block, learned everything as a second unit director under his father. He's on his way from New York to join our family, take over the film project with some oversight from me and Womble, and keep us within budget and out of trouble with far-fetched ideas."

"I like the idea of a carnival," Liz admits. "Reminds me of a college film course where the professor showed Orson Welles' *The Third Man*, photographed by Gregg Toland, with lots of distorted angles to show the sights and sounds of a carnival, but without the suspense."

"That's the idea, with lots of Leone's famous close-ups," Kim tells them.

"Where we can see the pimples and dimples on people's faces, expressions of surprise and excitement, everything you would expect from a carnival," Sandy replies. "But I'd like to correct the record here. Orson Welles may have been the star of *The Third Man*, but Carol Reed was the director, and the cinematographer was not Gregg Toland. It was Robert Krasker, who won an Academy Award for his brilliant black and white cinematography. I've watched it many times because It's one of my favorite films, in which each shot was so artistically composed."

"O.K; so much for *The Third Man*. How about the *Third Woman*? Where do I come in?" asks Greta scornfully.

"Impatient, are you?" asks Kim who, by now, stands behind

Greta and puts both hands on her shoulders. "In this film, you'll be a fortune teller; not a gypsy fortune teller; you're playing the part of someone who's impatient to meet each one waiting in line outside your tent."

"For what?" asks Greta.

"For you to tell them their fortune, predict their future, or give them a choice," answers Kim.

"What choice?" asks Greta.

"Keep those questions coming because that's the purpose of this meeting: to toss ideas around and form an outline, a story treatment, for our film," Kim declares. "You'll ask them if they would like their fortune told. If they agree, you gaze into your crystal ball, study the maps of the planets and stars reflected on the inside of your tent and predict their future. Everything you tell them will be based on their horoscope, in the same way you conduct your radio broadcast. If they decline to have their fortune told, you ask them what they would like to do or be for one hour."

"Wow. That certainly opens the door for your imagination to run freely. What happens if someone wants to make love for 60 minutes?" Liz inquires with some trepidation in her voice.

"That would depend on the parties involved, wouldn't it?" Kim answers with a grin.

"I can't wait to get in line with York at my side," says Sandy. "Where do I sign up?"

"Would you settle for second in line?" asks Greta. "I already have someone in mind for the first ticket holder to enter my tent."

"O.K., enough is enough," says Womble with a burst of laughter. "How about an idea or two from the male sex at Ridgefield, or don't we have any say in this art film?"

"Plunge right in," Kim tells him. "There are no restrictions on contributing anything here, no law that prevents anyone from offering something, no matter how ridiculous it might seem on the surface. Furthermore, as overseer, I don't care if you like me, love me or hate me. At the end of the film, all I want to know is that you and I gave it our best effort and made it something to be proud of."

"Mark told me Abigail had more work than one person could possibly handle, knew I was good at figures and asked me to be line-producer of our film project," Womble says slowly to allow everyone to digest his words. "He has approved a budget of two million dollars. So we'll have to innovate everywhere. He told me, 'Keep a tight hold of finances. Treat every dollar as if it was your last dollar.' Those were his exact words."

"We won't let him down," declares Kim assuredly, "That's a promise."

"I'm used to tight budgets after working under stress at the Pentagon," answers Liz. "If you need my help, just ask for it."

"Something comes to my mind about Greta always talking about the horoscope," Womble says. "I picture here as a fortune teller, too, and dressed in a dark-colored Middle Eastern jilbab, with an iridescent-gold silk khimar scarf around her shoulders."

"If someone like me should wish for a ride on a flying carpet to, let's say Paris, we could project photographs via rear projection," interjects York. "The result should be something close to the sights and sounds of Paris, from the top of the Eiffel Tower to the sidewalks of Montmartre, possibly ending at a marvelous Boulangerie-Pastisserie that bakes its own French bread and croissants. Perhaps slip whoever's on the flying carpet a chocolate éclair from Gabby's kitchen to increase the reality of the scene."

"And levitate the carpet with wires like they do with that aerial camera above the playing field of NFL football games. Make it roll to give the sensation of riding on a cushion of air," suggests Liz.

"Keep going, everyone," Kim encourages them. "Now's the time to give us your input so we can prepare a story treatment for Leone. Any other ideas lurking in your devilish, creative psyches?"

"I'd like to bring in Knute Runagrund, the retired tugboat

captain from Betterton," Sandy tells them. "Jack Johnson could build a set, an interior of a cabin, with a steering wheel and distinctive boat whistle. I picture Knute calling out the port to his passengers, with photographic images projected in the background, like a *theatre in the round.*"

'Move over Hecht-Hill-Lancaster," Kim says with a chuckle, returning to her seat. "If you want an acting part in this film, write down your ideas and don't worry about the exact words of dialogue. Just give us your intent so Sergio and I can figure out the best way to include it in the film."

Before Greta leaves the table, Kim takes her by her arm and leads her into Mark's office for a private talk. "We both realize that I'm the director of this project but not the director of this film," says Kim. "Nevertheless, I know what everyone has in mind for a good film about our family at Ridgefield. You're going to be the linchpin. A few segments will be scripted but you're free to improvise. It's important that you have the gist of what we're trying to achieve. What you do to improvise is crucial."

"You know that I'll do my best," says Greta, shaking Kim's hand and reluctant to let go of it.

"Over the next two weeks," says Kim, "give some *electricity,* as Billy Wilder calls it, to each scene in the story treatment. It can be an impulse, a reaction, something said off the cuff, a look of bewilderment, a grimace, anything that Howe can capture on film."

"If I understand you correctly," says Greta assuredly, "you want me to listen and respond, hoping something will develop organically; you're expecting to get some magic out of the chemistry. Do you think I can *pull it off?*"

"I wouldn't ask you if I didn't think you can *pull it off.* You're a good listener, probably from kibitzing with women as you styled their hair. But to make things easier, you'll have an electronic receiver in one ear so we can feed you info when needed. If you get stumped and need our help, put your right hand up to your ear and tap an SOS."

"Now, that's a relief," says Greta with a big sigh. "At least I'm not dangling on the edge of a cliff all by myself."

'And if you pay attention to Leone's direction, you might become a star."

Greta pauses to collect some confidence, smiles and thrusts her shoulders outward like a hen in charge of the barnyard.

"I'll promise you one thing," she tells Kim. "For anyone coming into my tent, they'll be in for a bigger surprise than opening a fortune cookie!"

# Chapter 7

Over the next two weeks Jack Johnson and his crew construct the movie sets needed inside and outside the sound stage for Ridgefield's first film, *Greta's Ludicrous Tent*. Concurrently, Womble arranges the rental of a small carousel, spinning tea cups and bumper cars. Leone manages to get all the cameras, lights, and dollies and a few specialists from a production facility in Baltimore eager to help get his project rolling along.

"To give the carnival an authentic look and sound," Womble tells Kim, "I've hired a bearded organ grinder with an antique symphonic Dutch organ to play typical carousel music that will spill out onto the carnival grounds."

"You might as well go all the way and add popcorn and barbecued chicken and sausage stands to give the smells associated with a carnival. That way, the entire cast of characters is completely at ease as they venture into the world of illusion."

After Leone arrives at Ridgefield and settles inside his trailer, Kim shows him a detailed story treatment and storyboard sketches made freehand along with clippings from old movie magazines to use as a guide for shooting some segments of their film.

"*Collaboration* is the keyword," she says, sitting in a chair that she swivels from side to side nervously. "You won't find much in the way of dialogue in this story treatment. We're going to *wing* it and attempt to create a piece of film, like a screen-test audition, that we can show to Mark and studio execs to see if we're on the right track. In our production, people from the Ridgefield family will act out scenes to be shot by a cinematographer in the documentary style of Billy Friedkin. Later we'll try to transform it into *film noir*.

"*Co-may tra-du-zee-o-nay*; how you translate into Italian, *Play it by ear?*" asks Leone.

"That's it. We'll make it up as we go along," Kim continues. "And James Wong Howe Jr. will join our production as cinematographer and be given the freedom to shoot whatever and wherever he feels will capture the essence of each segment."

A knock at the door interrupts their conversation as James Wong Howe Jr. opens the door and makes himself comfortable.

"Good timing, James," says Kim. "I know you both were pals in New York, so we'll dispense with introductions. Tomorrow, the moment of truth arrives finally and we'll begin shooting. We trust both of you and respect your talents. Get out there and make me look like the smartest person in the world for hiring you."

"*Whatsamattafayou*? my father would ask when someone doesn't understand him," Leone tells her, skimming over the first two pages, bringing them up to his nose to smell and scratching his head.

"Don't pay any attention to him," Howe tells her. "I've worked with him in New York and he's playing tricks with us. It's his way of teasing and telling us that he likes what he reads and smells so far!"

"Yea," answers Leone, laughing. "This stuff not only looks good on paper, it smells good too, probably from Kim holding it close to her body."

Kim and Leone turn their eyes to Howe and watch him turn several pages quickly as he begins to laugh at the characters that appear in the first few sketches.

"I love your plans for the opening sketch," Howe acknowledges.

"You want me to shoot a montage of activities around a carnival that dissolves into a crowd of people waiting in line to get inside Greta's tent."

"That's right. Her name will appear in blinking lights," Kim tells Howe. "To give our film it's special look, give me a close up like Sergio Leone Sr. would shoot, of only the bottom half of the letters on the top line and the top half of the letters on the bottom line. For our film try to leave something unfulfilled, so the audience will be looking for all the pieces of a puzzle subconsciously, if that makes any sense."

"Is there any dialogue from people waiting in line?" asks Howe.

"Yes, and some of their words are drowned out by the music from the organ grinder nearby. You can take liberty and have fun with the blinking lights reflected in the eyes of people waiting in line, some wearing sunglasses with various tints on the surface on their lens."

"If you want long, medium, and close-ups," Howe declares, "I'd like to use two cameras operating simultaneously. We'll use a 400-foot magazine attached to the Eyemo and a hand-held 35 mm camera used by newsreel combat cameramen. Each magazine will give us 4 1/2 minutes of film."

"Do it," Kim advises.

"We'll try to shoot everything in one take, if possible," Leone says. "It'll keep our costs down. Retakes are costly."

"I'll try to get as much good stuff on film as I can," Howe interjects.

"And let the editor use his talents and innovations in technology to make it into *film noir*," Kim answers.

"When you hear the clapboard," Leone tells Howe, "roll your cameras. Don't wait for me to shout 'action.' Got it?"

"I get the picture," Howe responds with a laugh. "Sounds as if we're *winging* it."

"Think always *Sergio Sr.*," says Leone, "and give me as many close-ups, without it being too obvious that our movie is modeled after my father."

"And the scenes inside the tent?" Howe asks, with some trepidation.

"There will be two to three people inside," Leone explains. "We want you to capture the expressions and reactions on their faces: a squint, a twitch, a fly that settles on a cheek unexpectedly. Your camera will see inside a person and know whether he or she is tense, or at ease, or broken-hearted. Less is more here, with dialogue kept to a minimum. Remember: Steve McQueen said he was always crossing out lines in his script because he was better when he didn't say much. He said the camera will say everything that needs to be said and say it better. Our film is based on innuendo and allusion."

"And what about the lighting inside the tent?" asks Howe nervously.

"Very little," answers Leone, "only a single candle on Greta's table. It's another opportunity for you to capture the play of light and shadows. Even a silhouette projected on the inside of Greta's tent has a certain beauty and mystery. Be aware of a wind chime that hangs over Greta's crystal ball. When someone enters her tent, a small gust of wind may trigger the chimes. Perhaps light from the candle will reflect off the chimes in awkward directions across the actor's face. I'm sure you'll take the ball and run with it when you see opportunities unexpectedly pop up."

"I get the idea," Howe says, nodding his head confidently. "Reminds me of Sven Nykvist, the great Swedish cinematographer, who said, and I'm paraphrasing here, 'I am captivated by light, which is used to dramatize the expression on a person's face. Because I'm interested in telling stories about human beings, the camera lens will show what they're feeling inside and why they're acting that way.' Before turning on my camera, I think about him and the importance of light. Sometimes, less is better."

"Looks as if we're on the same wavelength."

"One suggestion here,' Howe says. "Would you mind if I put

a small oriental incense burner somewhere on the table? The swirl of rising smoke might add a touch of mystery to the shot."

Leone pats Howe on his back and gives him a thumbs-up sign.

"We'll let the actors enjoy the fragrance, too." Leone says. "Maybe it will relax them during the shot."

The following morning, at 10 am precisely, Ridgefield is buzzing in anticipation of the start of their film project. Leone, with Kim always positioned nearby, gets confirmation that Howe and his crew are ready to begin shooting the opening scene of *Greta's Ludicrous Tent*.

"Everyone ready?" Leone asks, shouting and gazing quickly all around him.

Someone shoves a clapperboard in front of Howe's camera, which starts the take and marks the particular scene in the production.

"Camera is rolling. Action everyone! I said 'Action.' Can you all hear me?" Leone asks as he backs out of the scene.

Howe's Eyemo camera moves in for a close-up of Annette Welles Wagner, first in line. She's dressed in a dirndl with a shortened skirt to show off the longest and shapeliest legs in the world.

"I said 'Action,' Annette," Leone says again, much louder.

She realizes it's her cue to turn around and face her husband, Richard, standing in line behind her.

"I was told this carnival was something similar to a German Oktoberfest but don't see any beer halls around," says Richard, snapping the suspenders of his lederhosen.

"The beer will come after we see Greta, says Annette. "Hold onto your hosen, *mein schatze,* a few minutes more."

Their conversation gives the third person in line the opportunity to skirt around them and quickly enter Greta's tent before anyone realizes he's jumped the line.

"I know you," Greta exclaims at the top of her lungs for

everyone to hear outside her tent. "Everybody knows who you are. You're the filmmaker Barry Levinson."

"Please, not so loud. The deaf could hear you," Barry answers with a wide grin. "*Kinda* dark in here. Is that candle the only lighting you can afford? I've heard of being on a tight budget but really..."

"We're trying to achieve a dramatic effect here, *film noir*."

"I'm here to see if it's true what people are saying about Ridgefield and have my fortune told," says Barry.

"Right," Greta says, waving her hands over the crystal ball. "Take a seat. Get a load off your mind. I see clearly you're going on a long journey. You're going to Rock Hall."

"But I'm *in* Rock Hall," he exclaims.

"Do I lie, do I lie?" asks Greta, raising her head and glancing at the perimeter of her tent to see if anyone's peeking.

"I'm crazy about canaries and *wanta* go to the Canary Islands, off the northwest coast of Africa," he says excitedly.

"What you've said is only partly true. You were right about its location but wrong about seeing canaries there. According to my crystal ball, you're going to make a movie about a diner in Baltimore, with characters you knew from your days at Forest Park High."

"But I did that, over 30 years ago."

"Do I lie, do I lie?" she yells out so even the deaf buried in a cemetery nearby could hear her. "I see everything clearly in my crystal ball. I see Mel Brooks, who's telling me that he will put you in all his films. Besides being a great director, he says you're a *hellava* actor."

"Tell me something new, or I'm *outta* here."

"I'll get to the point. The best is yet to come. You're going to direct a small budget art film that will bring you another Academy Award. It's a story about a fortune teller, inside a tent of a carnival. She's a sight for sore eyes, but tells each of her customers their past, present and future. The entire film will be shot in 24 hours, on location at Ridgefield. To draw in nature-lovers, we might include the bald eagles, blue herons, Tundra swans and Canada geese all nesting next door at the Eastern Neck Wildlife Refuge."

"Interesting," mutters Barry under his breath.

"If you play your cards right, you may get the chance to direct it. I'm on the selection committee. The choice of director is between you and William Wyler."

"William Wyler? He's been dead for 40 years."

"Really? You're not putting me on, are you? That news never made it down to the Eastern Shore of *Murlin*. In that case, I guess you could become the director by default."

"No default for me, kiddo," replies Barry with a laugh. "My record speaks for itself. They don't hand you an Oscar by default. You get it the old fashion way. You have to *earn* it."

"On your way out, Barry, take one of those pamphlets in that rack by the door. Low-cost mortgage loans, new car financing, reasonable equity loans, reverse-mortgage loans, all of them are sponsors of our carnival."

"Fade out, cut and print," shouts Leone as Barry Levinson exits Greta's tent. "Well done, everyone. We're off to a flying start."

An hour later, everything is in place for the second segment to be filmed. Leone huddles with Annette and Richard Wagner, dressed like the grandparents of *Hansel and Gretel* and already seated inside Greta's tent.

The clapperboard is positioned in front of Howe's camera which is already running.

"I assume you know what you're going to do and say," Leone says nonchalantly to put them at ease. "After I back out of the way, go into your act. Don't wait for any commands from me."

"Be careful what you wish for," Greta tells them, adjusting her iridescent turquoise scarf around her shoulders. "It might come true. Do you want your fortune told or would you prefer to make a wish that, if it comes true, lasts only for 24 hours?"

Richard wraps his arm around Annette's waist and moves her closer to Greta's crystal ball.

"No flirting allowed inside Greta's tent, Richard," says Greta, rubbing her temples gently and alternating her eyes from their hands to her crystal ball. "I see that you are going to dance on stage with the *Rockettes* at the Radio Music Hall in New York."

"I don't dance," says Richard. "I play the piano."

"I wasn't referring to you, doodle head," Greta tells him. "It was your wife, Annette, the one with the most beautiful legs in the world. Now, do you want a wish or have your fortune told?"

"We'll take a chance on a wish," he answers. "I'd like to play *Die Walkure*, a composition written by my great grandfather, Richard Wagner, on the organ in King Ludwig's Bavarian castle. And I'd like to have my wife, Annette, come along and dance as a courtesan, a mistress with lots of luxuries heaped upon her, all of which she richly deserves."

"That's all within the realm of possibilities. I'm a fortune teller, not a magician. But for relatively simple wishes, I can accommodate you. Go back to Betterton, rent an organ and practice, practice, practice 'til you're blue in the face. Next month, you'll be playing the organ on stage at the Lyric Theater in Baltimore in a new production of Richard Wagner's *Die Walküre*, with a replica of the interior of King Ludwig's castle."

"Fade out and cut. That's a take. Print that baby," Leone shouts, smiling to everyone around him out until Kim gives him a gentle tap on his rear end.

"A goose to keep you loose," she says, "the kind men gave me in Rome, especially on a crowded bus."

An hour later, Howe and Leone are in a huddle and studying the story treatment for the next segment.

"*A-ten-see-oh- nay*," Leone shouts out in Italian. "Attention, everyone. So far, we're on schedule and within budget. Let's keep it that way, please."

For the next segment, Sandy and York are already sitting at

Greta's table. They're dressed in western outfits with white Stetson hats and cowhide boots as they stare into her crystal ball.

The clapperboard is positioned in front of Howe's camera.

"Film is rolling," Leone tells York. "We're ready whenever you are."

"We know that you're a fortune teller and not a magician," York says to Greta, pushing back his beige Stetson so the camera can capture his resemblance to Frank Lloyd Wright and the candlelight reflected in his eyes. "But according to the grapevine, you are known to occasionally possess some magical powers. If you can muster those powers, Sandy and I would like to take a magic carpet ride to Rome. I've always wanted to see the Forum Romano and Steppes España, and see how Rome managed to blend antiquity with modern architecture."

"For me, it would be the thrill of a lifetime to see *David* in the Academy of Rome," Sandy tells her, snuggling closer to York's body. "It must be 15-feet tall, in white marble from the quarries of Carrara. I've forgotten how many years it took him to sculpt it. After that, a visit to the Borghese Gardens would suit me perfectly."

Greta pauses and puts one hand under her jilbad and up to her ear.

"That's almost all possible," answers Greta," if you and York decide to play our game of make-believe. But if you go to Rome, you won't find *David* there. It's in the Academia Gallery in Florence, and it's 17, not 15 feet tall."

"That's what I like about working at Ridgefield," Sandy answers. "You scratch the surface of a colleague and Abracadabra, a genius appears."

"Getting back to your wish," Greta continues, "I'll ask Jack Johnson and his people to design and construct a set inside our sound stage, a replica of a magic flying carpet. We'll use rear projection to flash images of everything you mentioned onto screens around you. In the meantime, brush up on your Italian because we'll film this segment with words spoken only in Italian, with English subtitles."

"Ah, print that baby!" exclaims Leone. "Nice job, everyone. Wishes do come true if you want it bad enough. We'll film your magic-carpet ride after Jack Johnson finishes constructing the set inside the lab."

Fifty minutes later, Howe and Leone are huddling with Kim to go over the next segment featuring Reggie and Liz, seated inside Greta's tent with arms around each other like two love birds. They're dressed in red and white diagonally-striped jackets, looking like two human candy canes.

The clapperboard springs out of nowhere and in front of the lens of Howe's Eyemo.

"Anytime you want to begin, York and Sandy, do so, but look directly into Greta's eyes, not her crystal ball," Leone tells them.

"Between recording dates in New York," Reggie tells Greta, "I'd like to do something different for 24 hours. Liz and I have been rehearsing some songs. Can you arrange for us to be a *Singing-Telegram* Duo for *eharmony.com*, provided we're allowed to ad-lib here and there?"

"We'll sing messages of introduction," Liz adds apprehensively, "between two people interested in entering a relationship. Normally, individuals who contact *eHarmony* interact over the Internet. If we can pull it off, it's our way of giving them a unique way of starting a relationship."

"Nothing like music to lift the spirits of people," Greta tells them.

"*Wanta* hear a sample of our songs?" asks Reggie.

"Save them for your customers," Greta answers. "Go back to Betterton and practice chirping in the woods behind your Frank Lloyd Wright prairie-style mansion. Your wish will come true after we get approval from *eharmony.com*."

"Cut and print. That's a 'take it to the bank,' " shouts Leone.

"Only one more segment to go and we're still on schedule and within budget."

For the last episode of *Greta's Ludicrous Tent*, Howe turns on his Eyemo just seconds after the clapperboard appears in front of his lens.

"You can walk into Greta's tent anytime you're ready," Leone tells Knute. "Make sure the bird cage you're holding in one hand stays at waist level. Cameras are rolling everyone. We're ready anytime you want to begin talking to Greta."

"You're very old," says Greta, looking down into her crystal ball before he can get any words out of his mouth. "It's been a long day and so far I'm batting a thousand."

"My coat is old, over 40 years old," he tells her, easing into his seat and opening his battered pea coat. "But what is old? To me, it's just a three-letter word. I feel good for someone at 70."

"I see no imprints in the bridge of your nose. No need to wear glasses?"

"No glasses for me. I still see things clearly. Everything I want to see around me," says Knute, setting the cage on the table beside her crystal ball.

"You've brought along a pet. No pets allowed inside my tent."

"You may think it's a pet. You may call it a pet, but it's no pet. It's practically human."

"Oh say can you sing," squawks the parrot, fluttering its wings.

"Gertie, meet Greta. Greta meet my pal, Gertie, the smartest talking parrot in *Murlin*," says Knute proudly.

"In *Murlin*? You mean, in the world," squawks the parrot. "Show me more respect. I think I've earned it!"

"Gertie's got a mind and squawk all her own," Knute tells Greta, "and no one can ever predict what's coming next. We came from Betterton to see the world's foremost fortune teller."

"What you say is true," Gertie answers with a grin, "about me being the world's greatest. If you heard about me in Betterton, that's a miracle."

"*Miracle* was the name of the white Arabian stallion in Mel Brook's *History of the World, Part 2*. And we're hoping to have one this Christmas on stage at the *Hippodrome* in *Balmer*. *Wanta* hear our rendition of *Rudolph, the Red Nose Reindeer?*"

"Another time, perhaps."

"Then, we want you to tell our fortune. Will our show be a hit or miss?" he asks, crossing his fingers for good luck.

"What is your birth date?"

"The 10th of December. According to my mother, I was born under a full moon, the biggest baby ever seen in Olden, on the *nordfjord* of Norway."

"Somewhere during your life, something shrunk you. You must have been carrying a heavy load. What are you now, five foot two, eyes of blue?"

"You keep that up and you can join our troupe."

"According to the alignment of stars and planets and your birth date, it's going to be a hit, a big surprise, just like the one I'm going to level on you now. Even though you didn't ask me about it, there's something and someone else in your life that you've completely forgotten about, or never knew about, in the first place."

Knute is stunned temporarily. "That wasn't in the script. What's going on?" he asks.

"Go along with us, Knute," hollers out Leone, watching the action behind Howe's camera. "Look back at Greta and listen to what she has to say."

"You have me at a disadvantage," Knute tells Greta, covering Gertie's cage, "since I don't know what the hell you're talking about."

He leans forward and stares directly into her eyes as his nerves begin to get rattled in anticipation of hearing about something he's forgotten or never knew before. Inhaling the lavender burning in the incense burner helps to calm his nerves.

The flame of a candle on the table reflects off the glass of Greta's crystal ball and onto the forehead of Knute, who wipes off some perspiration and sighs. The wind chimes begin to give off a combination of complex overlapping Oriental musical notes, something Bernard Herrmann would have composed for a Hitchcock thriller.

"You've met the Wew twins, Ying and Yang?" asks Greta. "Notice anything special about them?"

"I've only talked to them once. Six foot three, on the lean side, wouldn't be able to tell them apart if my life depended on it. Pleasant young men of 40, I suspect. Didn't pay much attention, although I came away impressed by their intelligence in computer technology. They offered to computerize my tugboat if I decide to go back into business. I've been around people from all over the world and came away asking myself whether or not I may have seen them before."

"You didn't know they were born in Tibet, to a Chinese mother," she declares in a high pitched voice. She uses both hands to move some strands of hair that covered part of her eyes to the side of her head and behind her ears, exposing a pair of exotic jade earrings.

"And?"

"They were raised by monks, who rescued their 18-year old pregnant mother before the Chinese revolution swept through her village in China, in the same way Raul Wallenberg rescued some Jews from the Nazis' who swept through the ghettos of Hungary and Poland in World War II."

"What's all that got to do with me?" he responds tensely.

"*You* are their father!"

"What? You shouldn't kid around with an old geezer like me. My *ticker ain't* what it used to be."

"Everything I've told you is true."

"How do you know it's true?"

"Mark entrusted me to break the news to you and document it on film. He found it out when he hired them for Bethlehem

Steel (BS). Immigration officials had to do a background check since they applied for a green card for entry from Germany and were classified as 'essential personnel' working on government contracts."

"I'm dumbfounded," he answers, rising out of his chair and walking around it. "Stupefied."

"I suspect, and it's pure speculation on my part, that you were in your late 30's or early 40's when you met their mother in a Chinese port, probably brought her aboard your ship, and, I think you can fill in the rest, can't you?"

"Better take a seat before I fall down," he utters, collapsing into his chair. "With a little time to digest everything, you're probably right. But those kids certainly didn't inherit any of my genes when it comes to size and intelligence."

"I'm not so sure about that, Knute. Size is relative. Look what Napoleon did and he was only five foot two. As far as intelligence goes, you're brighter than you give yourself credit for. Otherwise you wouldn't have survived for 70 years. According to Mark, you have incredible gifts inside you, such as resolve and intuition. He liked you from the first moment he saw you pacing the sidewalk outside Annette's Antiques in Betterton. He saw some of the same attributes in you that he saw in his father. And he liked the twins twice as much after meeting them and seeing how quickly they adapted to America and contributed to the development of BS."

"And where is Soo Chow now? asks Knute sympathetically.

"In heaven. She died after giving birth to her twins, your twins."

Knute bows his head and says a silent prayer, as tears begin to form in his eyes. The candlelight reflects off his face into the crystal ball as Greta leans forward to gaze deeply into its center.

"I'm not making this up," she tells him. "It's all true. Cross my heart and hope to die."

"Have you told them about me?" asks Knute cautiously after gathering some strength.

"They're outside, listening to everything we've said to each other."

The Wew twins enter through a rear flap in Greta's tent and stand on each side of her circular table. A necklace is removed from each of their necks and placed on the table in front of Knute. It's two halves of a solid gold good-luck charm molded in the form of a North Sea salmon.

"I gave this gold charm to Soo Chow Wew a long time ago," he tells them, as memories begin to cross his mind. "The gold charm was a gift in honor of our accidental meeting in a small park, a walk through the flower gardens and pause for a cup of exotic tea. Birds were chirping everywhere."

He hesitates to wipe his brow and looks up at both twins.

"Our encounter ended aboard my ship. I was first mate, ambitious and out to see the world. I remember only one star in a dark blue sky; no big dipper, no little dipper," he tells them as tears run down his cheeks.

Unexpectedly, the flame of the candle beside the crystal ball flickers wildly, and Leone motions to Knute to wipe his eyes again, and to Howe to keep his cameras rolling.

"Sometimes it's better to let the characters do whatever they do best," Leone tells himself, "and let things take on a life of their own. Characters or actors should be allowed the freedom to express their impulses. That way, it's more spontaneous and creative."

A few seconds later, Knute removes a handkerchief from his back pocket, blows his nose into it then wipes his eyes, introducing some phlegm to his cheeks.

"Cut and print!" Leone shouts out at the top of his lungs, backing away from the scene. "That's it for today. A million thanks to everyone. We're off the ground with *Greta's Ludicrous Tent*. Now, it's the editor's turn to do his magic."

Leone circles behind Howe and his assistants and helps Greta out of her seat. "You were great, *hon*, but you may have a touch of psoriasis," he tells her, looking closely at her face, with red scaly patches from rubbing her cheeks and forehead during the eight-hour film shoot.

"Now, who's the mind reader here?" she tells him, misunderstanding the word *psoriasis*, which Leone pronounced quickly in three syllables, instead of four, so that it sounds as if he said: "*sore asses.*"

She scratches her head, puzzled for a second, then says, under her breath, "How in the hell did he know I have a sore ass from sitting so long in that wooden chair?"

Leone looks around for Howe, standing about 20 feet away and talking to two assistants. After Howe hands his camera to one of them and looks to be finished his conversation with them, Leone puts his arm around his shoulder and coaxes him away for a brief private talk.

"When I said 'That's it for today,' I wasn't referring to you," Leone tells him. "Please load two more magazines and shoot about eight to ten minutes of people meandering around the carnival."

"Short, medium and long shots of them enjoying the carnival rides as they sit on a tea cup, bumper car and carousel horse?" Howe asks him.

"We're on the same wavelength. We'll let the editor intersperse these shots between segments that you shoot inside and outside Greta's tent."

"This is where I have the most fun. The camera takes over and has a mind all its own. We just compose the shot and *let 'er rip*, if you get my drift."

At last it's the end of a long day of hard work. Throughout the nine-hour shoot, there was little chance for anyone to catch their breath. Everything directed by Leone is now labeled and stored inside the magazines that Howe and his crew shot. Now it's up to the editor.

"Man oh man," Leone says out loud, bursting with new energy, "if this audition is successful and I get the chance to direct a finished screenplay, I might win an Academy Award as Best Director."

After Knute is escorted out of the tent by the Wew twins, he shakes his head and tells them, "This was supposed to be acting out a scene, an idea, pure fiction and imagination. Was what happened in there for real?"

"Yes," Wing tells him, "it was all real."

"It'll take some time to digest everything, father," Ying answers, as both twins put their arms around Knute.

A week later, Kim confers with Leone inside the lab portion of Ridgefield's R&T Lab building.

"Looks like a small research lab at NASA with an electronic buoy on the launch pad instead of a rocket," Leone tells her in a high-pitched voice and raised eyebrows.

"It is a research lab, and you're right about the buoy," Kim declares, "which brings me to the reason for meeting you this morning. Mark, Womble and I have been looking over all the film shot by you and Howe last week. It's very obvious that you're capable of taking over our film project. The job of Director is yours, full-time, at a salary to be negotiated with Abigail. She holds the purse strings."

"That's all very flattering, but so far, all we've done is make *a* film, not *the* film. This was an audition, an experiment, something to learn from and move on to the next level."

"That's right, and that means hiring a screenwriter. Any suggestions?"

"I don't know what to say. I haven't seen the rushes and don't know what the editor has done to my film," answers Leone.

"Take my word for it. It was sensational and beyond what we expected," she says, hesitating to gather her next thought. "Try to make your decision to join our family as soon as possible because we'll have to process the paperwork to get your status of a sabbatical in New York changed to a green card as permanent resident. Although your work is not classified as 'essential to industry,' we'll try to expedite your application with immigration authorities. The sooner you join us, the better. Any time you're ready, you can move all your stuff permanently into one of our trailers with your name and new title emblazoned on the front door."

"*Como-say-dee-say*, how do you say in your country, where do I sign up?" Leone chuckles. "How can I thank you?"

"No need to thank me. It's you that saved the day for us," she replies. "Grazie."

"Multi-grazie, graziamento, mia amore," he answers and gives her a warm embrace and tender kiss on her lips.

This reaction could be the start of a beautiful friendship, but only time will tell how fast it develops into something serious. The linkage is there. Both are blessed with a Roman temperament and talent beyond description.

# Chapter 8

After two months of intensive investigation of the painting Mark discovered in the cellar of a deceased antiques dealer, Abigail catches him as he's about to leave his office inside the main house and gently pushes him back into his swivel chair. "I know you don't like to be pushed around," she tells him, "but it's better to take the news sitting down. Otherwise, you might fall down."

"Sounds serious," he replies. "I can tell by the way you're breathing."

"I took the painting to New York for the expert in Pollock's paintings to examine it under the microscope and spectrograph."

"And?"

"Guess what?" asks Abigail.

"Was it bad news, just like the Homer painting?"

"She was reluctant to confirm its authenticity because there was no documentation in any of Pollock's notes, letters and photos. Nothing. Zilch."

"I knew it was too good to be true."

"But damn it, I could see and smell that it was right and she was wrong," she says, removing her glasses as they begin to steam up. "I must have spent 80 hours studying and trying to figure out how Pollack may have applied the paint."

"Did you come to any conclusion?"

"It's my suspicion that he started in the center, dripping or splattering paint with several 3 or 4-inch bristle brushes, one for each color. I know from films that he often held two or three cans of paint in his arms and hands, and worked vigorously for a minute or two, then stepped back to see the results. If he was satisfied, he moved to the ends of the painting and continued the process, applying one color over another, in a spontaneous way. He must have used ten different colors of paint, with none a dominant color."

"*Figuring* out how he did it is one thing," says Mark. "*Proving* that he did it is another."

"The big break in proving the authenticity came about when I decided to get dirty," says Abigail assuredly.

"What are you talking about?"

"I put on a surgical mask, protective gloves and a surgeon's gown and went through every box of stuff you brought *outta* that cellar in Philly."

"That's gumption, which you have an abundance of, and?" he asks, motioning with outstretched hands to continue her *spiel*.

"It's an original by Jackson Pollock. In one of the boxes containing documents and records of Windsor Gallery, I found the original bill of sale, which confirmed my suspicions."

"What was written on it?"

"The Pollock painting was purchased by Bernard Feuerstein, owner of Windsor Gallery, on September 10, 1965 from Lee (Lenore) Krasner, for $1,200. It's signed by both the buyer, Feuerstein, and the seller, Krasner, who married Pollock in 1945 and died in 1984. Also, in an upper corner on the back of the stretcher, Pollock had written, in a light pencil: 'To Lee'."

"Are you serious or just pulling my leg?"

"Not when it comes to another discovery," says Abigail.

"I'm speechless," says Mark. "But you better stand back. I feel an eruption coming on."

"There's no way to describe the thrill of proving the authenticity of an important work of art. It's the opposite of your gloom about a year ago when you found a painting by Winslow Homer but couldn't prove it. You lose some. Now you've won a bigger one."

"I still don't know what to say, except a million thanks for another job well done. You might as well give yourself another raise and continue to spearhead this project by finding us a buyer."

"Should we break out a bottle of Dom Perignon to celebrate the occasion?"

"It'll taste better when we have a check deposited in our bank account."

"I've taken the liberty to put out a few feelers already," she discloses.

"Once again, you're always one step ahead of me."

"It's well known that Hollywood has many of the wealthy collectors of American contemporary art. I've narrowed possible sales to Steve Martin and Andy Williams, and spoken to their agents. After seeing a photo of the painting, each is ready to write us a check for two million."

"Dollars?" asks Mark, looking upward and closing his eyes momentarily to digest Abigail's revelations and thank God. "That's a nice dilemma to be in. What's your instinct say about how to proceed?"

"A coin toss to see who wins the Pollock."

"A flip of the coin? I'll buy that, and send this pen, a good luck omen, to the winner to sign his check."

"Your good-luck fountain pen? Isn't that the one you used to sign your check when you purchased the Edelfelt painting in Baltimore? If you don't mind my asking, how much did you pay for it?"

"Are you asking about the painting or the pen?" asks Mark facetiously. "What I paid is of interest only to the IRS when I file my tax return."

"I'll send the buyer your fountain pen, your Majesty," Abigail responds with a burst of laughter. "That money might be enough for Leone and Howe to get their film moving forward to the next step, whatever that is."

"However, I have another bit of news for you," she replies sheepishly.

"Oh, bad news?"

"Guess it depends on how you look at it. It was reported that in 2006, David Geffen sold his Pollock painting, titled *Number 5* and painted in 1948, for an incredible 140 million dollars!"

"Nah. Impossible."

"Impossible to you, but not to Geffen."

"As one of my seals, Monte Montgomery, used to tell me, 'I don't need the whole *enchilada* to make me happy.' In a recent email, he wrote that he's teaching seniors how to swim with their left or right arm, so they're amphibious."

"You mean ambidextrous, don't you?"

"Yes, I know the difference but not certain if Monte does," Mark says, leaning back in his chair and looking at all the photos lining the walls of his office that show the development of Ridgefield.

"As far as I'm concerned, I can live very nicely with the figure you quoted," he says, "and your suggestion to use the funds for that film project is a good one, too."

It's Christmas Day, around 9 in the morning, almost sixteen months after their marriage. Mark walks Jaime into the library at Cylburn to show him an eight-foot evergreen tree, beautifully decorated by his mother with tinsel, Christmas ornaments and twinkle lights. Ruth follows closely behind them and carries Baby Ruth, with head resting on her shoulder.

"There's nothing like the exhilaration that comes from having our family together again," Sara tells them. "And this time is so special because it's our first Christmas with my two grandchildren.

Today, I feel as though I could lift the world and turn it topsy-turvy."

"Like an upside-down cake?" Ruth asks with a laugh.

"That's the idea," Sara answers. "My heart is about as content as it's ever been in my life. God has blessed us beyond measure. Wish my husband could be here to enjoy all of you, too."

"He'll always be with us, mom," Mark says graciously. "I bet he's bragging to everyone within distance of his voice about his two grandchildren."

After Mark finds a present for Jaime to open and play with the toy inside, he retrieves a camera from the grand piano and begins shooting a sequence of photographs for their scrapbook. He scurries around the room, shooting long and short shots and pausing occasionally to angle his camera to achieve an unexpected image. He ends up eventually on the floor, shooting up at everyone as if he's John Frankenheimer filming race cars and their drivers in *Grand Prix*.

Even Jaime begins giggling at his father's antics with the camera. When Mark bends down to show him his camera, Jaime tries to open his mouth wide enough to put his lips around the lens.

"No, son," he tells him. "It's not something to eat."

"Can I help with the preparation of dinner?" Ruth asks Sara. "Mark can look after the children. How many guests are coming?"

"I've invited Mike Bloomburg and Lola Albright, who are part of my family and have been for several years," she answers, taking Ruth's arm and walking to the kitchen. "The maid will help out by setting the dining table. Time to use our Stieff sterling flatware and Spode china."

Around the second week of March, almost a year after his first interview with Jack Dunn, Chubby Bender is dressed in a loose-fitting uniform of the Daytona Beach *Islanders* and walking down a long dark tunnel leading from the clubhouse to the baseball field of Jackie Robinson Stadium, formerly known as City Island Stadium. The cleats of his spikes scratch the concrete floor and echo off the concrete-block walls.

Once onto the field, his eyes squint a little as he tries to adjust to the bright Florida sunshine. He hesitates a moment and digs his cleats into Mother Earth, which brings a sigh of relief. He's made it to spring training and pounds his glove with his right fist, followed by a tug at his waist belt to bring his pants up an inch or two.

"I'm in spring training with the *Oryuls'* rookies," he tells himself. "It's just the first step, but a big one."

Spring training for the Baltimore Orioles Class-A affiliate officially started a week ago, and Chubby's reporting one week late, which is not a good way for a rookie to begin his professional career. He pounds his glove again and again to break it in, then keeps adjusting his baseball cap down. By the time he reaches the batting cage, it's down to his eyebrows.

"Hey, kid, where do you think you're going?" asks Joe Klein, the short, stocky, bald-headed 60-year old General Manager of the *Islanders*, wiping some dust off his bifocals.

"*Reportin'* to Mr. Klein," answers Chubby slowly in his eastern shore twang.

"That's me, kid," says Klein, adjusting his visor with drop-down sunglasses. "What's your name?"

"Chubby Bender. Mr. Dunn signed me and told me I'd begin my career by playing for the *Islanders*. He said to report as soon as possible."

"Is that a fact? You may be one of Dunn's boys, but I'm the one who says who plays and who doesn't here."

"I passed a statue of Jackie Robinson at the south entrance to the ballpark. Maybe one day they'll put one up for me," Chubby says brazenly.

"What did you say?" Klein asks, looking him over from the toes of his spikes to the tip of his cap.

"Forget it. I was muttering to myself."

"*Whadaya* weigh?" asks Klein, slapping Chubby's shoulders to get a sense of his muscles.

"185."

"How tall are you?"

"Five foot ten."

"Don't think you fit the build of a power hitter from the looks of your physique," Klein says pompously. "I want you to meet the manager of the *Islanders*, Hank Majeski Jr."

"Let's see what you can do in the batting cage, kid," the bumptious Majeski says. "This is spring training, *kinda* like boot camp for new recruits. No time to lose down here. Grab yourself a bat and take ten swings."

Majeski turns his body around to face the infield, just as his father did as a manager for over 20 years in the 1950's. Hank Sr. was known as one of the best fielding third basemen of his era, who coaxed his son into coaching and sent a number of rookies on their path to the big leagues.

"Give him ten fast ones and vary the location around the plate," Majeski hollers over to Carl Runk, the batting practice pitcher for the *Islanders*.

Chubby steps into the batting cage nonchalantly with the bat laying on his right shoulder. He looks down at home plate and his spikes barely scratch the dirt.

"I can tell right off that he's no hitter," Majeski mutters to Klein. "He doesn't dig a toe-hole to anchor his right foot so he can push off it for added power. He just scratches the dirt like a farm hen looking for a kernel of corn."

Runk fires a quick series of three fast balls and Chubby swings awkwardly and misses each by a foot, which angers both Klein and Majeski, both leaning against the batting cage netting to study his stance. Out of the next seven pitches from Runk, Chubby manages to foul-tip three that strike in front of the plate and bounce backward over the catcher.

"No, no, no. Be *smat*," Majeski shouts in his Staten Island brogue, a combination of Polish and Irish upbringing. "You just killed three worms in front of home plate. *Git* the bat away from your chest and cock it, otherwise you won't even see the ball crossing the plate and definitely won't get any power. You're swinging like an old lady using her umbrella to shush away rabbits eating lettuce in her *gaden*. You keep that up and you can send your mother a *postcad* telling her when you're coming home."

"I can do better with a little practice," Chubby tells Majeski, spitting out some phlegm over one shoulder. "Just got off the train and never had a chance to loosen up."

"One of Dunn's wonders, huh, kid?" says Majeski, unwrapping some bubble gum and jamming it into his mouth. "Put the bat down and field some grounders at third base."

Chubby tosses his bat towards the dugout and heads down the third base line. He takes his position about five feet beyond the infield grass, scratches his cleats into the dirt in front of him and nods that he's ready to handle whatever is hit to him.

Cy Davis, the *Islanders* infield coach, stands about 20 feet away from the left edge of the batting cage with a fungo bat in his hands, awaiting a signal to begin hitting grounders to Chubby.

"Okay, move him around some," Majeski yells over to his coach. "Let's see if he's a better fielder than a hitter."

Out of ten grounders hit to him, Chubby catches three, bobbles three and misses four completely. "Hey kid, anybody ever call you *butterfingers*?" asks Majeski, laughing and walking slowly with Klein towards third base. "You've shown me you can't hit or play the infield? If Jack Dunn signed you, he must have seen something special about you. Don't tell me you're the wonder boy, Roy Hobbs, the best damn pitcher in baseball?"

"As a matter of fact, I am," boasts Chubby. "But the name's Chubby Bender, not Roy Hobbs, the best damn pitcher in baseball."

"The best what?"

"Pitcher. I'm a knuckleballer from Easton," Chubby tells them. "Mr. Dunn said that you'll teach me the way the game *oughta* be played, the way your father taught you. You'll know how to get the best *outta* me, smooth out the rough edges on my mechanics until the *Oryuls* call me up for the last month of their season."

Klein and Majeski turn to each other and have a big belly laugh.

"That kid's got some *kinda* bravado, don't he?" Klein declares.

"He'll need it," Majeski replies, with a disappointing sigh as he beckons Chubby over.

"You've come a long way from, did you say, Easton? Mr. Dunn must've seen something in you, otherwise he wouldn't have signed you. Get the hell out in right field and start warming up in the bull pen with Coach Dempsey. In five minutes you'll be throwing batting practice to our *regs*."

"*Regs?*" asks Chubby, with a puzzled look.

"Our regular players," Majeski utters, shaking his head back and forth. "Don't tell me it's the first time you heard that expression? Where in the hell have you been playing, on Mars?"

Five minutes later, as Chubby heads to the mound to begin throwing batting practice, Hank huddles with Dempsey who jogs from the outfield bull pen and takes his position behind home plate.

"How's he look, Demp? Is his ball moving?"

"Christ, his fast ball's moving all right, but couldn't break a pane of glass. I wondered why his ball kept getting bigger after it left his hand, then it *hit* me," Dempsey declares, laughing out loud. "Got good control. From what I've seen so far, I feel sorry for this cocky farm boy."

"All right, kid, let's see your fastball," Hank yells over to Chubby. "Try to throw it by our *regs*, if you can."

"You number three, four and five guys: take three swings and get outta there," shouts Majeski to three of his players waiting behind the batting cage. All three are bonus babies who were the best hitters in the middle of his lineup last year and everyone, especially themselves, expects more production since they're no longer rookies.

Jim Gentile Jr., a left-handed power hitter scheduled to bat third after hitting *.325 last year*, jumps into position at home plate, cocks his bat and hits the first three pitches from Bender over the centerfield fence, 375 feet away.

Howie Moss Jr., a right-handed slugger scheduled to bat cleanup after hitting .340 last season, follows Gentile and nails three pitches from Chubby over the left field fence, 330 feet away.

Pete Pavlik Jr., another left-handed hitter not known for power but who recorded an on-base-percentage of .440 last season, follows Moss and crushes Chubby's three fast balls over the right field fence, 325 feet away.

All three hitters are *loosy-goosy* as they huddle behind the batting screen and tease each other about which one hit Chubby's pitches harder and farther.

"Hey, *Demp*, I thought you said he had good control," says Majeski disgustingly." His ball's always going toward your target but never reaches your mitt."

"Balls down here must be juiced," Chubby hollers down to Dempsey, who's still in a catcher's crouch behind home plate, "or maybe it's the thin air here."

"Juiced? Thin air?" asks Dempsey, raising his mask until it's positioned on top of his head. "The only things juiced are oranges, not baseballs, and the only thin air here is what's between your ears!"

"Well, kid, we've seen what you don't have to strike out a batter, which, so far, is all *gabage*," Majeski shouts back at Chubby. "Show me *whateva* else you have in your pitching arsenal and do it fast, otherwise you'll miss your train back to Easton tonight."

"You mean I can now throw them my knuckleball?" Chubby asks him in anticipation of getting the chance to finally show his money pitch.

"That's what I mean, kid. You can even throw the kitchen *zink,* if it'll *strike 'em* out."

Suddenly, Chubby's composure turns to ice as he takes his

left hand out of his glove and uses both hands to rub down a new baseball with some rosin. He grips it in his right hand, digging his fingernails into the stitches of the cowhide cover. He takes a deep breath, lets it out slowly and nods his head confidently after the catcher gives him the sign for a knuckleball. A cunning smile covers his face, knowing this is the pitch that will make him famous. He swings his right arm once in a windmill windup and releases the first in a series of three knuckleballs to Gentile, anxiously waiting to continue blasting away at Chubby's pitches.

"Strike one, two, three and you're *outta* there, Gentile," Dempsey quickly bellows like an umpire but without any hand signals.

"*Damndest* thing I've ever seen," asserts Gentile, flinging his bat away in disgust. "They should sign this kid *pronto*. All three of his knuckleballs were floating all over the plate."

"You weren't concentrating on the ball," says Moss to Gentile. "You were still thinking about those liners you hit over the fence. I'll show you what to do with his knuckleball. Watch *me*."

"Strike one, two, three and you're *outta* there, Moss," bellows Dempsey again. "You missed all three by a foot."

"They dance up and down," declares Moss, looking strangely at his bat. "Maybe I need a butterfly net. One instant his ball goes to the left and the next, to the right. It's a flutter ball."

"You guys are all wet behind the ears," says Pavlik, jumping into the batting cage and eager to take his *cuts* at Chubby's pitches. "You guys, pay attention. I'll show you how to make contact."

"Are you ready?" Chubby asks Pavlik, waiting until he takes a few practice swings and steps into the batter's box.

"Ready and able," hollers Pavlik. "Show me *whatya* got, farm boy!"

Chubby shrugs off the slur, digs his fingernails into the stiches of the baseball and swings his arm twice in a windmill before letting loose three strikes right down the middle of the plate. Pavlik swings and misses with such force that, after the third strike, he twists his legs and falls to the ground.

"All of you guys are wet behind the ears," says Dempsey. "You'll never hit a knuckleball by lunging at it. Wait for it to cross the plate. And you weren't watching Chubby's release point and changes in speed. He hardly worked up a sweat against you meatheads!"

"Hey Demp, is there any phlegm on the *boisbol*?" asks Majeski.

"No, skipper," exclaims Dempsey, "only rosin as it flutters and moves through the strike zone, not to the strike zone. I guess I owe him an apology. He's cocky, all right. Good trait for a closer."

"Hey kid, bring your ass over here a minute," Majeski yells to him.

Chubby jogs over and stands at attention, looking eyeball-to-eyeball in the manager's face.

"Your knuckleball doesn't have any *giddy up* but it does have *giddy out*!" Majeski tells him, taking his pitcher's glove off his left hand and checking it for a foreign substance.

After he smells the leather and rubs his fingers all over Chubby's glove, Majeski hands it back to him.

"Is that good or bad?" asks Chubby.

"It's good, kid, real good. You're not on steroids, are you, or any performance-enhancing drugs?" Hank asks him like a prosecutor questioning a suspect in court.

"I take 1,000 milligrams of Vitamin C every day, to prevent colds from developing. I learned it from reading about Nobel Prize winner Linus Pauling."

"Don't believe it will prevent a cold but it may shorten one," Majeski tells him. "Vitamin C will boost your immune system and repair tissues in your body, too. Trust me on that."

"I will," Chubby says, pounding his fist into his glove.

"And by the grace of God, we finally have a middle reliever or closer," says Majeski, pointing to Chubby's chest. "Hit the showers and report to Mr. Klein. We'll take a chance and give you a contract to sign, but I have one question: When you couldn't hit a ball to save your life, misplayed grounders at third and had our three best hitters rip your fastball over the fence, why weren't you discouraged?"

"Why should I be discouraged?" asks Chubby. "I still hadn't shown anyone my knuckleball!"

Majeski walks over and puts his arm around Klein's shoulders. "That kid is *smat* and fearless, the right mental make-up for a closer. I think Mr. Dunn may have sent an angel to help us win a pennant this year."

The following day, Andy Musser, the broadcaster for the *Islanders*, is leaning with one shoulder against the chain-link fence in right field, holding a miniature tape recorder about the size of a pack of cigarettes in one hand and spots Chubby Bender running wind sprints.

"Hey, farm-boy, number 33," he shouts over to him. "After you finish your workout, can you spare a minute or two?"

"You talking to me?" Chubby asks with his thumb pointing to his chest.

"You're the only one running winds sprints."

Chubby jogs over, removes his cap, wipes some sweat from his forehead and introduces himself.

"Bender's the name, spelled B-E-N-D-E-R. You can call me Chubby, for short," he tells Musser.

"Musser's the name, spelled M-U-S-S-E-R. You can call me Andy, for short. You're the first player I've seen for the *Islanders* who beat a broadcaster to the ballpark on a hot and humid day. But that's not why I asked you over. What's all this buzz around camp about a farm boy from Easton with the best knuckleball since Tim Wakefield of the Boston Red Sox?"

"Don't know what you're talking about, sir. I'm from Easton and I throw a knuckleball, but so far, I haven't proven anything yet."

"Been throwing it long?"

"Sixty feet six inches."

"I'm not referring to the distance between the mound and

home plate. I'm asking about the first time you started throwing the knuckleball."

"Well, I've wanted to play baseball ever since I was old enough to stand on my own two feet," answers Chubby with a wide smile. "That was a long time ago. Not very interesting stuff, really. If you want something worthwhile, why don't you ask who taught me how to perfect the knuckleball?"

"Okay, who taught you how to perfect the knuckleball?" asks Musser, grinning and moving the recorder closer to Chubby's mouth.

"Many along the way, but Jim Honochick and Hoyt Wilhelm gave me the best advice and showed me the way to grip the ball and use different arm angles to release it and throw batters off balance. Then, there was my adopted family at Ridgefield, outside the town of Rock Hall, who gave me a place to practice and perfect everything. They were very encouraging and even got me an interview with Jack Dunn Jr. of the *Oryuls* in Baltimore. Everything happened so fast after that."

"Interesting."

"But I haven't proven anything yet. I'm just waiting for the season to start and doing everything I can to help the *Islanders*. It's an opportunity to do something I've wanted to do all my life, and that's play baseball. The Good Lord will take care of the rest and hopefully, I'll be in an *Oryuls* uniform in late September when they call up promising rookies to the big leagues."

"Did you know that Dempsey's raving about you in the clubhouse right now?"

"What's there to rave about?"

"He's explaining the movement on your knuckleball in terms of physics, mathematics and aerodynamics."

"I never paid much attention to that stuff," says Chubby.

"Ever heard the expression: *he worked the axis*?"

"Never."

"Dempsey's in the clubhouse trying to explain to Hank Majeski the $x$, $y$, and $z$ coordinates of Calculus 101."

"You lost me, sir."

"He says '*x*' is the horizontal line where your ball moves left or right, '*y*' is the vertical line where your ball moves up and down, and '*z*' is the depth where your ball moves in and out as it breaks the plane of the plate."

"That's way over my head, man. All I try to do is get the sign from the catcher and get the knuckleball to the spot where he's holding his catcher's mitt. As far as I'm concerned, there's no *x, y* or *z*'s involved. That's all *cocky-dooly!*"

"One last question. *Whataya* eat before a game?"

"I always eat one hotdog at the ballpark, with Tabasco sauce and paprika."

"Is that where you get the flutter in your knuckleball from?" asks Musser, glancing at the timer on his recorder.

"Nah," says Chubby. "I just like my dog a little spicy."

# Chapter 9

It's noon on Memorial Day and Mark and Ruth have an emergency appointment with their pediatrician in Chestertown. Although it's a holiday, they have convinced their family doctor to examine three-year old Jaime and one-year old Baby Ruth for a running nose, fever and diarrhea.

Outside their home at Ridgefield, about thirty minutes before noon, Mark is opening the driver's side of his car as Ruth straps her children into the back seat for the 20 minute drive through Rock Hall and into Chestertown.

"Let me drive into town this morning," she tells him. "That way you can sit in the back seat between the kids and play with them a little and watch for deer near the trees along the road. They scare the hell out of me when they burst out of the woods."

"Why don't you admit that you simply enjoy driving my father's Mercedes," he tells her with a chuckle. "Nothing like a Mercedes 500, even if it's an '83."

"Still looks like it just came out of the showroom."

"He kept it running in top condition, like everything he owned."

Keeping her eyes mainly focused on the road into town, she looks occasionally in the rear view mirror to catch a glimpse of

Mark with his arms around their children, strapped in their safety seats.

Two minutes later, as they approach the town limits where Eastern Neck Island Road becomes Main Street, Ruth reduces her speed from 45 to 25 mph. Three blocks after passing the Town Hall on her right, she grips the steering wheel as her car begins to move slowly across Sharp Street, where Durding's Ice Cream Parlor, Jake's Haberdashery, Java Rock Coffee House and the Methodist Church form the corners of the town center.

Unseen by anyone, a speeding car on her left runs a stop sign and slams with full force into the front half of her car and sends it spinning almost 120 degrees clockwise until the front section faces the Java Rock Coffee House. The impact immediately releases the airbags in the front seats, but offers no protection from a side collision. The dashboard folds like the bellows of an accordion and is pushed two feet to the right where it wraps around the empty right-front passenger seat. The horn somehow remains pressed, alerting all within hearing distance.

The front frame of the car has buckled and ripped away from its welded corners. Several components from the front half of the Mercedes now lay in the street. The fan motor whose impeller blades spin and scrape the surface of the inside housing, giving off an eerie screech. The water radiator sputters as hot steam escapes slowly from punctures in its fins. The Mercedes hood ornament, the hallmark three-pointed star, now lies by a curb. The smell of petrol surrounds the car and a spark could ignite the liquid leaking from a ruptured fuel line.

"Don't move a muscle until I can check out the kids," Mark shouts frantically to Ruth as he releases the harness straps around his children and takes them into his arms.

The babies are crying after being shaken up so abruptly, but begin to feel comfortable once they are secured in their father's arms.

On the front deck of Java Rock Coffee House, a senior citizen sits slouched in a green plastic patio chair under a red, white and blue-stripped umbrella. She's nursing a cup of hot coffee as the collision unfolds right before her eyes. They almost bulge out of their sockets as she spills the coffee cup and reaches for her phone to speed-dial 911.

Fortunately, the Rock Hall Volunteer Fire Department is less than a mile away and its rescue vehicle is dispatched immediately to the scene.

The siren of the rescue vehicle blasts into everyone's ears and frightens the babies to a point where they are now screaming at the top of their tiny lungs. The decibel level of their crying almost matches the siren's level, so that even after the siren is turned off, the screaming and crying continue from their mouths.

A minute later, a young man with muscles bulging out of his short-sleeved shirt uses the Jaws of Life to cut open the rear door. The grinding action of the diamond-tipped blades cutting through metal creates a terrifying high-pitched sound. Ruth is still sitting in the driver's seat, held upright by the front air bag. After Mark and his children are extricated from their car, he looks closely at Ruth and realizes for the first time that she is immobile. The collision has taken her life.

Everything happened too fast, like an explosion caused by a mortar shell in combat. There was nothing he could have done differently to save her life. This time his instincts and intuition are of little help. The collision snapped her neck. He tries to console the children as best he can.

After the babies are taken out of his arms by two attendants of the rescue squad, Mark looks around at the intersection, and his body begins to shake uncontrollably. He goes into shock and falls in a heap to the ground, as if instantly struck. He begins to experience a series of convolutions and eventually curls up into a fetal position.

He squirms until a rescue volunteer kneels down beside him and straps an oxygen mask to his nose and mouth. Pure oxygen from the canister attached to the mask helps him to regain his senses. A few minutes later, he's sitting on the ground, looking upward at the sky and trying, with all his might, to scream out to God.

"Why not take me? Why Ruth?" he yells at the top of his lungs. Then, after catching his breath, he attempts to release more anger. But no sounds come out of his mouth, wide open with distorted lips. The horror and silence at this instant has more visual impact than the loudest scream anyone could make under these circumstances.

His body stops quivering as he begins to drift into a quick flashback of combat four years earlier, in Iraq, when Rusty rolled over him and died from a broken neck, too. But this incident is far worse. It's the love of his life, his beautiful wife, Ruth, and the end of an all too brief era of happiness.

After Mark and his children are secured inside the rescue vehicle they are driven to the Chester River Hospital in Chestertown.

As Mark is pushed in a wheelchair into the emergency room behind two nurses who carry his children in their arms, cardiologist Dr. Joe McLain recognizes him from his visits to the hospital to see Judy Ridgefield two years ago and immediately gives instructions to a nurse to telephone Ridgefield with news of the accident.

Although he's not the physician on duty in the emergency ward, Dr. McLain is respected as a take-charge individual in emergencies. After a thorough examination, he orders the attending nurses to administer some medication immediately; for the children, pills to dry up a running nose, reduce their fever and diarrhea and for Mark, tranquilizers and blood thinners to correct an erratic heart.

Later in the afternoon, Sara pokes her head into his private room and finds him and his children resting. His mother is a nervous wreck and was driven to the hospital by Lola, who follows in her footsteps.

"What can I say to you?" she asks him in almost a whisper, as tears flow down her cheeks.

Lola grabs her around her waist to keep her from falling over.

"Can I get you something to drink?" she asks. "You could be dehydrated."

"Yes, that's a good idea. If you don't mind, I'll take a seat close to Mark."

"I haven't had much time to digest everything yet," Mark tells her, "but now that I see you here, I can't help thinking of the time you and Dad came to see me after Vera's murder in this hospital room," says Mark, pressing his thumb against his wrist to check his pulse.

"If there's anything that you need me to do," says Lola, "just tell me."

"I can feel my heartbeat is erratic," he tells them. "Hopefully in a few hours it will return to normal."

"We'll be spending the night at Ridgefield," Lola tells him. "Let me know if you need anything. You can lean on me."

"What about your work with Mike Bloomburg?"

"It'll be there when we get back to Baltimore," she tells him. "My work with Mike is not really work at all. He's a joy to be around. In fact, he's approached me about becoming a partner in the firm. How's that for a quick rise in the legal profession?"

There's a knock on the door and detective Patrick "Pappy" Paprika, who goes by the nickname of 'PP,' of the Kent County Sheriff's Office, hands him a note from the head nurse.

"This is not the time and place to play cupid; don't get spicy with me, Paprika!" says Mark, unraveling the paper and quickly handing it back to him. "My eyes are blurred. Would you read it for me?"

"It reads: 'Good news travels fast. Bad news travels faster. We're here for you whenever you need us. May God watch over you and your children. Abigail.' "

Mark moves his head backward into the soft pillows and closes his eyes.

Detective Paprika nudges his shoulder several times to get his attention and asks Sara and Lola to leave the room; he must discuss something privately with Mark.

"From the looks of the damage to both cars, it appears that the speeding car must have been going over 45 in a 25-mph zone, and the driver never applied his brakes. There were no skid marks in the intersection," Paprika explains slowly. "Also, the driver had a blood alcohol level more than two times above the legal limit, with a touch of cocaine included."

Mark is still too dazed to digest everything and drops his head to his chest.

"I'm sorry to be the one to have to give you this news," Paprika continues, apologizing for adding to his pain and misery. "By the way, the driver had to be cut out of his seat and gave his name. I think he said, 'Maxwell Floyd.' Ever heard of him?"

"No, but I can't wait to get my hands on him," says Mark, who raises his head suddenly, opens his eyes widely and growls, exposing his teeth. Both hands begin to clench into fists.

"Revenge won't bring back your wife," Paprika continues. "Besides, you'll have to get in line. He's in the recovery room, guarded by a police deputy, after admitting he was 'juiced' from whiskey and cocaine at Waterman's Restaurant, about three blocks away from the point of impact. He said he was in a hurry to get back to the sloughing shed to look after *peelers*, whatever that is. He also goes by the nickname of 'Pretty Boy' Floyd."

"Now, that's a name I recognize," answers Mark with anguish.

"Well, he won't be pretty anymore. His head went through the glass windshield," admits Paprika. "He should've worn his seat belt. According to the doctors treating his injury, he'll be confined to a wheelchair for the rest of his life. He's now a paraplegic."

Paprika hesitates to allow him time to absorb his words.

Mark lowers his head until his chin touches his chest. He holds his breath for about 30 seconds; it's an exercise to reduce anxiety and dispel hot flashes that randomly appear. Perspiration forms on his forehead as Detective Paprika disappears and Dr. McLain suddenly stands at his bedside.

"You won't be going home today," says Dr. McLain. "Your

EKG shows an erratic heartbeat, called atrial fibrillation or *AFib*. It's probably due to the accident unless you've had this condition and never knew about it; it puts a stress on your heart. We'll give you some medication and a small dinner around 6 pm. It's important that you do not take nothing, ah anything into your stomach after 8," says Dr. McLain, trying to speak and review his charts at the same time.

"I think I know what you're going to do with me tomorrow morning. What about my two children?"

"We'll keep your children close by, with nurses ready to assist you. Since your erratic heartbeat is presumably due to the accident and hopefully not something you've been experiencing over a period of time, electroshock should restore your heartbeat back to its normal rhythm. The procedure is scheduled for tomorrow morning at 7."

This news is little consolation to Mark as he reaches for his cell phone to call Abigail. "I thought we'd be coming home," he tells her grimly, "but my erratic heartbeat complicates things. I'll call you tomorrow morning after undergoing an electroshock treatment to correct the *AFib*."

The following afternoon, Mark and his children are back at Ridgefield where his home is destined to be transformed into a mausoleum.

Five days after Ruth's death, a funeral mass is held on Saturday at noon inside St. John's Catholic Church in Rock Hall, with Father Paul Campbell presiding. Butterflies begin to stir inside his body as Mark gazes at Father Campbell, standing alone on the altar. He can't help thinking about his father's funeral mass two years ago. Eventually his mind seems to be operating on automatic pilot as he drifts in and out of two funerals.

After the gospel is read, Father Paul nods his head to Liz, who walks to the center aisle, genuflects and turns to face the small gathering of family and friends. "We need not fear or be angry about the loss of Ruth Wayne Hopkins, for she has gone to a far better place," Liz reads from a card gripped tightly in one hand. "Ruth was unique. Beautiful on the outside, twice as beautiful on the inside. She turned down an opportunity to go to Hollywood for a screen test and instead joined American Airlines for a chance to see the world. She was a hometown beauty voted unanimously the Queen of the Harvest Moon Festival two years ago. She showered us with her kindness, good spirits and *Joie de Vie*. That joy will live on in the life of her husband and children."

She hesitates a few seconds to gather her breath and nods toward her husband, Reggie, who leaves his seat to stand beside her. "Mark has asked me to read this part of the eulogy to his wife," he says slowly, in a most comforting voice. "Ruth Wayne Hopkins, whom we have grown to love, is gone but will never be forgotten. We should not disgrace ourselves by running away from the fear of seeing a loved one die. We should face fear, look into its eyes, and know that God is guiding us and lighting the way ahead. He will judge the living and the dead. He will neither deceive nor be deceived. God gave her to us for a short time and has chosen to take her to a higher place. Ruth is the lucky one. She is with God."

After Reggie and Liz return to their seats, Father Paul surveys the church and notices a hand raised by someone in the last pew. "If you'd like to address the gathering, please come forward and be heard," he tells the young man, who rises from his seat and walks slowly down the aisle of the church.

It's Bud Wayne, the brother of Ruth, who has been granted special permission by the circuit court judge of Kent County to leave the Patuxent Correctional Institution in Jessup to attend his sister's funeral. He's dressed in his orange-colored prison-issue jumper, free of shackles, and walks slowly to the front railing of the altar.

"While locked up behind bars, I've had plenty of time to reflect on Ruth and realize how special she was to me. With her passing comes a final chapter in her life but not an ending. She will forever be with me in spirit to guide me, as she always tried to do, in her own special way."

He opens his Bible and begins to read: "Matthew, chapter 18, verse 21. Peter came to Jesus and asked, 'Lord, how many times shall I forgive my brother when he sins against me? Up to seven times?' Jesus answered, 'I tell you, not seven times, but seventy-seven times...' "

He closes the bible, looks down at its cover for a few seconds to say a silent prayer and gather his strength. "I thank God and the circuit court judge for giving me permission to attend my sister's funeral. As I pay my last respects to her, I pray that God will have mercy on her soul and guide her into a better life hereafter."

"He looks anemic to me," Mark whispers to his mother as Bud passes close by and makes his way back to his seat.

"I guess the rumors about him becoming a 'born-again' Christian are true," Sandy tells York, sitting in the second pew behind Mark, his mother and Lola.

Father Paul concludes the funeral mass by administering a blessing to everyone. "At the request of her husband," he acknowledges, "the burial will be private, however everyone is invited to a reception at Ridgefield immediately following this service."

The bell in the church steeple tolls for five minutes and continues at five-minute intervals for the next hour.

The reception begins around 1 pm inside the sound stage of Ridgefield's Research and Test Lab (RTL); the front half, which includes a small stage, is cordoned off by a long curtain. Along one wall is a table beautifully decorated by Annette with some antiques from her shop in Betterton. The center piece is a twenty-inch high white porcelain tundra swan with a cavity in its back that holds a bouquet of multi-colored roses. Assorted gourmet dishes of finger food, prepared by Gabby and Manny, include: sweet fresh claw meat from Bluefin Bay crabs with a touch of Alfredo sauce on a wafer of wheat toast, medium-size shrimp sprinkled with a drop or two of Tabasco sauce on pumpernickel bread, avocado and Maytag blue cheese imported from Newton, Iowa all spread onto an Oreo cookie, along with bowls of fresh fruit carefully placed between chilled buckets of champagne.

Lois and Clowie are the first to arrive and begin to hand out a one-by-two-inch oval patch, hand woven by Clowie with *RWH* in capital letters.

"Just remove the paper backing and stick it on your lapel," Clowie tells them. "It's something to remember Ruth by. The idea was borrowed from sports teams who honor one of their fallen members. You can sew it on later, if you'd like."

About a half-hour after everyone settles down, Reggie makes his way to the stage, checks his guitar to make sure it's in tune, and motions to Liz, Sandy, Andrew and Frances Muller to join him on stage.

"Before getting underway with our music," Reggie says, "let me introduce two new additions to our combo: Andrew and Frances Muller, brother and sister act from Muller's Seafood Café on Bond Street in Baltimore. I think you're going to enjoy the phrasing they bring to our musical medley dedicated to the memory of our dear friend, Ruth."

"Everyone is welcome to sing along," says Sandy. "The words will be flashed up on a screen at the back of the stage."

"The first song is *Someone To Watch Over Me*," says Liz, "written by George and Ira Gershwin, with a few word changes to suit the occasion."

*"There's somebody I'm longing to see, I hope that Ruth turns out to be, someone who'll watch over me, I'm a little lamb who's lost in the woods, I know I could always be good, with someone who'll watch over me."*

Andrew with his harmonica, and Frances on the piano, continue playing in the background and segue into the next song in the medley. "And now," says Reggie, stepping to the microphone, "we'd like to play: *Till There Was You*, a beautiful ballad written by Meredith Willson."

> *"There were bells on the hill, but I never heard them ringing, no*
> *I never heard them at all, till there was you.*
> *There were birds in the sky, but I never saw them winging, no, I*
> *never saw them at all, till there was you.*
> *And there was music, and there were wonderful roses, they tell*
> *me, in sweet fragrant meadows of dawn, and dew.*
> *There was love all around, but I never heard it singing, no, I*
> *never heard it at all, till there was you!"*

"And lastly," says Sandy, "you all know them as the pride of Betterton and our newest recording artists, Knute Runagrund and his parrot, Gertie, singing their rendition of Irving Berlin's *Always.*"

By now, everyone is familiar with their recent success on stage at the Hippodrome Theatre in Baltimore, in which Knute sings all the following words except the word, *Always,* which is squawked by Gertie:

> *"I'll be loving you Always, with a love that's true Always,*
> *When the things you've planned need a helping hand,*
> *I will understand Always.*
> *Days may not be fair Always, that's when I'll be there Always,*
> *Not for just an hour, not for just a day, not for just a year but*
> *Always."*

During the reception, Manny tries to be as unobtrusive as possible, taking photos of everyone without their knowing it and pausing only when Gabby hands him an assortment of hors d'oeuvres.

A few minutes after the music on stage ends, Sara walks slowly over to Lois and Clowie, standing near the stage. "Would you mind giving me a few minutes alone with this gorgeous lady?"

Sara asks Clowie. "There's something I'd like to talk over with Lois confidentially."

"Be my guest," Clowie answers. "It's a beautiful day outside, so you may want to stroll up to the rip-rap along the shoreline of Ridgefield. It's very peaceful when you're near the Chesapeake Bay."

"I've been wanting to speak with you, too," Lois answers as they walk arm in arm across the room and out an exit.

"Let's take Clowie's suggestion and walk to the shore," says Sara. "The Bay seems to be beckoning me."

"I had the same feeling."

When they reach the shoreline of Ridgefield, both stand relaxed and inhale the fresh breeze blowing gently over the waves.

Sara puts her index finger into her mouth and then raises it above her head.

"Never could quite figure out how someone can tell the direction of the wind with one wet finger in the air," she tells Lois with a grin.

"Unusually warm for this time of the year, don't you think?" Lois asks, holding up one hand to shade the sun from her eyes. "Plenty of watermen still out on the Bay."

"I wanted to thank you for joining the board of Bethlehem Steel. You've been a big help to my son, so he tells me. He's going to need everyone's help even more now that his wife is gone."

"It's not a one-way street. We're helping each other by sharing information, whether it's technology or mutual sales."

"Speaking of sharing," says Sara, "I'd like to share something with you that even my son doesn't know about. You and I are related."

"How?"

"You descended from Tom Carnegie, Andrew's younger brother, and I descended from Margaret, Andrew's only daughter. A lot happened after they were all born in Dunfermline, Scotland, and now is not the time to go into our family tree. I just want you to know that you could be either my niece or my cousin. Of course, we're a generation apart."

"Are you kidding me?" asks Lois.

"Even my husband didn't know that I came from the Carnegie clan in Allegheny City. I met Mark's father while we were taking a course in business administration at Hopkins. He was so wrapped up with his goal of one day taking over his father's mill, I thought it best not to complicate things with family history. I doubt if it would have made a difference anyway. He had enough ambition for both of us and was so talented and hard working."

"Remarkable."

"I always wished," says Sara, "that I could have done more for my husband, but the mill seemed to come first. It was my rival because he was so devoted to his work."

"You kept the family together. That's quite an accomplishment."

Sara turns to Lois and turns the collar of her blouse upward.

"You are so beautiful," she tells her. "When you and Mark began to conduct business together in art and antiques, I was hoping it would gravitate into something more personal, but Mark had his eyes on Ruth."

"And I had mine on Clowie. She's an incredibly-gifted lady."

"Really?"

"She can take a design by Coco Chanel, Yves Saint Laurent or Givenchy, add her own splash of originality and produce a dress fit for any actress. She already has a few of her costumes in the collection of a museum."

"Why haven't we heard more about her?"

"Because she hates publicity and prefers to remain incognito."

"Seems like we're both learning something here today," Sara tells her as she takes hold of her arm. "The twists and turns of life. We are all guided by the Good Lord. Maybe we'd better be getting back to the reception. Again, I just wanted to thank you for all you've done and will do. I'd love to see more of you, especially since we're related. Feel free to drop in at Cylburn whenever you want to take a break from your work at the mill."

"Before we go back inside, maybe you'd like to hear something I've never told anyone."

"And what would that be?"

"Why I like Mark and admire him so much. Most of our forefathers climbed their way out of poverty with very little education and achieved success by investing in things."

"Things?" asks Sara.

"I'm referring mainly to our patriarch, *Andra* or *Andy* as he was called, whose first real job at 15 was delivering telegrams around Allegheny City at all times of the day and night. Fast forward to training himself to be a Morse-Code telegrapher, railroad station manager and by thirty, an investor in businesses like the telegraph right-of-ways, railroads and timber lands."

"Don't forget his coal, iron and oil companies, where their products and services were in demand," says Sara.

"I was coming to that," says Lois. "My point is that, most of the time, he had insider knowledge to hedge his risk. He never invested first in an individual or partner. On the other hand, Mark invests in people. *That* is what I like best about him."

"I hadn't thought about it before," says Sara. "Now that you mention it, Andrew was good with numbers and Mark is good with people."

Around 3 pm, Lola noticed that Sara and Lois have left the reception and takes Mark by the hand and walks him over to the men's room.

"Slip into something more comfortable, Mark," she tells him. "You'll find your clothes inside. We're going horseback riding in the Refuge."

After changing into his old riding jacket and pants that Lola brought from Cylburn, Mark is stunned when she opens the door to a horse trailer parked beside the R&TL building.

"Surprised?" she asks him. "Actually it's Sandy's idea, to take a ride to the Refuge. Tom Bowman loaned her two horses from his *Dance Forth Farm* outside Betterton. So, *saddle up*, partner, or, as they say in Hunt Valley, *Tally ho.*"

Within fifteen minutes their horses mosey through the woods of the Refuge, next door to Ridgefield. "Seems as if they've been here before and know exactly where they're going," Lola admits, patting the neck of her stallion.

"I doubt it, but more like instinctive. Wouldn't surprise me if this was an old horse trail. So peaceful here. I can see why birds and waterfowl would migrate to the Island. I should spend more time here, with my children, too."

They reach a small clearing within the forest where the horses stop to feed on a grassy area.

"Might be a good place to walk a little and feel the earth below our feet," suggests Lola as she dismounts and pulls a pamphlet out of her jacket. "According to my handy guide, there's more than 500 acres of forests. The Island is about 2,285 acres and begins at the mouth of the Chester River, with six miles of trails."

"Don't think we have time for more than a mile or two today," Mark utters as he dismounts and walks his horse beside hers. "We'll have to come back again. I think I saw a deer with a white tail."

"The guide says there are white-tail deer," she declares with a laugh. "I wonder how long it took someone to think up that name."

"There goes a baby fox. No, it can't be a fox because it's climbing a tree. Must be a big squirrel."

"Wildlife includes beaver, red fox and the endangered Delmarva fox squirrel, which is probably what you saw," she tells him.

"Obviously. However, did you know the tundra swan flies over 3,700 miles from Alaska to migrate on the Island, from October to March?" says Mark. "They're all white, except for their black bills, legs and feet."

"The rhythmic flapping of its wings," she says, reading from her guide, "produces a tone that earned it the name of *whistling swan*, with a wing span of 77 inches. In August, the ospreys begin to migrate farther south and the blue-winged teal, ducks with bright iridescent blue or green patches on their wings, take up residence here, along with the tundra swan."

"We might get lucky and see one of the threatened southern bald eagles living around these parts," admits Mark.

"Do you know how to tell the difference between the southern and northern bald eagle?" Lola asks him suspiciously.

"No. How?"

"The southern ones always end their *screech* with *y'all*," she replies with a burst of laughter.

For a brief moment, Mark is relaxed and enjoying the company of a beautiful woman. "What does your guide say about the American Indians who lived here hundreds of years ago?" he asks.

"Around 1300 AD," says Lola, "the first tribe to live and fish here was the Woodland Period Indians, then around 1608 Captain John Smith met the Ozinie Indians, who were related to the Algonquin-speaking Nanticoke."

"You'd make a good guide for the Island reserve if you ever decided to give up your day job. By the way, how are things at your law firm?"

"You really want to know?"

"Yes, I want to know."

"Handling litigations alongside Mike Bloomburg is terrific," she admits, smiling, "but I enjoy taking care of a wonderful woman at Cylburn and, when I can fit it into my schedule, riding horseback in Hunt Valley."

"Perhaps it's time to get back to Ridgefield," says Mark, "and return these stallions to Tom Bowman in Betterton. Are you planning to spend the night here?"

"Sandy's invited me to stay in her newly decorated apartment," says Lola. "In the morning, after breakfast with Annette, Richard and Sandy I'll drive back to Baltimore."

For the next five days, Mark changes his entire routine of work so that he can spend as much time as possible with his two toddlers. He is besieged, overwhelmed -- in a good sense -- by everyone in the Ridgefield family who offers a hand to lift him out of the first stages of his depression and bereavement.

The second Monday in June, Mark jogs around the 50-acre farm of Ridgefield, falling several times when he pushes himself and sweat creeps into his eyes. By the time he completes a 30-minute workout, he looks as if he's been dragged through the field by a team of horses. A quick shower can clean up the dirt, but bloody hands, elbows and knees from scraping gravel require treatment to prevent infection.

On Tuesday he excuses himself from having breakfast with the Ridgefield family, preferring to work out in the fitness center. He begins his routine with a five-minute bout of pounding both fists into a heavy compact duffle bag, as if it's a boxer charging into him. Ten minute sessions on the rowing machine and 60 reps of pumping 40 pounds of iron quickly follow, all without uttering a word.

After his early Wednesday morning workout in the fitness center, he jogs across the middle of the farm and retreats into the woods of the Wildlife Refuge. Soon he spots a bald eagle and its eaglet resting side by side, with their talons griped and curled around a dead limb jutting out of a 30-foot high hickory tree.

"Wish I could climb up and get a new perspective of life from your perch," he tells the bird, propping his body against a tree trunk about 30 meters away, a quiet spot where everything seems frozen in time. "Better yet, I wish that God would give me the strength to spread my wings and soar with eagles like you. Have you seen any great blue herons or green-backed ones lately?"

He waits for a response; even a nod of the eagle's head would be some acknowledgement, but they're concentrating on something that has captured their attention. He pauses to study their white head, neck and tail, and the blackish-brown back and breast, yellow feet and beak.

Seconds later, the eagle and eaglet spring away from the dead limb with an incredible burst of energy. For the first time, he tries to measure their wing span.

"Must be seven feet, at least," he says to himself. "Look at the way they soar with their feathers separated. No wonder those Indian warriors put an eagle feather in their hair as a symbol of great strength."

He turns his head and follows the flight of the eagle and eaglet, soaring upward across a meadow. "Fly all the way to heaven and tell Ruth how much I miss her," he calls out as tears begin to form in his eyes. "At this instant, I close my eyes and visualize in my mind a picture of me holding her tightly and listening to the ballad, *I See Your Face Before Me.*

The following lyrics stream through the forest as if they were sung by a wood nymph:

*"In a world of glitter and glow, in a world of tinsel and show, the unreal from the real thing is hard to know, I discovered somebody who could be truly worthy and true, yes, I met my ideal thing when I met you,*

*"I see your face before me, crowding my every dream, there is your face before me, you are my only theme, it doesn't matter where you are, I can see how fair you are, I close my eyes and there you are, always,*

*"If you could share the magic, yes, if you could see me too, there would be nothing tragic, in all my dreams of you, would that my love could haunt you so, knowing I want you so, I can't erase your beautiful face before me."*

# Chapter 10

Afterdtwo weeks of his typical morning workout at Ridgefield Mark stands inside his office, facing a hole in the drywall with an empty frame around it. "I remember you," he says. "I put my fist right through the 5/8-inch drywall when I lost my temper after losing out on the Winslow Homer painting in California. Ruth overheard me and said, ' You shouldn't feel discouraged. The disappointment will soon pass away.' "

When Mark steps back from the wall, he notices Womble and Abigail, stroking the autumn-colored fur of her kitten, might have overheard him. "Ruth was right," says Abigail. "Sorry. We weren't eavesdropping but wanted to see what's new. My kitten meowed when it heard the tapping of your computer keypad a minute ago."

He motions them into the room. "Take a seat in your Eames lounge chair," he tells Abigail, "and Womble, the ottoman's all yours."

Mark leans back in his swivel chair and pounds the padded armrests with his fists. "If only I hadn't changed places with her," he tells them angrily, "she'd still be alive."

"Too many 'if's,' " says Womble. "You also could ask yourself, 'what if the children didn't have a fever and running nose?' We know all about the 'what if' syndrome, don't we? Nothing good ever comes out of second-guessing yourself."

"I was thinking about that short cut down Boundary Avenue," says Mark, "which bypasses the center of town."

"You and I know that we are in God's hands," says Abigail, "and trust he will watch over us."

"I've decided to take the kids to Cylburn, look after my mother and give her a chance to spoil her grandchildren. I might be away for several weeks. In the meantime, could you both continue to take care of everything at Ridgefield? It's time to get away from here. But feel free to call if you need me."

"What about a follow-up at Aberdeen?" asks Womble. "Kim and Liz are ready to put a prototype of their electronic buoy into the Bay, somewhere near Edgewood Arsenal. We owe it to them to get approval from Aberdeen and see how it performs."

"Good point. I was about to ask you to take on that responsibility and run interference for Kim and Liz. Would you take charge of their project and arrange face-to-face meetings between representatives of Edgewood and Ridgefield? While Liz is capable of confronting military officers with her Pentagon experience, Kim may need some support. No one is going to throw their weight around with you backing them up. They should have more respect for Kim and Liz, knowing you won't take no without an explanation. We have a good product here that should be tested in the Chesapeake Bay, and tested now. The fact that we brought the case of the missing mustard-gas canisters to their attention should give us an edge. They owe us something. It's time to collect."

The following day, the twentieth of June, Mark is inside his bedroom at Cylburn, unpacking a suitcase. At the bottom is one of Ruth's extra-large pullovers with the American Airlines emblem across the front. She wore it over her uniform on cold, damp trips from Heathrow Airport to her London hotel. For the next three days, he'll wear it everywhere, even to bed.

Downstairs in a cozy solarium near the kitchen, Sara is sitting on a sofa, babysitting Jamie and Baby Ruth. When Mark sees her with his kids, he begins to laugh for the first time in a long time.

"Wish I had a camera handy to take a picture of you with Baby Ruth tucked in your arm and Jaime on a rein. It would make a great greeting card," he says.

"Been a long time since I had a child in one hand. Never more than one," she tells him. "Good to see you laughing again."

"I keep thinking this is all a nightmare, and I'll wake up and everything will be like it was before the accident."

"The pain and suffering will pass, and you'll be left with beautiful memories of your life with Ruth. It was the same for me when your father died. I'd like to think that they're together and he's showing Ruth around heaven."

Mark doesn't want his mother to see him burst out in tears, so he leaves the room and walks slowly into the library. In a far corner, beside a Dutch armoire, his closes his eyes and massages his temples, hoping flashbacks of the crash that still haunt him will fade away. "Stupidity, that's what it was," he cries out. "I will never forgive that bastard for getting himself drunk and killing Ruth."

"You'll never be happy until you find forgiveness for those who injured you," says Sara in a soft voice. "I had the same feelings about wanting to strangle those two brutes who failed to give your father oxygen when he had his heart attack in the mill."

He backs away from the corner and gives his mother a big embrace, strong enough that she grimaces slightly. "I can't help constantly dwelling on the crash. We were going only about 20 miles an hour. If we had been a second slower or quicker, Ruth would be alive. Everything happened so fast."

"The Good Lord says to love your enemies," says Sara, "and do good to those who do you the most harm. I heard that the driver is now a paraplegic; he'll have to live with pain the rest of his life. You can begin to remove some of *your* pain by gradually extending a hand of atonement; Reconciliation instead of retribution."

She pauses to wipe some tears coming down her cheeks.

"A friend told me at your father's funeral that people are not always going to make the right decision or do the right thing, but the way you handle the aftermath, the consequences, will define you as a person. Those words are something for you and me to think about. And remember: the human spirit can overcome everything."

While Mark and his children are at the Hopkins estate, Abigail is busy, working inside Mark's old office. As she shuffles some bills on her desk and logs off on her computer, Womble pops his head in the doorway.

"Couldn't do it without you, always within arm's reach or a phone call," she says. "Mark made a good decision when he hired you over a cup of coffee at Java Rock two years ago. My right-hand man, that's what you are, with an uncanny intuition and a way to head off a crisis before it develops. You'll find an increase in your salary next week."

"I'd like to take some credit, but you and Mark hired very good people," he tells her proudly. "I just try to keep everyone on their toes and do it with a little wit and nudge of encouragement. Did you see the prototype that Kim and Liz are developing in the R&T lab?"

"You mean the electronic buoy with sensors to monitor pollution in the Bay?"

"Precisely. It's powered by solar energy, looks like a miniature Atlas rocket with funny-looking nozzles for sucking up liquids. I wouldn't be surprised if one day it answers all questions asked of it. They mentioned something about 'speech recognition technology,' and research by a pioneer, Dr. Frederick Jelinek, of Hopkins. Kim and Liz are working on a secret research study that they won't disclose at this time. They deserve a raise, not me. They're the ones who are making history here at Ridgefield."

During the last week of June, Mark's life at Cylburn has

Joseph John Szymanski

grown grotesque, a combination of deep depression during the day and nightmares that keep him from getting a good night's sleep. Flashbacks usually begin with his experiences in Iraq, when his armored vehicle was struck by a missile and overturned, leading to the death of Rusty, his SEAL mate. Then segments of his implication in Vera's death, suspicious circumstances around his father's heart attack at the mill and images of Ruth being held erect by airbags exploding around her are played over and over again in his subconscious.

On the last Saturday of June, Mark is alone in the kitchen at 7 am and slams the refrigerator door closed. Seconds later an antique mantle clock with a large glass face falls off the top of the refrigerator and crashes to the ground, scattering parts all over the kitchen floor.

"Never liked that clock there," he bellows. "No place for a clock. Don't want to be reminded of time."

He picks up the wooden case, watching more parts from the inside mechanism fall around his feet and lifts it as if he's about to throw it against a wall. After coming to his senses, he sits down as his shoes crush some glass on the floor. At this instant, the room is filled with an eerie silence, as he buries his head in his hands and begins to cry uncontrollably.

Over the next few days, his bereavement worsens. He's makes it known to everyone that they can celebrate the upcoming fourth of July with fireworks by themselves. He has enough fireworks burning inside him and realizes he's much too short-tempered and bitter to face any celebration. No one is exempt, even God, from the brunt of his anger when he tries to recite his daily prayers.

"Why has God chosen to give me success and wealth with one hand and take away two loves with the other?" he asks himself, walking around the grounds of Cylburn. "There doesn't seem to be any escape from pain and suffering. How much can one person be expected to endure?"

In a far corner of Cylburn Park, he sits under the shade of an old oak tree with his back against its trunk and runs his fingers through his hair. Mumbling begins and he can't make much sense out of it. "Am I going crazy or something?" he asks himself. "I don't know if I can go on with my life."

He retreats further into isolation. He is close to a behavior that clinicians might classify as insanity, with suicidal thoughts. When medication or psychotherapy is suggested by Mike Bloomburg, the Hopkins family lawyer, Mark abruptly hangs up the phone. Despite his mother's oversight and Lola's periodic visits, Mark remains encapsulated inside his self-imposed fortress of depression.

Around the middle of July, on one of her visits to see Mark and his mother, Lola brings along Marnie Rivers. This beautiful 32-year old psychologist has many of the same attributes as Ruth.

"She's too good to be true, very likable and charismatic," Sara tells her son. "Lola insists that you give her a chance to help you."

With continuous urging from Sara and Lola, Mark's one-on-one meetings with Marnie begin to have a noticeable impact, if only in halting the direction of his grief. She gains his confidence and, through psychotherapy, allows him to reconnect with his wife and father.

"Your therapy may be working," he tells her. "Yesterday I pictured myself on the phone, a conference call with my father and Ruth, trying to cram in all the things I wanted to tell them before they died. It was hectic, similar to my telephone calls from Iraq, when I had only three minutes to talk to my family. Today I told them how Jaime and Baby Ruth were outgrowing their clothes, how they were beginning to take to the water in the pool just as I did at their age, and had a good appetite for mom's home cooking."

"That's a good start. It's part of the unraveling process."

"Did you know we were planning to take the children to Disneyworld in Florida?" he asks Marnie impulsively, without thinking. "Of course, you didn't know that." He pauses then continues, "How long must I endure these nightmares? Images of Ruth keep fading in and out of my mind. When you talk to your wife every day for almost two years, you don't suddenly stop talking to her because she's dead. And then there is the added misery of seeing Dad everywhere in this house."

"The misery will pass and fade into an awakening. It's good that you've managed to reconnect with him on a spiritual level."

"I remember a dream last night in which my father was leaning over my shoulder in the kitchen, watching me stir oatmeal in a pot. I must have been around ten. When I became a teenager, I was much taller than him, so he could never look over my shoulder again."

"That's a good incident to remember. Your subconscious is resurfacing and a recovery is near."

"I doubt if I'll ever recover completely. It's taken me two years to accept his death, but I still try to speak to him as often as I can. Get his advice. Let him know that we still think about him and love him."

"In a way," Marnie says, "connecting directly with Ruth and your father is better than any drug I could recommend for your rehab."

"Now, I realize how similar my action is to Abigail's conversations with the spirit of her mother," he says. "At first I didn't believe it when she told me she gives her mother updates about her life at Ridgefield."

Mark takes Marnie by her arm and ushers her over to the large portrait of his grandfather sitting proudly on his favorite hunter.

"Every time I look up at this wonderful painting by Sir Alfred Munnings, I see my father, not my grandfather, sitting there, staring down at me and asking me to hold tight and take over the reins of Bethlehem Steel. He taught me how to work. My mother taught me how to enjoy it."

"You're on the path to recovery, Mark," she responds. "Keep talking to your loved ones. Let nothing stand in your way of happiness."

He takes her arm again and walks her over to the grand piano.

Spread out on the top lid are over 25 photographs of the Hopkins family, each in a sterling-silver frame.

"Here's one of my favorites," he tells her proudly, "Dad graduating from Hopkins with a degree in metallurgy at the age of 21. And there's one of him at 40, when he had complete control of the mill and installed more efficient processes for the production of cold-rolled steel."

"He reminds me of Bill Holden when he made the film *Picnic* with Kim Novak," she tells him joyfully. "What a handsome man."

"And a heart to match. I've spent many hours thinking about what he's done for mom and me. I hate to think where I'd be today if it wasn't for him flying by helicopter with our family attorney, Mike Bloomburg, to the hospital in Chestertown."

"Were you involved in a serious accident?"

"Serious, yes. Accident, no. Can you imagine waking up in the front seat of an automobile from an overdose of drugs given to me for a sexual encounter by a woman I hardly knew, who was murdered by her husband and still sitting upright in the driver's seat with her throat cut from ear to ear?"

"Was this real or a nightmare?"

"Both. To make a long story short, without my father bringing Mike to the hospital and hiring an incredible private eye by the name of Virgil Tubbs, I might not be here today."

"Try not to dwell too much on the negatives. Put your mind and heart at ease by enjoying flashbacks of the good times in your life, especially those with your father and Ruth. It's time for you to rejoin the human race. Isn't that what your father and grandfather would tell you?"

As Mark begins to pull himself upward and out of depression, he's aware that he was a victim of his own making. Encapsulated, isolated, withdrawn from family, friends and fellow workers, even from his children.

"Getting these monsters out of my psyche has to end sooner or later, so why not sooner?" he asks himself. "There's no joy in feeling sorry for yourself. It's time to get up off the floor and get back in the fight, and perhaps God will make me stronger than I ever imagined."

Early on the first of August, after a shower and breakfast, he and his mother are sitting at the breakfast nook as he pours her a second cup of hot coffee.

"Haven't said much to me this morning," she says. "Something must be brewing in your mind."

"Would you mind looking after the children? I think it's time to take a step in another direction, this time upwards," he tells her.

"Are you going somewhere this morning?" she asks with some trepidation.

"I'm driving to Rock Hall to see Pretty Boy Floyd," he says.

"I thought he was about to go on trial for driving under the influence, possession of cocaine, excessive speed and who knows what other charges," says Sara.

"I didn't tell you that his lawyer made a plea deal with the Criminal Court Judge," Mark says. "In exchange for a plea of guilty, he will have his driver's license terminated for life, pay a hefty fine and perform 200 hours of community service. On the surface the judge's decision may seem unrealistic but it was rendered from a humanitarian standpoint. He said that nothing would be gained by putting a paraplegic behind bars."

"What will you do when you see him?" she asks."

"Not sure, but at least it's time to stop feeling sorry for myself or blaming others."

"Whatever you do," says Sara, hoping he will not seek vengeance, "ask God for help to see things clearly and do the right thing. Bitterness will get you nowhere."

"That'll be on my mind as I drive down to see him."

"If all goes well, perhaps you can have a look in their sloughing shed, a 'maternity ward' as Szymanski calls it," Sara says jokingly. "If you find any peelers that have sloughed into soft crabs swimming around, perhaps you might bring some home for dinner."

Two hours later, he's standing beside Bonnie Bratcher Floyd as they peer through a screen door of the sloughing shed, a separate building about forty feet behind her house. As Bonnie tries to pull open the door he keeps it closed so that he can pause to watch her husband in his wheelchair, attending to peelers swimming in tanks of Bay water.

"Not a pretty sight," she whispers. "Lately he doesn't hear me when he's tending to his peelers, even if I speak loudly. Sometimes he seems to look right through me, as if I'm not there. He's in a different world. His life is soft crabs and the open Bible in his lap. He reads a few lines and keeps repeating them, his way of memorizing the passages."

"Is he a born-again Christian?"

"Don't know what that means," she answers.

"He seems to be mumbling something about being 'reborn.' Might be referring to the peelers swimming in the tanks."

"He's confined to that wheel chair like Bud is confined to his prison cell," says Bonnie. "Sometimes I'm beginning to think I'm bad luck for them."

"Get that notion *outta* your head fast. You're a good woman and you've come a long way in tough times. You've made the best under the circumstances. In reality, Pretty Boy and Bud took advantage of you."

"At least Pretty Boy married me although DNA tests eventually showed my son, asleep inside his crib in the main house, was not his, but Bud's. However Pretty Boy *is* the father of our baby due in about five months. That's for sure."

"Congratulations, Bonnie," says Mark, nodding his head with relief, "but still a bit confusing."

"Just when I thought everything about our life was wonderful, Pretty Boy made a bad decision to rush home and drive his car while drunk. Now he's also married to that wheelchair and spends much of his time inside the sloughing shed."

"Is he able to move around without pain?" he asks.

"Not really," says Bonnie. "He tries to hide it and gets therapy three times a week. He has good strength in his arms. Lucky he's lean."

"I see you have a ramp leading into your house. Do you have a chairlift in the bathroom?"

Yes, plus a government caregiver to help him and our baby," Bonnie answers.

"I can't see his face clearly," says Mark. "Does he have scars from crashing through the windshield."

"Yes, but he's still a very handsome young man," answers Bonnie.

"I don't feel like facing him today," Mark tells her quickly. "I need time to think about him."

He turns away and walks to his car. When he reaches for the door handle, he looks upward and says a silent prayer: "Oh, merciful father above, forgive me, please, for thinking of myself, and give these deserving souls the benefit of your grace and goodness."

Afterwards, he does an about-face and walks slowly back to Bonnie.

"I can't leave without offering to help you and Pretty Boy and especially your baby," he tells her. "If, at any time, you need something or someone to help you keep your soft crab business afloat or money for medical expenses or unforeseen hardships, don't hesitate to call me at Ridgefield."

"I'll keep you in mind, Mark. It must have been hard to face us. Please come back again. By the way we've got a half dozen soft crabs that just sloughed and were put in the cooler. Would you like to take some home for dinner tonight?"

"If it's not too much trouble," he tells her. "My mother loves them almost as much as I do."

After opening the cooler, Bonnie removes a cardboard box containing a half-dozen soft crabs.

"Want me to clean them for you?" she asks.

"No, just lay some newspaper or cardboard over the crabs and sprinkle a layer of ice on the top to keep them cool. Be sure those *Callinectes Sapidus* are on edge and don't touch the ice. A 45 degree-angle prevents fluid from escaping out of a peeler's mouth and gills."

"I've been putting them at an angle without knowing why," says Bonnie. "And what's *Cal-li-nec-tes*?"

"Beautiful Swimmers. That's what scientists and marine biologists call the Atlantic blue crab. Actually, *Callinectes* means 'beautiful swimmer' in Greek, and *Sapidus* means 'tasty' in Latin. I learned how to handle soft crabs when I went crabbing with my Dad and know what's good to keep 'em alive until you have them for dinner. Tonight, my mother will sauté them in butter, lay 'em on a slice of whole wheat toast with a thin layer of Hellman's mayonnaise, lettuce and tomato."

He takes a $50 bill out of his wallet and stuffs it into her pocket.

"Before you go," she says, "I can't speak for my husband, but I'd like you to know what others have told me."

"Which is?"

"To err is human, to forgive divine."

"Tell that to Ruth, not to me," he says with a touch of resentment. "Just when I felt the hand of God on my shoulder, the devil must have reached up and grabbed me by the seat of my pants. I guess forgiveness will have to wait for another time. Only God can forgive Pretty Boy."

At the end of August, Cumberland Federal Correctional Institution (FCI) is the new home for Bud Wayne, who has been transferred from Patuxent in Jessup. He still remains in solitary confinement for the murder of his first wife, Vera, while Rachel Able, his new wife whom he married soon after going to prison, manages Swan Haven Marina, in accordance with the terms of their pre-nuptial agreement.

Although Ruth and her sister Jean are equal partners with

their brother, Bud, it is Rachel's time to shine by showing a profit in tough economic times. She resolves to keep a tight grip on expenses and knows when to make a long-term rental deal with boat owners who need mooring at the marina. "Been a month since I saw Bud at his new home in Cumberland," Rachel tells herself, inserting some correspondence into a manila folder and closing a file cabinet inside her office at Swan Haven Marina. "Maybe it's time to close up the marina at noon and pay him a visit."

After a four-hour drive by car over the Bay Bridge and at least four major highways, Rachel notices a handsome officer behind the reception desk as she signs in at Cumberland FCI.

"Your driver's license, please?" Officer Meadows asks her with a smile. "It'll be returned when you sign out."

Rachel is quickly escorted to the visitor's room and notices her husband, dressed in his prison orange jumpsuit, already seated across from a glass enclosed visitor's booth.

"Who are you?" Bud asks, holding a telephone in one hand and watching her ease her shapely five-foot, eight-inch body into her chair.

"Cut the act, Bud," she says after picking up her telephone and hearing his question. "I haven't changed that much since I was here a month ago, have I?" she asks, feeling a bit edgy.

"No one to talk to anymore," he says slowly with his head, swiveling from side to side.

"It was a choice of taking care of the marina or seeing you, so I chose the marina. We're still turning a profit despite tough times," she answers. "Isn't that why you asked me to marry you and manage the marina in the first place?"

"Manage the marina? What marina?" he asks, rolling his eyes and head around, confused and bewildered. "It's only me and God and the Bible from now on. I've read the Bible over and over because it brings me some peace of mind."

"What's happened to your hair? It looks like it's falling out," she admits.

"My hair? The doc says it has to do with," he suddenly stops talking, opens a Bible and reads the words written on a scrap of paper, "A combination of thyroid, nutrition and stress, causing a hormone imbalance, known as *Androgen DHT, di-hydro-testosterone.*"

Rachel looks closer at his eyes, which are glossy and dilated. "You're not making a lot of sense," she says. "You should get a blood test and talk to a dietician about the food they're serving you."

"Huh?" he utters, grabbing the sides of his head with both hands. "I feel another headache coming on."

He leans his head backward and moves it around haphazardly, sniffing the air. "You smell something burning? Rubber burning?"

"You look like you're hallucinating," says Rachel. "Are you paying attention to what I'm saying?"

"Attention?" he asks. "That's what my mother always asked me."

"Are you putting on an act? That won't help to get you *outta* prison any sooner. You're confined for another 20 years, no parole, remember?"

"Remember what?" asks Bud, rolling his head around his shoulders.

Rachel rises abruptly from her chair, slams the telephone receiver down on the table top and walks to the exit door. "I'm *outta* here," she murmurs angrily. "I've got enough to worry about trying to run the marina single handedly. I've no time to get involved in your state of mind."

As she reaches the exit door, she turns to have another look and watches him fumble through the pages of his Bible. He drops it to the floor and begins to massage the temples of his head furiously, using alternating hands as if he's in an uncontrollable seizure. "Is he putting on an act or really flipping his lid?" she asks herself.

Back at the reception desk, Rachel notices a different receptionist at the sign-in, sign-out counter.

"You weren't here when I signed in ten minutes ago," she says, noticing no wedding ring on her hands.

"That's right. Officer Meadows is on a coffee break. Anything I can do you for?" asks Sergeant Sylvia Take.

"I'm Mrs. Rachel Wayne," she tells her, signing out on the visitor's log book and spinning it around so that it now faces the Sergeant.

"You weren't here very long this afternoon, Mrs. Wayne," she says, noting the times she signed in and out on the log book.

"Might be a good idea to have the prison doctor take a look at my husband, Miss Take," she says. "He wasn't making any sense today. Very incoherent."

"I'll make a note and pass it along to my supervisor right away," she answers, handing back her driver's license.

A few days following her visit to Cumberland, Rachel is opening a number of bills in her office when the phone rings a long time before she picks it up. "This is Doc Holliday at FCI in Cumberland," he tells her. "I've some bad news, concerning your husband."

"How bad is bad news?"

"When you were visiting him three days ago, did he say anything about smelling burning rubber?"

"Not that I can recall," she answers quickly.

"After you left the facility," says Holliday, "Bud could hardly make it back to his cell. He was incoherent and talked about smelling burning rubber. We rushed him to Maryland General Hospital in Baltimore where they did a CAT scan and MRI and found evidence of a brain tumor. One of the symptoms of this disease is the patient smells burning rubber."

"Is this really the prison doctor?"

"Affirmative," says Holliday. "The cancerous tumor is small but always fatal. It's called 'Glioblastoma Multiforme, GBM.' "

"How long does he have to live?"

"That's the million dollar question. It's up to God," he replies.

"George Gershwin died from it at the age of 38, six months after he was first diagnosed with the cancer. I'm sorry to be the bearer of this news. Wish I had more time to answer any questions but there's another caller waiting to talk to me."

"I don't know whether to laugh or cry," she says loudly, dropping the phone down and falling backward in her swivel chair. She pauses to gaze at a large photograph of Vera hanging on the wall near her desk.

"Vera, if you can hear me," she says, "revenge is sweet, but retribution is sweeter."

Beginning with the first week in September, Lois stops by Cylburn to jog with Mark around the perimeter of the Hopkins mansion before starting her day at the office. The physical exercise is beneficial to them, as Mark begins to look at her in a different and much brighter light. Despite the similarities of Marnie and Ruth, Mark begins to emerge from the cocoon of depression and is attracted to Lola. The chemistry between them leads him to realize how deeply she really loves him and has loved him since they first met two years ago in Betterton at Annette and Richard's wedding.

"Cozy, having a cup of coffee with you after a morning jog around Cylburn and a quick shower," Lola tells him, munching on a banana-nut muffin. "I love this part of your house, a breakfast nook overlooking your Mother's flower garden. Gemutlichkeit, which means 'cozy' in German."

"Where did you learn that word?"

"From the dances at the Rathskeller, the beer hall at the Fifth Regiment Armory," she boasts. "It's history now, closed a few years ago, but we had fun dancing and eating wonderful German bratwurst and drinking draft beer imported from Bavaria."

"I'm seeing a new side of you, definitely more tender than the stunning attorney overloaded with legal briefs."

"Why, Mark, that's the first kind word I've heard from you in a long time. Don't know whether to thank you or Marnie for it."

"No need to thank us. I've been thinking more and more about you and me."

On the last Wednesday in September, at the end of two weeks of regular morning workouts with Lola, Mark is disappointed when she fails to show up or call him. "I was hoping to take her to a German pub to celebrate the beginning of *Oktoberfest*," he says to himself.

Around 4:30 in the afternoon she telephones and asks if she could drop by around 7. About three hours later, the maid opens the front door as Mark walks out of the library and glances down at his wristwatch and scratches his head. "I missed you this morning," he says, kissing her cheek. "You didn't show up or call me."

"No, I didn't. Not this morning. There's something that I wanted to talk over with you, and now may be the right time."

"Sounds serious."

She takes a deep breath and gazes in his eyes. "As Admiral David Farragut said: 'Damn the torpedoes; Full steam ahead.' I have a confession to make," she says, walking him back into the library. "I've admired you from the first moment we met two years ago at this very spot after you asked me about my perfume. I always admired you and Ruth and the happiness you brought each other. It is not my intention to step into her shoes; I couldn't begin to fill them anyway. She was very special, a good friend and impossible to replace. But, after a reasonable length of time, you're entitled to a fresh start in life. I believe it's time for me to share your life; every hour of every day. I want my chance to make you happy, too."

Mark takes her in his arms and realizes how deeply she cares for him. "I can't explain the things that are jumping around inside me," he says, giving her a passionate kiss. "I remember the words you told me two years ago in Betterton, which gave a new meaning and purpose to my life."

"If you didn't understand me, I was just proposing to you," says Lola. 'If you turn me down again, I might shoot myself!"

"This is the right time for us, and it may surprise you to know that I'm not stunned, not in the least," says Mark. "Come upstairs. I want to show you something in my bedroom."

"You're not rushing things a bit, are you?" she asks.

"Yes and no," he answers, escorting her up the staircase, down a short hall and into his bedroom. "I want you to see a painting."

"If you're thinking of showing me your Renoir," she says, tugging his arm, "I've already seen it."

On a far wall of his bedroom is an equestrian painting by George Ford Morris, measuring 36-inches high by 28-inches wide (see photograph).

"Do you see the resemblance of this elegant lady to you?" he asks, putting his arm around her waist, "It's actually Mabel Garvan, on her imported hunter *Alert,* painted in the early 1920's by one of America's foremost sporting artists. My father bought it as a wedding present to my mother, but don't ask me what year that was."

"It's so beautiful, Mark," she tells him. "My resemblance of Mrs. Garvan is close and the forest could pass for Hunt Valley."

Mark is interrupted by the ringing of a telephone on a nearby table. "Mr. Hopkins, this is Dr. Izzy Youish," Mark hears through the transmitter. "I'm the pathologist in the coroner's office of Kent County who performed the autopsy on your wife."

"Yes, I've heard of you. I can't honestly say I was looking forward to your call. Please, hold the line," he says, pressing the phone to his chest.

"It's the coroner, Dr. Youish," Mark tells Lola quietly. "It must be important."

Mrs. Francis P. Garvan on imported hunter, *Alert,*
by George Ford Morris (American 1873-1960)

"Sorry for telephoning you so late in the day," Dr. Youish says. "But I have some news about the autopsy performed on your late wife. We discovered that she had an advanced stage of pancreatic cancer that apparently went undetected and undiagnosed. Although I'm not qualified to render a prognosis, I can tell you, it could have meant a long and painful period of chemotherapy, radiation treatments and toxic medicines, with no guarantee of success."

"I know you wouldn't be kidding me, but are you certain about this discovery?" Mark asks with alarm in his voice.

"Yes, I'm positive," he says. "Her instantaneous death, the result of a broken neck, albeit tragic and premature, may have been a blessing in disguise. I'm very sorry to have to tell you this, as I've heard such good things about you and the work you're doing at Ridgefield. May God watch over you and your family. And forgive the late night call, but I thought that you should know immediately the results of our tests."

Mark is speechless. His mind is temporarily frozen. He lowers the phone slightly away from his ear, then hears Dr. Youish call out his name.

"Mr. Hopkins, are you still there?"

"Yes, I was about to hang up the phone."

"I hesitate to tell you this last thing because of the way you might interpret it, but Ruth was about two months pregnant. I'm not qualified to say whether or not either one would survive Ruth's chemo treatment, but feel it was a blessing that both died instantaneously, without any pain."

"That's easy for you to say," he says, slamming the phone down and slowly turning away from Lola as tears begin to roll down his cheeks.

Realizing it must have been troubling news from Dr. Youish, Lola puts her arms around his waist and leans her head against his back.

"When you find a new love in your life," he says softly, turning his body and letting her forehead rest on his chest, "it may be the right time to make your dreams come true."

"When I first met you in Betterton and you were involved with Sandy, you explained that you were not ready to settle down," says

Lola, kissing his hands. "Then you met Ruth; you said that it was a twist of fate. Somehow, I think it was a gift from God, something divine. Your life with Ruth was about as close to perfection as possible on earth. I want our love to be as good as it can be and I intend to spend the rest of my life proving it to you."

"You don't have to prove anything to me," Mark says, with a tear in his eye. " You've already shown how much you love me and my mother."

Although Mark would deny it, over the last several weeks the thought of ending his life bounced in and out of his mind. It was this telephone call about Ruth's cancer and Lola's revelation of her love that has restored his faith in God and pulled him back from the doorstep of suicide. Depriving his children of the love and care that only he could give them somehow always kept him from stepping *over the edge*. It's clear to him that he still has the necessary knowledge and will power, traits were ingrained in his psyche from his studies at Hopkins and officer's training as a Navy SEAL, to go forward with his life. Never again would he dwell on the aspect of ending his life or doubt his faith in God. He now had too many reasons to begin a new life with Lola.

"It's what Ruth would want me to do, too," he says.

# Chapter 11

On the last Saturday of September, Lola has arranged a surprise birthday party for Mark at Cylburn. Everyone from Ridgefield is there, their first chance to see Mark after an absence of many months. It's a celebration and a reunion of good friends.

"Ridgefield just wasn't the same without you," says Abigail. "In honor of the occasion, we have a special birthday present."

After opening the box, he finds an original wall-hung sculpture, about 16 inches wide and 22 inches high, of a section near the roof of an old barn, with two chickadees, one perched on a rusty nail below and to the left of another peeping out of a knothole in the wooden wall.

"It's called 'Caretakers,' because they eat insects and are well-loved backyard birds. The chickadee is a plump little bird, with a distinctive black and white head and acrobatic maneuvers, remindful of the agility of a SEAL like you."

"Remarkable carving," says Mark. "Almost as if they're alive. Who carved it?"

"Don Briddell, one of the best students of the famous Ward Brothers of Cambridge, Maryland," Abigail answers. "I can't imagine any of them carving it better than Don Briddell. Everyone here at Ridgefield pitched in to buy it directly from his Overboard Art Gallery in Mt. Airy."

"Where's that?"

"In Howard County, about 100 miles from Rock Hall."

"Pardon me for breaking in," Greta says with a little hug, "but according to the alignment of the planets and stars, you're destined for a big comeback. I envision you as a particle about to collide with another one inside my crystal ball."

"Are you positive?" Mark asks facetiously.

"You're the one that's positive and the other particle is only partially negative, which means you're attracted to each other and about to create a new and lasting love interest."

"Have you been peeking into my private life?" asks Mark, as Kim puts her arms around both of them.

"Welcome back to the human race," Kim tells him. "We missed you terribly at Ridgefield. Although you'll probably not heed my words, I've been waiting to tell you that everyone here is willing and ready to share your workload."

"Everything seemed to move a step slower," admits Liz. "To be sure, it was probably what you would have wanted us to do, meaning 'get it right the first time.' We all got a chance to stop and smell the roses and to realize how lucky we are to be alive and working at Ridgefield."

"Might be a good time to announce our engagement," Lola tells Mark with an embrace.

"Attention, everyone. Gather in," says Mark. "Greta is right when she just told me I was on a collision course with a new love interest. Lola has consented to be my wife."

Sandy finds an old leather belt with five jingle bells attached to it, holds it high in the air, and rings it merrily. A few minutes later, she notices that it's four o'clock and tells everyone to quiet down.

"We've all been invited to Camden Yards at Oriole Park to see Chubby Bender in an Orioles uniform," she says proudly. "It's the September call-up of players chosen by the front office for their success during the past season. Chubby had a big year for the *Islanders* at Daytona Beach, where he was voted 'Rookie of the Year' in the Class A League. In interviews with the press, he's given Ridgefield credit for providing the facilities to develop his pitching talents. He's left us tickets for tonight's game against the Yankees. Who knows? He might even get in the game, and it would be nice to see history in the making."

Three hours later, everyone is leaning over the wall to shake hands with Chubby and meet some of the top players on the Orioles rooster. Manny's fingers are shaking so much he's snapping some photos twice when pressing the shutter release on his digital camera. Nevertheless, he manages to capture Chubby as he introduces his teammates to everyone from Ridgefield. However, because he can't get on the field, Manny gets carried away and decides he wants a low shot looking up at Chubby with his teammates and asks Womble to hold onto his legs as he hangs upside down over the short fence along the third base line of left field.

"I've seen a lot of news photographers take a shot with their camera but never upside down," answers Womble with a big laugh, "but if it's what you want, let's do it before we get arrested or hauled off to a sanitarium."

After taking over 20 shots with his body held upside down by Womble, Manny beckons Chubby over so he can speak confidentially with him.

"You've got a tear in your orange stockings," Manny whispers to him.

"I know. Doesn't mean a thing. Been wearing them for the past month and won 16 straight games in relief. I'm superstitious and won't change them until I lose my next game!"

After extending good wishes to Chubby, Manny turns to everyone hanging over the fence and declares, "Next week, all of you will be in photographs on exhibit inside the R&R Refuge gallery at Ridgefield."

Around the middle of October, Mark is sitting in a small conference room at Bethlehem Steel, smiling at Lois Carnegie and Dr. Joost de Wal seated across from him.

"I detected a sense of urgency when you telephoned me at Cylburn last night and asked to meet us this morning at 9 o'clock," Mark says to Lois as he looks at his wristwatch.

"It *is* a matter of urgency, otherwise I wouldn't have asked you all to be here," Lois answers, turning to face Joost. "Did you know that I'm on the board of Carnegie Steel?"

"Yes, I'm well aware," Joost replies, smiling and nodding his head.

"I bet both of you didn't know that an NFL franchise could be awarded to Los Angeles, which means a new stadium to seat 90,000 hungry fans."

"A stadium?" asks Dr. de Wal with a puzzled look. "Perhaps one day we'll see Ajax play there in a soccer match."

"It won't have a dome over the stadium since it's in sunny California," she answers.

"Hungry fans?" asks Mark.

"They're hungry for an NFL team to call their own," Lois answers. "But the construction project will have more I-beam steel than two battleships. And Congress wants the owners and developers to use as much American-produced steel as possible, provided the cost is close to the figures submitted by Baoshan of China, Nippon of Japan, Tata of India, Severstal of Russia, and ThyssenKrupp of Germany."

"Interesting," Mark says. "We got the Wew twins away from ThyssenKrupp just in time to help us here."

"Very interesting," Joost replies, nodding his head with a cunning smile, as if he's two steps ahead, already formulating a plan of action.

"Carnegie Steel could fulfill the terms of the contract with the owners," Lois continues, "but we will need a partner to produce everything they need on schedule. So here's a proposition from Carnegie for your consideration.

"First, Carnegie Steel (CS) and Bethlehem Steel (BS) will unite to form Carnegie-Bethlehem Steel (CBS Steel), with Carnegie as managing partner. It's a deal similar to one used in the aerospace programs and patterned after Northrop-Grumman, the managing partner, with Lockheed-Martin and other subcontractors as partners."

"I follow you so far," says Mark, sipping from a glass of water.

"The production of I-beams and anything of a steel nature," Lois continues, "will be divided between the two mills. However, because you have an automated robotic system designed by the Wew twins already in place, you should be able to turn a bigger profit than Carnegie. Nevertheless, at the end of the contract, after all costs are tabulated, Carnegie and Bethlehem Steel will split the profits equally."

"Looking at the big picture," Joost tells them, "I envision a contract that could keep us fully employed for at least six months, with enough profit to keep the mill solvent for a year."

"How soon can you get us the specs and materials lists so we can begin the proposal process?" Mark asks Lois, jotting down some notes on a legal pad.

"Everything you need to make your decision is inside this packet, but we have only a week to give the owners of the stadium our agreement for CBS Steel to be the sole source of steel," says Lois.

"By the way, where is the new stadium to be constructed?" asks Mark.

"It's taken everyone almost 15 years to pick a site," answers Lois, "but they've chosen the old Hollywood Race Track. It's in the middle of the city, with good access to freeways and the LAX airport."

"I bet that'll cost a pretty penny," says Joost.

"I've heard 1.5 billion for the land and stadium," says Lois, raising her eyebrows in astonishment.

"Well, that means Joost will have to get the Wew twins in

here as soon as possible and see if we can fulfill our part on time and within budget," says Mark, scratching his chin. "My sixth sense tells me that there should be a clause in the contract with CBS Steel to protect each side of the partnership in the event something unforeseen develops and one side cannot fulfill its obligation. Trust is one thing. Control is another."

"I'll have lawyers at CS examine this point," says Lois, "and write the conditions to protect each side."

"It's an intriguing proposition," says Mark. "Thank you for giving BS an opportunity to participate with CS. Reminds me of the 'good old days,' as my father called it, when our forefathers were making steel in Pittsburgh."

On Christmas Eve, Mark and Lola arrive at Ridgefield for a holiday celebration inside the sound stage of the R&T Lab building. "Santa told me to make sure everyone has a good look inside your Christmas stocking," says Mark with gusto. "You'll find a bonus check for a job well done."

"Frankly, I'd rather have one of those voluptuous James Bond girls inside my stocking," Womble utters to York, standing next to him.

"What about Eloise?" York asks him.

"Don't think I know her."

"Ask Mark. Once you meet and get to know her, she'll fit one of her legs nicely in your stocking, with a little help from you, of course."

As York and Womble end their repartee, Lola takes the microphone away from Mark. "Now for some news that can't be put inside your stocking," Lola says with tears in her eyes. "We've set a wedding date, June at Cylburn. Dreams do come true."

"Some more news that certainly no one expected," says Mark, gripping the microphone tightly. "Lola and I want to spend more time with my mother. So we'll be leaving Ridgefield. Our departure doesn't mean that we won't be paying you a visit. Also, unforeseen problems along the shoreline of Bethlehem Steel at

Sparrows Point will require all my energy and attention. A crisis has surfaced there. It entails pollution from waste disposal of coke byproducts started months before World War II, when the plant was operating under the direction of the government. I'm very pleased that Lola has agreed to join the board of BS and handle the pending lawsuits. Residents living around Sparrows Point claim an increase in odors coming from ground waters below the earth is due to contamination with naphthalene and thick coal tar. Billions of dollars are at stake here, possibly the survival of the mill itself."

Mark backs away from the microphone and looks down sadly at the stage floor to gather his next thoughts. "Therefore, I am announcing my retirement from Ridgefield, effective the first of July. Everything will be under the control of Abigail and Womble. But I'll expect all of you to carry on the work we started together here."

There is silence inside the sound stage. Everyone is stunned by Mark's decision to retire from Ridgefield at the age of 29. Seconds later, a round of applause erupts. Whistles and cow bells ring and echo off the concrete-block walls.

"I'll always have you in my heart," he continues, "and will leave a contract with Abigail for each of you to sign, guaranteeing you a job at least for the next two years. After that, we'll have to play it by ear. Oh, just so you'll remember this Christmas as something special, we have a little gift for you," he declares, handing each employee a box. Inside is a ROLEX *Oyster Perpetual DATEJUST* wristwatch with the bezel engraved with the words: *You Can Be Better than You Are.*

Three months later at noon on the first day of April, Mark is standing in the kitchen of Cylburn when the telephone rings. He answers it, munching on some raw carrots that Lola has just set on the small dining table.

"*Hey...hell...hello.* Is that you, Sandy?" he asks, looking down at the caller id on the receiver.

"Yes, it's me, but are you all right?" she asks quizzically. "Your voice sounds as if your mouth is stuffed with food. Are you munching on something?"

"Nibbling on some carrots. Good for the eyes. What's up, Doc?" he asks.

"Do you know what day this is?"

"I know it's the first of April."

"It's also the chance of a lifetime."

"I would never forgive myself if I passed up the chance of a lifetime," he answers quickly.

"Tom Bowman called me with a proposition for you," she says, "but you have to make a decision before we hang up the phone."

"You have my undivided attention. I'm even beginning to hold my breath a little."

"Tom has secretly been granted permission to deliver the first foal from the great *Rachel Alexandra* at his breeding farm, Dance Forth Farm, outside Betterton. He's willing to sell you a one-third share of *Rachel Alexander's* foal, expected within the next two hours for $200,000. He'll guarantee a healthy foal, but the money has to be in his bank account by noon tomorrow. He didn't give me any explanation, and I didn't ask him why the rush."

"And who is the sire who impregnated *Rachel Alexander?*"

"*Storm Cat.*"

"Is this an April Fool's joke?"

"This is for real, Mark. Cross my heart and hope to die."

"Opportunities like this come only once in a lifetime," he says. "I'm looking at your bronze cast of *Storm Cat* as we speak. He is a fabulous thoroughbred that won the hearts of the horse-racing community. His grandsire was Northern Dancer, who descended from Native Dancer, the 'Gray Ghost of Sagamore,' owned and bred by Alfred G. Vanderbilt II."

"I'm familiar with Sagamore, established in 1925 by Margaret Emerson Vanderbilt."

"But did you know she gave the farm to her son for his

twenty-first birthday?" asks Mark, "Now Sagamore is owned by Kevin Plank, the *Under Armour* guy. As for *Rachel Alexandra*, I'll always remember my mother and father telling me over dinner at Haussner's Restaurant about how she outran all the bigger boys during her racing career."

"I wish you could talk to Tom directly, but he's reluctant and bound by the secrecy of having *Rachel Alexandra* in labor -- not to mention the risk of delivering a healthy foal. Are you ready to give me your answer?"

"A foal by *Storm Cat* out of *Rachel Alexandra*? Count me in. Get the details of his bank account and tell him I want to buy two-thirds for $400,000, and I'll wire the money to his account tonight."

While Mark and Sandy are conversing, Tom Bowman is standing inside an observation room looking at the playback on a video monitor. It shows that, during the night, the mare has already expelled about three gallons of chorioamniotic fluid, from the amnion inside her womb. This first phase of labor allows the inside sac, the amnion, with the fetus inside it to start through the birth canal.

"Well, *Big Hossey,* it's ShowTime," he says to himself in a comforting southern accent and moves his face almost against the glass pane of the observation window to see every movement around her dilated cervix.

A few minutes later, he swings open the wooden door of the large foaling stall with cameras recording everything taking place inside.

*Rachel Alexandra*'s body begins to quiver nervously as she notices Tom entering her stall and nods her head as if to say "It's about time, Doc." She slowly moves her hind legs a few inches farther apart to begin the second stage of labor, called 'activation.'

He watches her uterine contractions increase and her cervix, the lower part of her uterus, dilate further. "All signs look good, *Big Hossey,*" Tom says out loud, noting that the waxy secretion around her nipples is gone and milk begins to drop from them. "No time for second-guessing. God help me, please. This is not the first foal I've delivered, but it is the first birth for this mare."

Another element suddenly enters his mind: Secrecy. Only Tom Bowman knows and he's not talking to anyone about how, after 50 years as a veterinarian, he managed to get possession of *Rachel Alexandra*, who was impregnated by *Storm Cat* in May at Spendthrift Farm in Kentucky. After almost 11 months to the day, she's about to give birth inside his breeding farm outside Betterton, Maryland.

"Oh, *Big Hossey*, take it easy," he tells her as the feet of her foal, still encased in the amnion sac, protrude out of her cervix, followed by the body.

"Best delivery I've ever had," he boasts with a slight chuckle. *Rachel Alexandra* turns her head to look back at her newborn foal for the first time, then glances over to Tom, lifting her head and wheezing.

"I knew the best way to deliver your foal was to let you deliver it naturally, without interference, and monitor your progress," he responds.

The mare takes a breather and allows her foal to get used to its surroundings.

Tom notices that the umbilical cord is broken, which he treats with iodine, and the foal is standing on its own four wobbly feet.

"Welcome to Maryland and Dance Forth Farms," he says ecstatically. "You may not know it, but since you're a colt and one of the most perfectly-proportioned foals I've ever delivered, we'll call you *Stormy Alex*.

"My brother-in-law, Tom Szymanski, a trainer of thoroughbreds and wheeler-dealer in horse paintings in Marriottsville, should be given credit. He's the one who suggested the name."

The last phase is the expulsion of the membranes as *Rachel Alexandra* removes all traces of placenta from herself and her foal, who begins to nurse on her nipples. "Stormy Alex," he tells the foal, "your mother's milk contains colostrum's, essential antibodies that you'll need, so be patient. Rome wasn't built in a day and neither will you." He begins to laugh at himself, feeling foolish that he's talking to a new-born foal, who doesn't have a clue what he's saying, but at least Tom enjoys the sound of his voice inside the foaling stall.

Seconds later, after her foal stops nursing for another breather, *Rachel Alexandra* turns her head to get another, longer look at her chestnut-colored foal. "How's my baby boy?" she seems to ask the vet, followed by a low nicker, a robust neigh and an emphatic whinny!

"Thanks be to God," says Tom, watching the mare admire her foal. "Giving you the freedom to graze in the pasture and go to water whenever you wanted, plus the two-a-day walks has paid off."

He takes a digital camera hanging on a post nearby and quickly snaps several photos for his files. Although camera monitors around the foaling stall have recorded everything taking place inside the stall, Tom enjoys the act of taking live close-ups and says to *Rachel Alexandra*, "Two weeks ago, your udder descended and the milk veins under your belly grew large and stood out. Then, seven days ago, the muscles in the croup area shrunk due to the relaxation of the pelvic muscles and ligaments. Your tail and hip muscles dropped a little, and only five days ago, your teats filled out and the nipples became shiny and tight. And no signs of edema anywhere. It's a miracle from God when everything goes perfectly."

Tom remembers the bronze of *Storm Cat* that Sandy Welles created two years ago and decides to continue snapping more photos for her. He says out loud, "Based on these close-ups, I'll commission Sandy to make a clay model of this mare and her foal. It'll make a nice addition to my art collection."

After returning the camera to its post, he reaches over one shoulder to pat himself on the back. Despite his age, approaching 72, he still has the willpower to carry on with his breeding work.

"I never thought I would ever have the guts to say it, but this is truly a moment of infinite happiness," he tells himself as tears begin to form in his eyes. "No major complications up to this point. Praise be to God."

Money matters rarely cross his mind and are normally the least of his worries, except for now, when he pauses to catch his breath and realize he has risked everything on the foaling of a mare from *Rachel Alexandra*. One miscue, one accident, could have spelled disaster and doom.

"You've given a new meaning to April Fool's Day," he tells *Rachel Alexandra,* who will probably spend the next phase of her life producing foals instead of racing down the stretch of America's greatest tracks. "On behalf of me, *Stormy Alex*, and the world of horse racing, thank you!"

He hesitates long enough to draw in a deep breath and release a big sigh, then removes a cell phone attached to his belt and telephones Sandy.

"Did you have any success with Mark?" he asks.

"Affirmative, but he wants to buy two-thirds for $400 grand. He said you'll have the money in your account tonight."

"It's a deal. Tell him we have a beautiful colt named *Stormy Alex* that will be registered in Maryland. Also advise him that the Maryland legislature passed a law that will increase the purses of horses who win and were born in Maryland. This is one step that will stem the tide of breeders leaving the state for greener pastures in Pennsylvania, Delaware, New Jersey and Virginia."

"Maybe you should talk to Mark directly," says Sandy.

"When it comes to big money matters, I'm no good and break out in hives. Plus, I'm a vet and breeder who enjoys the breeding process and knows when to let others handle big finances. I'll have my hands full administering antibiotics and the next stage of caring for *Rachel Alexandra* and the weaning of *Stormy Alex*. I have to check the immunoglobulin levels of her colostrum's, take a culture of her uterus, and work-up a complete blood count (CBC) on her foal.

"You know something, Sandy," he continues, "up until now, Dance Forth Farm was a good breeding farm of about 133 acres, with well-drained pastures. But, after the birth of *Storm Alex,* this farm and my life will never be the same. I've made history here today and want something to remember this day. Photos are helpful, but I want you to make a clay model of *Rachel Alexandra* and her foal, cast it in bronze so I can touch it and feel the excitement again and again."

"In that case, I'll include you with a stethoscope around your neck. At five-foot six-inches and weighing about 140 pounds, you remind me of Charley Grapewin, the feisty old backwoods codger named Jeeter Lester in John Ford's *Tobacco Road.* Always amusing, a bit eccentric and totally dedicated, that's what you are."

"For an old geezer at 72, my hands are still steady, my eyesight sharp, except for using bifocals to read the fine print on contracts, and my mind is working better than ever."

After Tom Bowman ends his phone call to Sandy, he puts both hands into the front pockets of his pants and pulls them outward.

"Not a dime or a buck on me," he tells himself with a big laugh, "but certainly that'll change. With God's help, I'm going to retire and hire that bright young grad, Tom Bass, recommended by Dr. Dean Richardson at Penn's new Bolton Center of Veterinary Medicine in Kennett Square. I'll let him take over much of the routine work here and talk to Mark about my managing the early years of *Storm Cat* from now on."

After leaving the breeding stall, he walks across a dirt road towards his office and slowly surveys his breeding farm. He knows that the rolling hills here will keep *Stormy Alex* in shape and build stamina and muscles, plus there's plenty of grass, rich in limestone, particularly calcium, that will give his bones the strength of steel.

Tom removes a corncob pipe from his shirt pocket, slaps it against the palm of one hand to clean out any bugs and puts it in one corner of his mouth. "Invincibility. MacArthur had it and I still have it after 50 years as a vet."

As for Mark his time and money is still invested in people and a sport that needs constant support for survival. Racing is as much about people as it is about thoroughbreds, from the stable boy who cleans out the stall, to the trainer, jockey, veterinarian, all the way up to the owner.

However, the payoff down the road for him and Tom Bowman, who are entering the Sport of Kings on a scale unimaginable to them, is huge. Both realize the potential for riches will come at Keeneland's September yearling sales in Lexington, if they decide to sell *Stormy Alex* at auction.

Ever since the Darley Arabian, the Godolphin Arabian and the Byerly Turk were exported from the Middle East to England three hundred years ago, all modern thoroughbreds trace their genes back to these three stallions.

One of the most legendary horse-breeding and racing stables in the world is Godolphin Stable, owned by Sheikh Mohammed bin Rashid al Maktoum, the current ruler of Dubai and Prime Minister of United Arab Emirates. If he or another oil-rich Middle Eastern royal family, study *Stormy Alex's* pedigree and want this colt for their stable of prominent race horses, they will bid fiercely for *Stormy Alex*, and the yearling could easily fetch a record price at auction.

It's well known within the horse-racing industry that in 2006 Sheik Mohammed offered $17 million to Elizabeth Valando, owner of *Nobiz Like Showbiz,* for the breeding rights to her stallion. She turned him down without an explanation.

There's also the case of *Smarty Jones,* whose owners, Roy and Pat Chapman, in 2004, sold 50% of his breeding rights for more than $20 million to Three Chimneys Farm, a preeminent horse breeding farm established by Robert and Blythe Clay in 1972, in Midway, Kentucky. When *Smarty Jones* retires, he will join *Seattle Slew, Silver Charm, Genuine Risk, Point Given* and *Big Brown* there.

Consequently, if *Stormy Alex* is put up for auction next year at Keeneland, with *Storm Cat* as sire and *Rachel Alexandra* as dam, he could conceivably break all existing records for a yearling and fetch $25,000,000 or more.

Two weeks before his wedding to Lola, scheduled for the last Saturday in June, Mark sits on the front steps of the main house at Ridgefield as dawn is breaking over the Chesapeake Bay.

"Feels like old times," he tells his golden lab, lying with her head resting on his lap. "After a two-hour drive from Baltimore last night, I couldn't fall sleep. Those damn northeasterly winds always howl as they blow through the vinyl siding, and you weren't any help with your tip-toeing around during the night, too."

He begins to massage her neck, unaware that a figure is looming nearby. It's only when a large shadow is cast on the ground that they look upward together.

"I thought I'd find you here, looking out at the Chesapeake Bay," Womble tells him.

"You'd make a good cat burglar," says Mark with a chuckle.

"Deep in thought, are you?" asks Womble, plopping his body beside him.

"I've been thinking about how lucky it is to get back into the human race. Two years ago I proposed to Ruth out there on the sandy beach of Ridgefield Farm, and in two weeks Lola will become my bride. So much has happened in such a short time. God continues to bless me. After moving all my gear to Baltimore, I'll miss this place and people like you. No hard feelings for stealing her away from you, is there?"

"Stealing who away?"

"Lola."

"I found her intriguing and talented with a fabulous personality. On a scale of 1 to 10, I'd give her a rating of 10 plus."

"And so what happened?" asks Mark.

"You did. She's had a serious crush on you for a long time and kept it to herself. You're a lucky guy."

"And you're a good sport. Perhaps you'll let me play cupid and line you up with an extraordinary lady living in town, only a few minutes away. Would that interest you?"

"Not until you tell me more about her," says Womble, wobbling his head.

"Her name is Eloise. She's around 38, and you're 42, so you're similar, age-wise. She's five foot ten and you're six foot, so you're similar, height-wise. She has a bust of 42 inches and you have a chest of 44 inches, so you're similar, top-wise."

"Tell me something about her character, please."

"She is frank, honest and knows how to double a dollar. Over a year ago she asked me to appraise a bronze statue of a nude woman, a gift from a boyfriend whose wife didn't want a better looking nude in their house. Eloise opted not to pay for an appraisal and quickly accepted my cash offer of twelve-hundred dollars and started to collect toy mechanical banks that have doubled in value."

"Anything else I should know about her? What makes you think she might be interested in meeting me?"

"You ask too many questions," says Mark. "If you'd like to meet her, I'll tell her that you're coming over for some peaches although they won't ripen on her trees until mid-July in Maryland. The rest is up to you. But don't be surprised if she meets you at the back door of her house, wearing only a negligee."

"Make that call, please. I can't wait to see her ... peaches. I'm dying to know how she supports herself and I'm not referring to her size 42-inch bosom."

An hour later, Womble is knocking on the rear door of Eloise's home on Main Street, only a five-minute drive from Ridgefield Farm and two blocks from the blinking yellow light in the center of Rock Hall.

"I'm Womble Weinstein from Ridgefield," he says proudly, noticing her flimsy negligee. "Mark said you have some peaches for me and thought I should get to know you."

Eloise grips the door and leans forward to have a closer look at his face. "You remind me of someone but I can't quite recall who it is," she says. "Well, just don't stand there with your eyes popping out of their sockets. Haven't you seen a woman in a negligee before?"

"I wasn't sure if you're real or an illusion until you spoke to me," he says nervously. "You're gorgeous."

"Would you like a cup of fresh coffee?"

"Please," Womble says slowly in two syllables and follows her through a small living room and into her kitchen. He pulls up a chair at her pink Formica kitchen table. "I'm surprised that you're not married, considering all the equipment you have..." He stops in mid-sentence to take a closer look at her voluptuous figure and continues, "...in the kitchen. It's very cozy. Have you lived here long?"

"Three years," answers Eloise, switching on her automatic coffee maker. "The mortgage was paid off last year, so I wasn't forced into foreclosure when the recession hit our town."

"So you're a woman of independent means?" he asks.

"That's a matter of perspective. What are you at Ridgefield, a private investigator?"

"I'm more like a night watchman working the day shift. It's my job to keep everyone on their toes and see that everything *smoes fruidly*, ah flows smoothly. Ever since Mark said that I should get to know you, there are strange feelings stirring around inside me," says Womble, watching her pour him a cup of coffee. "It has to do with anticipation mixed with physics and chemistry. Maybe I'm in a magnetic field or the Bermuda triangle."

"You don't waste any time beating around the bush."

"When you're my age, time is too precious to waste beating around the bush."

"And your age is?" asks Eloise.

"Over 30."

"How much over?"

"Not much," answers Womble, taping his chest with his fists.

"I'm in excellent shape, physically and mentally speaking, with not many obvious or hidden vices."

"Now I remember who you remind me of; your confidence and demeanor is the same as Warren Buffett."

"You know Warren Buffett?"

"No; very few people get to know him unless you want to pay a million bucks to have dinner with him. But I've read everything I can on the Internet about the Wizard of Omaha, hoping to learn something about his philosophy of investing in stock and art."

"Unbelievable."

"No, it's believable; trust me," she says. "That's how I got carpal tunnel syndrome (CTS); spending too many hours at the computer."

"That reminds me of the 10-hour days working on Wall Street with derivatives, ah swaps," explains Womble. "I made over a million in commissions but had a nervous breakdown when the market suddenly collapsed just as I decided to risk everything and become a player too. Overnight I lost it all and was back at ground zero."

"You don't show any signs of regret or disillusionment. On the contrary you seem to have a positive attitude about it."

"That's because I decided to step away from Wall Street and find another line of work. One afternoon while having a cup of coffee at Java Rock Café, I met Mark. He told me that life is complex and full of ups and downs; to get up off the ground and get back into the fight, not run away from it. He must have seen something special in me and offered me a job at Ridgefield Farm."

"I feel the same way after Mark bought a bronze nude from me two years ago," she says. "I put his money into some banks; not the kind you're thinking of but toy mechanical banks, bought in estate sales and at auctions like eBay. A specialist on *The Antiques Roadshow* said that these collectibles are gaining in popularity and price."

"It seems as if we have a lot in common, Eloise. By the way I like the sound of your name. Would you consider it presumptuous if I invited you to see my cabin in the Pocono Mountains, near Stroudsburg some weekend?"

"Is that an invitation to see your etchings, with no strings attached?"

"No etchings and nothing attached," he says, laughing. "I have a weekend cabin there, with a hot mineral spring nearby. Just bring your bathing suit. Those thermal salts might benefit your wrists and fingers with CTS."

"How about this weekend?" she asks. "As you said before, 'time is too precious to waste.' "

Two days later, at noon, Eloise and Womble are walking hand in hand in the woods of the Pocono Mountains, dressed in casual polo shirts and jeans. Each has a small pack. "The mineral spring is a just over the hill ahead," says Womble, leading her up a medium grade to the hilltop. "There's something spiritual about this area. Here you can feel closer to God."

"This is my first trip to the Poconos. I never realized how beautiful it is; a perfect destination to get better acquainted, which reminds me of something I read by Robert Browning: 'Ambitious men climb and climb with great labor, and incessant anxiety, but never reach the top.' Do you think he was referring to you?"

"Absolutely," answers Womble, realizing Eloise is no ordinary woman. "Expressions from your lips continue to surprise me."

"The view is magnificent," she declares, putting a hand to her forehead to shade the sun in her eyes.

"It certainly is," he adds, turning her around and giving her a kiss on her lips. "Welcome to Pocono Summit."

They walk a short distance further down a gentle slope and find the hot mineral spring. "It appears to be about twice the size of those fancy swimming pools you find in *Architectural Digest*," says Eloise, trying to gauge its size. "Are there any bears around here that I should be made aware of?"

"No bears, but maybe a wolf like me."

"You're more of a golden retriever or hound dog," says Eloise, grinning.

"We can change our clothes over there behind that dense brush. That's our private bathhouse here in the woods."

A few minutes later both are sitting at the edge of the mineral spring as large bubbles from deep within the earth rise all around them. Eloise senses the movement of his eyes and lets her body slide until it floats. At this point Womble's mind plays tricks with him as he watches an optical illusion created by the sun reflecting off the bubbles rising around her body as it floats in front of him.

"Alexander Pope said 'A person who is too nice an observer of someone close by, like the one who is too curious in observing the labor of bees, will often be stung for his curiosity.' "

"If you're referring to me, then I don't mind getting stung," he says, leaning his back against a bank of earth.

"I believe your libido is acting up," says Eloise, laughing.

"That's possible. Yesterday I had a plate of raw oysters for lunch, which could account for my behavior today."

"I read that Sigmund Freud linked sexual desire to all constructive human activity resulting from eating more than six oysters. How many did you consume for lunch?"

"One, two, three, four...more than six," says Womble, counting the number on the fingers of his hands.

"I wonder if he likes me," Eloise asks herself, "and if so, will he ask me to spend the night in his cabin? On the other hand, if he doesn't ask me, should I ask him or would that be carrying our first date too far?"

Womble has the identical thought but adds: "If we have sex, she'll have to first sign an agreement between two consenting adults!"

After two hours of soaking in the mineral spring, they walk down a dirt path through the woods with dappled light filtering through the trees as squirrels dash around them in search for food.

"Was that a whippoorwill whistling?" asks Eloise.

"No, that was me imitating a Hermit Thrush," he tells her. "It's a shy, secretive woodland bird, who sings a single high, flute-like note followed by a rapid series of rising and falling notes. It means that my cabin is straight ahead; I call it *Sleepy Hollow*."

"For some strange reason that is hard to explain," says Eloise, "I'm thinking of an old Gershwin ballad called "I've Got A Crush On You.""

"Don't you mean 'thrush' on you?" asks Womble, who begins singing the song with one word changed to express his delight that Eloise made the trip with him to the Poconos.

*"I've got a thrush, ah crush, on you, Sweetie pie, all the day and night time, hear me sigh, I never had the least notion that I could fall with so much emotion. Could you coo? Could you care, for a cunning cottage we could share? The world will pardon my mush, 'cause I have a got a thrush, ah crush, my baby, on you."*

At this point only time will tell what lies ahead for these lovebirds, walking down a small grade to a cabin that looks like a birdhouse sitting on a knoll barely visible through the trees. Their attraction to one another was inevitable; one thing is certain: they're definitely on the same wavelength and close to a love nest.

# Chapter 12

Back inside Ridgefield's lab, Kim and Liz are engaged in double-checking their design and preliminary 'workbench' tests of their electronic buoy and other related activities at Ridgefield.

All of a sudden Little Mac McBride, taking notes like a secretary, begins singing songs that Sam Cooke recorded in the 1950's.

When Liz hears his distinctive voice crooning a rendition of *You Send Me* and *Wonderful World,* she interrupts her work and phones her husband, Reggie, to arrange an audition at his studio outside Betterton.

After the close of work that day, Little Mac stands somewhat nervously in Reggie's studio, watching him adjust a mic and music stand on a small stage in the rear of his grand room .

"Liz told me she overheard you singing some of Sam Cooke's songs," Reggie explains. "I'll say one thing right off the bat. You've got the looks of a singer. You must be about five foot eight, 175 pounds, a sparkle in your eyes, pearly-white teeth and a million-dollar smile on your face. It's called 'good stage presence,' and you definitely have it. Now let's see what kind of instrument you have on the inside. While I'm checking the wiring and electronic hookups, tell me something about yourself."

"Not much to tell. I grew up in *Balmer*, in the rough neighborhood near Druid Hill, and always sang gospel music with my father in our Baptist Church," Little Mac explains.

"Soul music?"

"*Yea*. You could call it that."

"A very good way to start out, a strong foundation."

"My father, 'Big Mac,' could imitate Nat King Cole. We had his recordings and some of Sam Cooke's, and played them all the time, even during lunch and dinner."

"Imitations are a good way to start out, but I expect you to be yourself."

Reggie hears someone knocking at the front door and when he opens it, Richard Wagner, retired Washington College (WC) professor of music, walks through the doorway, his head almost touching the top of the door frame.

"I was in the area and thought I'd drop by to see what you're up to lately," he tells Reggie. "If I'm intruding, give me a swift kick in the rear end and I'll hit the trail back to *Annette's Antiques*."

"Perhaps you can listen and give me your opinion of Little Mac's voice," says Reggie, adjusting his playback console so that Sam Cooke's voice is removed from the track of one of his recordings.

"Little Mac, I forgot to ask if you can read music," says Reggie, noticing a puzzled look on his face. "Don't worry about it. I'll teach you how to read music but no one can teach you how to sing. *That* has to come from you. In the meantime, you can play it by ear. Listen to the entire sound track and sing along if you want. This is an informal audition. Ingenuity and intuition are characteristics I'm looking for in addition to a good voice and intonation."

"What about the rise or fall in the pitch of his voice?" asks Richard.

"Yes, that's important, too. I'm hoping to find a way to include Little Mac with Liz and Sandy, who performed two years ago at the funeral reception for Mark's father at Cylburn. Maybe they could develop into a trio. In this business, innovation is the key to success."

At the end of 30 minutes, Reggie looks at Richard and both give a thumb's up sign. "Liz was right about Little Mac," says Reggie. "This kid's got talent, but he can't always imitate Sam Cooke. We've got to compose some new songs for him. Perhaps you and I can write something original, but in the style of Cooke and Nat King Cole so he feels comfortable when he sings it. *Whataya* think?"

"Count me in," says Richard. "I'm going ballistic watching Annette dust her antiques although her tap dancing around her shop always arouses me. She really has the most beautiful legs in the world."

"Forget women for a moment," says Reggie. "I was asking you about writing something for Little Mac."

"And I said 'Count me in'," answers Richard, laughing. "Would our partnership be 'Perdue and Wagner' or 'Wagner and Perdue?' Our names don't have the *zing* of Rodgers and Hammerstein. But this twenty-first century and contemporary music, like contemporary art, is all the rage. Besides, I've always wanted to write something special since I retired from WC and discover a newer version of Sam Cooke. Maybe Little Mac's our boy!"

"Before you leave, tell me something about your hobbies," Reggie asks Little Mac.

"Hobbies?"

"That's what I said. You know, psychologists say one's hobbies are the best insight into a person's character and ability."

"Guess you could say that singing is my hobby."

"Well, singing is only one-half of it. If you don't have the passion and resolve to keep improving, singing will remain a hobby. On the other hand, If you want to reach the level of a professional singer, we'll show you the way, but it will all be your doing."

Over the weekend Reggie and Richard write an original arrangement of a medley of Sam Cooke and Nate King Cole's most popular songs, and call it *Ode to Wendell Phillips*. It's an homage to Cooke and Cole's early years of study at Wendell Phillips Academy High School in Chicago.

After several practice sessions at Reggie's studio that include Little Mac, Liz and Sandy, the subject of adding the four members of the *Betterton Breeze* to the ensemble is broached.

"They're freshmen at Chesapeake College during the week and working for Jack Johnson on construction projects around town on the weekends," says Sandy.

"They have a natural *Doo-Wop* rhythm and harmony," Reggie says, "and could give a nice balance to the vocal arrangements. I remember them from the Harvest Fest in Rock Hall two years ago."

"That means the group would grow to seven vocalists. If we keep adding on, we'll soon be the *Tabernacle Choir*," Liz says with a big laugh.

"But we could do some interesting things with the harmony and counterpoint," says Reggie.

Two days later Reggie ends a two-hour rehearsal of Little Mac, Liz, Sandy and the *Betterton Breeze* by opening a letter that was sticking halfway out of his hip pocket and left everyone anxious about it.

"There's a possibility of an audition next month at the Hippodrome Theatre in Baltimore," he tells them. "I think they're looking for new talent for one of their upcoming TV specials, *Search For Tomorrow's Stars*. We'll need a good name for our group. Any suggestions?"

"Why not call ourselves, *The Betterton Beach Boppers*?" Liz asks, grinning. "It's a take-off from the vocal group of yesteryear called *The Beach Boys*. Simple and recognizable."

"If I can get my two cents in," Sandy asks, "how about calling our group the *Betterton Better-Tones*?"

"All good ideas, but I wouldn't rush into it," Reggie tells them, "Let's sleep on it for a few nights. And one more thing. We still need a lot of practice to be successful as a team. Remember what Vince Lombardi said? 'Practice doesn't make perfect. Perfect practice makes perfect.' "

"And Mark told us when we were training to run the relays," Jesse says, "there is no 'I' in 'team.' He drilled that slogan into us from his days as a SEAL."

Mark parks his BMW near the side entrance of the R&T Lab building and says to himself, "Only one week before my wedding and I hope the weatherman continues with his prediction of nothing but sunshine for the next five days. June is busting out all over."

As he reached the front door, he pauses to gaze around Ridgefield and catch another glimpse of the Bay with its waves sparkling in the sun.

"I was here last week, which seems like yesterday," he tells himself, "but this time I have good news for Kim and Liz. Hope I don't upset them by dropping in unexpectedly."

Inside, off to one corner, Kim and Liz are bending over a drafting table and studying some blueprints of their electronic buoy. A slight gust of wind causes one edge of the print to lift slightly upward. They see Mark and motion him over to join them.

"What a surprise," Kim remarks. "You look as if you're ready to parachute from an airplane with your one-piece orange jumpsuit."

"No one told us you were coming," Liz replies. "We would have baked you a cake. Something on your mind?"

"We've been given the green light finally by the Environmental Protection Agency (EPA) and Corps of Engineers (CE) to install a prototype of your electronic buoy off the shore of Edgewood Arsenal at Aberdeen Proving Ground," Mark says proudly, as his eyes survey the interior of the entire lab. He's astonished to see a transparent 10-foot high, 10-foot diameter, circular opaque plastic curtain in the center of the lab. From his experiences as a SEAL, it reminds him of a makeshift shower curtain large enough to give privacy to an entire squad of men.

"Now, what's all this talk about a secret project you're working on inside your lab?" he asks them somewhat nervously. "I thought I should drive down from Baltimore to see how you're spending my endowment and inheritance. If you want to keep me in the dark, just say so, but sooner or later, you'll have to unveil it. Why not now?"

"We wanted to tell you when the time is ripe," answers Kim.

"Like now," interjects Liz.

"There are two parts to our secret project," Kim declares proudly, pulling away the curtain so he can get a look at what's hidden behind it. "The first is the electronic buoy that you funded, the one operated mostly by solar power."

"I thought it was powered totally by solar energy," Mark responds hastily.

"We redesigned the electronic system," interjects Liz, "to include changes in wind velocity and atmospheric pressure. We've taken an *Atmos* clock apart, studied the principles of its operation and patents filed in Washington, and applied the same technology to our buoy. It will run concurrently with the solar cells, but generate additional power from the winds coming up the Chesapeake Bay, wave action of tides moving in and out of the Bay and changes in atmospheric pressure."

"But the best part of the electronic buoy is that it gathers samples of the water, processes the test data, such as nitrogen and potassium content, and sends it immediately to our control center here at Ridgefield," Kim boasts. "In effect, it's an intelligent buoy, which is the first part of our secret research in a nutshell. I guess now that you have the government approvals, we don't need to wait any longer to install it offshore at Edgewood."

Mark runs his fingers through his hair and stares in amazement at their electronic buoy.

"I think Womble mentioned something about your buoy

looking like an Atlas rocket, but I had no idea about how far you've progressed with the prototype. It looks as if it can talk."

"It can," says Kim.

"In that case, in the vernacular of Mohammed Ali, 'Show me what ya got,' Smart Buoy!" says Mark, raising his fists and imitating Ali's boxing stance.

"Put me in the Bay, step *outta* my way and make my day!" says the buoy in a strange computer-generated voice.

'*Oy vey*," says Mark, with his knees buckling. "I'm bowled over as if a car hit me. It's almost human."

"Not almost; all human," says the buoy in a louder voice, followed by a puff of air from its midsection that could be a belch or a fart.

"The second part of our research began after watching watching the maintenance man use his industrial vacuum, about the size of a 10-gallon trash can, to clean up the mess around here," says Liz proudly. "It dawned on us to use the same principle, so we invented a marine vacuum cleaner to detect, collect and process heavy metals, such as mercury, near the shores of rivers such as the Susquehanna and Patapsco. All the waste products are sucked up through hoses into a lab on the mother ship overhead, then reprocessed and used in other applications," says Kim. "Much research lays ahead, especially how to maximize the suction when using multiple hoses that lead into a mega vacuum."

"Instead of a trash can, there's a ship overhead," Liz continues, "with a chemical lab on board which will identify the chemical elements, separate and deposit them in individual containers for use in other applications."

"You should get it all documented and file a patent before someone gets wind of your ideas," he orders them. "Looks like a 'win-win' situation. Well done. You can expect a raise in your next paycheck. I'm proud of you and your efforts. There's no way to explain the exhilaration I get from hearing about your ideas for making the Chesapeake Bay a better Bay."

"For two years," says Liz, "we've been talking about an

intelligent electronic buoy with sensors for this and that, right? Well, it's time we gave our baby a new name, something recognizable, that might put Ridgefield on the map, from an Internet standpoint. From this time onward, we're going to give our 'buoy' a new moniker, '*eBuoy*.' We're taking a page out of eBay, the biggest marketplace for buyers and sellers of every kind of goods. Everything except for our *eBuoy*."

"I like it," Mark exclaims slowly in three distinct words.

"He likes it," Kim echoes in a louder voice.

"Get it registered as soon as possible," he says.

"It's been accomplished," Liz confesses with a chuckle. "Feeling so confident about the name, we had to find out if it was registered. It turns out that ebuoy.com is registered already, but an even better designation, ebuoy.org is now a registered website for Ridgefield's electronic buoy."

"What about merchandising?" Kim asks. "Shouldn't we be thinking about generating some income by marketing our buoy?"

"I assume you have something in mind, otherwise you wouldn't bring it up when we're ready to adjourn our meeting," replies Mark with a smile.

"As a matter of fact, I have a few suggestions. First, we get the Chinese to produce a miniature buoy in plastic to put on a shelf or in metal to use as a paperweight. Secondly, for the filthy rich collector, we make a limited edition of our eBuoy, designed to open like a Faberge-egg, revealing a surprise inside."

"And the surprise?" asks Kim.

"A photograph of you and me in a bikini," says Liz, laughing. "Actually, the buyer should decide what is placed on the inside."

"How about a miniature object d'art in plastic of Greta staring into her crystal ball?" Kim suggests. "With a coin slot on the side. When a quarter is feed into the slot, out comes a postage-size note with your fortune printed on it, something like the paper inside a fortune cookie."

"If it were made into a paperweight, it would be a reminder

to people that the Bay needs protection and everyone's help," Liz tells them.

"I better tell Gabby," Mark interjects, "that I'm spending the night and to break out the champagne for a celebration, a christening of *eBuoy* and merchandizing ideas to promote our film."

Later that evening, Mark sits in his old office, now Abigail's, trying to catch up on some emails. He smiles, noticing a 'What's Up Doc' inquiry from his buddy, Monty Montgomery, in Southern California. He lets the phone ring a long time before answering it.

"Sorry to call you so late in the evening, but I thought you'd like an update on your wife's estate," the Kent County Recorder of Wills, Scarlett Stewart, tells him apologetically. "Among the assets in the probate of your late wife is a 1/3 interest in a marina identified as Swan Haven Marina in Rock Hall. Tomorrow morning, I'll forward a copy of the letters of administration, in which you're named the executor and beneficiary of her estate."

Mark is temporarily floored but soon remembers that Ruth told him that she, her sister Jean and brother Bud, each held title to 1/3 interest in Swan Haven Marina.

After hanging up the phone, he makes a note to discuss his inheritance with everyone at tomorrow's breakfast. There are some traditions that he refuses to change, such as a briefing after breakfast.

The next morning the Ridgefield family finishes their breakfast and anticipates Mark's briefing. "Now that you've filled your tummies," he announces playfully, "it's time to fill your mind with an interesting phone call I received last night. According to the Registrar of Wills, I've inherited a one-third ownership of Swan Haven Marina, which means Ridgefield owns it since everything I own is funneled into RIDGEFIELD LLC. Now, off the top of your heads, give me your ideas of what we should do with a marina."

"A marina?" asks Sandy excitedly. "I can't help but picture

Knute Runagrund at the helm of a tug boat pulling into Swan Haven Marina. I always wanted him to be a part of Ridgefield. Here's our chance to welcome him aboard."

"I see it as an opportunity," says Liz, "to use a part of the marina for deployment of our electronic buoys."

"With ownership comes responsibility," interjects Lola, "which translates into time and energy. Wasn't it your intention to return to wheeling and dealing in art?"

"Mark, before you explain anything further," says Womble, a voice of reason, "your ownership would be a minority one, entirely dependent on the individual or individuals owning more than 50% of the marina. If you want to improve or change performance, profitability and potential for further development, you have to get approvals from those owners. If you intend to keep your one-third ownership, my advice would be to buy the one-third ownership of Ruth's sister, Jean, since Bud will remain in prison for the next 20 years and has always contended that he'll never sell his share while alive."

"You've given me differing views, but it just dawned on me that we're missing the boat," says Mark. "We've forgotten Jaime."

"What's a two-year old have to do with the marina?" asks Kim.

"When Vera died," says Mark, "Jaime inherited her interest, so he owns one-half of Bud's ownership, which is a one-sixth interest in the marina.

"In that case," interjects Womble again, "you should still buy Jean's share of the marina. That is, if you want to develop Swan Haven Marina into something special." He looks at everyone seated around the table and continues, "A bird in the hand is worth two in the bush."

"You're still the master of clichés, Mr. Weinstein," admits Mark and hands him a plate of cold pancakes. "Here, have another pancake in lieu of a raise in pay!"

"Take Womble's advice," Abigail says, "and buy controlling interest and develop the marina so that Jaime and Baby Ruth can work there as they grow up and support us when we're senior citizens. If it's not getting too personal, what does your ownership amount to right now?"

"From an accountant's standpoint," says Mark, "here's the answer: When the Wayne patriarch and matriarch died unexpectedly, Bud was 18, Jean, 19, and Ruth, 20, so each inherited a one-third interest. Bud, however, was given the title of manager by his two sisters along with permission to run the marina, take a reasonable salary each month, and divide any profit three ways at the end of the year. Now, at the age of 25, Bud married Vera and they managed the marina together. Vera was pregnant at the time and led Bud into believing that he was the father of her baby, Jaime."

"I'm beginning to see this story as a movie for Leone and Howe," Kim interjects.

"After Bud murdered Vera," Mark continues, "and was sentenced to jail for perjury, Vera's estate was probated. She left everything to Jaime, including her half-share of Bud's one-third ownership share of the marina. That means that Jaime owns one-sixth of the marina."

"This is getting too good for a movie," says Womble. "I would love to develop it into a television series, something like *Days of Our Lives* or *As the World Turns*."

"It's going to get better still," says Mark. "Soon after Bud was sent to prison, he realized that the marina needed a new manager, not Bonnie Bratcher, a baby sitter with whom he had occasional sex and who was not capable of running a marina much less her fragile life. So Bud made a deal with a former girlfriend and astute business woman, Rachel Able, who agreed to marry him with the stipulation that she would be paid $1,000 a month as a basic salary, plus a bonus of $1,000 a month for 22 years for keeping the marina viable. At the end of that period, when Bud is released from prison, she agreed to divorce him and be handed a *golden parachute* check for $264,000. If at any time during the 22 years, either Bud or Rachel decide to terminate their agreement, either could file for divorce and Rachel would not receive the *parachute.*"

"Should I send out for some Chinese food?" asks Abigail lightheartedly. "I can't stand the suspense without nibbling on an eggroll."

"Now," Mark continues, "one year after Bud and Rachel's marriage, I adopted Jaime and a week later, married Ruth. One year after giving birth to Baby Ruth, Ruth died and left her entire estate to me, which amounts to her one-third share of the marina. Therefore, I own one-third plus one-sixth, which equates to exactly one-half ownership of the Swan Haven Marina. And to further complicate matters, I've heard through the grapevine that Bud has a malignant brain tumor."

"We'll need some time to digest everything, Mark," says Kim. "In the meantime, we should make Ridgefield into a brand name. With all the talent around here and wonderful projects to show the world what American ingenuity can do, Ridgefield could develop into a brand name, like George Lucas' *Lucasfilm*, Steven Spielberg's *Dreamworks*, or Bernard Arnault's *LVMH*, which includes *Hermes* and *Louis Vuitton* luxury goods."

"Nothing wrong in thinking big," says Womble. "In fact, over the weekend, after consulting with my new partner, Eloise, the lady with the big peach trees, we're on the verge of taking out a business license to represent up and coming stars in and around Ridgefield. We're thinking of forming a personal-rep agency for intellectual properties, starting with Reggie and his vocal group, the *Better-Tones*; Knute and his parrot, Gertie; Greta and her *horror-scope*; and Leone and Howe, juniors, as a film team. We've extended an invitation to Lola to join our agency as legal-eagle."

"There absolutely must be something in the water around the Chesapeake Bay," says Abigail. "What you said makes a lot of sense, provided you establish your agency under the umbrella of Ridgefield LLC. I foresee a billboard that reads: ***eBuoy* powered by *iRidgefieldTechnology*.**"

"Along the lines of creating a brand name," Kim declares, "I'd like to see someone create a color that would signify Ridgefield, the way Tiffany has a distinctive blue, Valentino a red, Home Depot an orange and Lowes a dark blue."

"You sly dog. I bet you already have a color in mind, don't you?" says Mark.

"Green, the color of money," Kim says with a chuckle.

Later that evening, Mark is sitting alone on the top step of the front porch, gazing at the *Turneresque* sunset with its flaming yellowish-orange sky over the Chesapeake Bay Bridge, seven miles away. He senses that his days at Ridgefield are coming to an end unless Szymanski comes up with another book.

"I heard through the grapevine," he says to himself, "that he's working on a novel titled *The Lousy, Down-and Out, Filthy Rich.*"

His concentration on the sunset is interrupted when Mother Goose and her seven young goslings parade from under the porch, forming a semi-circle in front of him. A few moments later, Jen comes running from the shoreline, carrying a stick in her mouth, about the size of a ballpark wiener.

"No canister tonight, Jen?" Mark asks her. "The beach is looking a little cleaner these days."

Jen drops the stick, nods her head and says, "You got that right, pal."

"By the look on your face," he continues, "you're telling me we've come a long way, but there's much more to be done to clean up the water in the Bay. "

Jen turns her head several times in the direction of Mother Goose and her seven goslings and says, "She's come a long way, too, thanks to your repair job on her broken wing."

"People still need to be made aware of the importance of the Bay and the impact of pollution, otherwise no one will have a clean place to work, live and play," Mother Goose says, as her goslings turn their heads toward Mark.

Mark picks up the stick that Jen carried in her mouth and

dropped next to him. He begins to read the writing on it as Jen uses her front two paws to dig a hole to bury it in.

"Hold off, girl. This is not a bone meant for burial. There's some writing along one side."

"What's it say?" asks Jen, looking up and bobbing her head.

"It doesn't say anything," Mark answers slowly. "It reads, 'Magic Wand. Make a wish and it will be granted within 10 seconds!' "

Suddenly, from somewhere off the shore of Ridgefield Farm Mark hears a thundering voice, causing him to drop the stick. "Moses? Can you hear me?" says the Spirit, rising out of the Bay with its arms flapping in the air like a goose frightened by the sound of a hunter's gunshot.

"Oh, no. Don't tell me it's the Spirit of the Chesapeake Bay?" Mark utters loudly. "You're back again?"

"I never left. After all, they don't call me 'the Spirit of the Chesapeake Bay' because of my blue eyes. I'm here to do good things and lead the way towards a cleaner, more useful Bay. I see in my log book you're doing the same thing and about to install electronic buoys to monitor the pollution."

"That's right, but as I told you before, there's no Moses here."

"Then you must be Mark Hopkins?" asks the Spirit. "You're back again? I thought you moved to *Balmer*?"

"I may have moved away, but my heart is still here."

"Guess you know a good thing when you see it."

"What's going on? Why are you asking for me?"

"To fulfill your wish. We're getting near the end of the trilogy and I want to make your wish come true, for a few shekels as tip, of course."

"The Good Lord has given me a new life, with Lola and our children," says Mark, "so my wish would be for others."

"I'm waiting, but can hold my position in space only a minute or two longer. I have other house calls to make."

"I wish," says Mark, "for a peaceful world without terrorists to allow my friends in Betterton, Rock Hall and Aberdeen to continue their good work."

The Spirit's voice becomes incoherent, spitting gibberish, and his body vibrates and shakes nervously, jiggling up and down and around.

"Looks like he's experiencing an electric shock," Mark says himself.

"Excusez-moi, scusa, perdon, entschuldigung sie bitte, quin ni," the Spirit answers in quick succession. "Please. It'll take a few seconds to process your wish. In the meantime, have a look at a series of flashbacks of your life on the Bay since you came back from Iraq."

The sky begins to darken slightly as images move from left to right above the spirit. Flashbacks begin with:

- His dive off the top deck of the New Bay Belle to save Sandy's life.
- The interplay of Pretty Boy Floyd, Bud and Vera Wayne and her ultimate murder that incriminated him as a suspect.
- The sale of a rare dagger, which he discovered in Iraq and was sold for $500,000 to an American museum.
- His purchase of Ridgefield Farm with a R&R Refuge for Red Cross Vets who served as medics and a research lab to develop an electronic buoy to monitor pollutants in the Chesapeake Bay.
- His father's fatal heart attack and murder by a rival suitor interested in buying his steel mill.
- His great love affair with Ruth Wayne.
- The discovery of a canister of mustard gas on the shoreline of Ridgefield that led to the court-martial of a corrupt Army officer at Edgewood Arsenal, Aberdeen Proving Ground.
- His investment of $2,000,000 from the sale of a Pollock painting discovered in the cellar of an art gallery, into a film project.

- The development of Chubby Bender, a 19-year old farm boy, into a pro baseball pitcher with a nasty knuckleball.

The Spirit puts one hand up to his nose to close his nostrils and blows, causing water to spurt out of his ears. "Moses, ah, Mark, are you still there?" asks the Spirit.

"I'm still here."

"I can hear you much better now that I got the water *outta* my ears. Check your emails for tracking the status of your wish. But I heard through the grapevine that you still don't have a good ending for *ABERDEEN.* May I offer you a little spiritual advice?"

"By all means."

"A good way to end a story is with a message to the reader, something like the fortune written on a strip of paper inside a fortune cookie; perhaps a message such as: 'You Can Be Better than You Are.' "

"Interesting, but give me something with a little more punch," says Mark hurriedly.

"I remember reading a book about the life of Abraham, the prophet," says the Spirit with conviction.

"You mean to tell me that you can read a book? I thought you only read tablets, like Bayer, Tylenol and Nuprin," says Mark facetiously.

"I'll tell the jokes if you don't mind. Anyway, they're caplets, not tablets. Tablets are what Moses received from God listing the fifteen commandments."

"Wasn't he carrying only two tablets?" asks Mark.

"I must ask Moses if anyone ever called him a big *schlemiel* for dropping one of the tablets he *schlepped* around the Mount of Olives. *Und zo,* you *wanta* hear my advice for an ending with some punch or not?"

"Please, go on," says Mark. "The suspense is killing me and the reader of this novel."

"Abraham said: 'It is true that you may fool all the people some of the time; you can even fool some of the people all the time; but you can't fool all of the people all the time.' "

"I wasn't expecting a lecture," says Mark. 'The author is looking for words with a punch to end ABERDEEN on a high note."

"You mean like this," the Spirit answers, hitting the highest note only a tenor could possibly sing.

"Words, Spirit. He's looking for words."

"In that case, if I were Szymanski who, according to his editor, Mike McGrath, has an abundance of gumption and aspires to be a storyteller along the lines of Preston Sturges, I would end the trilogy by declaring: 'Whoever doesn't take the time to read *BETTERTON, ROCK HALL* and *ABERDEEN* can be fooled all the time!' "

"Very profound; that's an inevitable conclusion. Are those your last words for me?" asks Mark.

"Isn't that a mouthful?" asks the Spirit. "I'm *outta* breath and my arms are killing me from flapping like a goose on a windy day. But since you asked for it, here are my last words and you can carve them in granite for the world to see and read: "Always tell the truth, never be cruel and resolve to be better than you are."

The Spirit disappears as a bolt of lightning strikes the waves below the spot where he was suspended in space. When the sound of thunder reaches the porch of the main house of Ridgefield Farm, Mother Goose nods to her seven goslings to gather in.

"It's getting close to bedtime and I have a bedside story to tell you about the Chesapeake Bay and the sunsets over the Bay Bridge. There are no sunsets like those over the Bay," says Mother Goose, leading her goslings in a single file; all march in step and flap their wings, a form of applause that *ABERDEEN* is finally coming to an end.

Before disappearing under the porch, Mother Goose looks over to Jen, who begins licking Mark's chin and wagging her tail. He gives her a big hug and puts his forehead against hers;

Jen's cold wet nose tickles his chin. "I love you, Jen," he tells her. "We'll never be apart again. Tomorrow, I'm taking you with me to Baltimore."

**THE END** (*OR IS IT?*)

# GLOSSARY GUIDE

(Compiled by the author and inspired by Gordon Beard who published his "Basic Baltimorese" in 1979, '90 and '99.)

| Pronunciation (Slang) | Correct Spelling |
|---|---|
| *Aba-deen* | Aberdeen |
| *amblanz* | ambulance |
| *Anne-Arunnel* | Anne Arundel |
| *anytink* | anything |
| *ap-tight* | appetite |
| *arn* | iron |
| *arster* | oyster |
| *arthur* | author |
| *Ay-rabb* | Arab |
| *baffroom* | bathroom |
| *Bawlamer, Bawlmer* | Baltimore |
| *beero* | bureau |
| *betcha* | bet you |
| *Bethum Steel* | Bethlehem Steel |
| *Betterin* | Betterton |

| | |
|---|---|
| *bee-in* | been |
| *Blair* | Belair |
| *bob-war* | bobbed-wire |
| *boisbol* | baseball |
| *bootiful* | beautiful |
| *boybin* | bourbon |
| *bray-edd* | bread |
| *burn* | born |
| *Chalee* | Charlie |
| *Chesspeake* | Chesapeake |
| *Clumya* | Columbia |
| *complected* | complexioned |
| *corner* | coroner |
| *corter* | quarter |
| *Curt's Bay* | Curtis Bay |
| *curup* | corrupt |
| *curyus* | curious |
| *curyusty* | curiosity |
| *dare* | there |
| *dee-smissed* | dismissed |
| *doll* | dial |
| *Droodle Hill* | Druid Hill |
| *dubya* | w |
| *Dundock* | Dundalk |
| *eelight* | elite |
| *eht* | eat |
| *es-choo-air-ree* | estuary |
| *excape* | escape |
| *falue* | flu |
| *fur* | fire |

| Fert McKenny | Fort McHenry |
|---|---|
| fillum | film |
| fur | for |
| Furd | Ford |
| furty | forty |
| gaden | garden |
| gabage | garbage |
| Glennin | Glyndon |
| goff | golf |
| goldie | goalie |
| Greenmont | Greenmount |
| guvner | governor |
| hafta | have to |
| har | hire |
| harber | harbor |
| harble | horrible |
| harred | hired |
| Harrid | Howard |
| Harrid Street | Howard Street |
| hellava | hell of a |
| Hippdrum | Hippodrome |
| hosbiddle | hospital |
| hoss | horse |
| i-deer | idea |
| igger | eager |
| iggle | eagle |
| ig-nerent | ignorant |
| incabate | incubate |
| Inna Harber | Inner Harbor |
| inner-rested | interested |

| | |
|---|---|
| *inner-restin* | interesting |
| *jiggered* | jagged |
| *jogerfee* | geography |
| *jools* | jewels |
| *keerful* | careful |
| *kidneygaden* | kindergarten |
| *kroddy* | karate |
| *Liddle Itly* | Little Italy |
| *lie-berry* | library |
| *lig* | league |
| *Luck's Point* | Locust Point |
| *Lumbered Street* | Lombard Street |
| *mavalus* | marvelous |
| *mare* | mayor |
| *member* | remember |
| *mezz-aline* | mezzanine |
| *moran pie* | meringue pie |
| *Murlin* | Maryland |
| *Naplis* | Annapolis |
| *neck store* | next door |
| *na* | no |
| *notink* | nothing |
| *ode-a-see* | odyssey |
| *orning* | awning |
| *Oryuls* | Orioles |
| *pa-lease* | please |
| *Patapsico* | Patapsco |
| *Patomic* | Patomac |
| *pawtrit* | portrait |
| *postcad* | postcard |

| | |
|---|---|
| *payment* | pavement |
| *Plaski* | Pulaski |
| *plooshin* | pollution |
| *po-leece* | police |
| *quairyum* | aquarium |
| *quarr* | choir |
| *Recerstown* | Reisterstown |
| *roolty* | royalty |
| *rower skates* | roller-skates |
| *rown* | around |
| *Sagmor* | Sagamore |
| *sec-er-terry* | secretary |
| *Sigh-a-nai* | Sinai |
| *sil-lo-kwee* | soliloquy |
| *smat* | smart |
| *sometink* | something |
| *sore* | sewer |
| *sore asses* | psoriasis |
| *Sparris Point* | Sparrows Point |
| *spicket* | spigot |
| *Talzin* | Towson |
| *tarpoleon* | tarpaulin |
| *tink* | thing |
| *tuhmar* | tomorrow |
| *Tulla* | Tallulah |
| *twunny* | twenty |
| *upair* | up there |
| *umpair* | umpire |
| *urshter* | oyster |
| *Vandabill* | Vanderbilt |

| | |
|---|---|
| *varse* | worse |
| *vollince* | violence |
| *vydock* | *viaduct* |
| *warder* | water |
| *Warshtin* | Washington |
| *Westminister* | Westminster |
| *Wataya* | What do you |
| *whirl* | world |
| *winder* | window |
| *wit* | with |
| *wrench* | rinse |
| *Wuff Street* | Wolfe Street |
| *exlent* | excellent |
| *x-raided* | x-rated |
| *ya* | you |
| *yella* | yellow |
| *yesterday* | yesterday |
| *yewmid* | humid |
| *yewmity* | humidity |
| *yur* | you're, you are |
| *yurp* | Europe |
| *yursell* | yourself |
| *zackly* | exactly |
| *zinc* | sink |

| **Correct Spelling** | *Pronunciation (Slang)* |
|---|---|
| Aberdeen | *Aba-deen* |
| ambulance | *amblanz* |
| Annapolis | *Naplis* |
| Anne Arundel | *Anne Arunnel* |
| anything | *anytink* |
| appetite | *ap-tight* |
| aquarium | *quairyum* |
| Arab | *Ay-rabb* |
| around | *rown* |
| author | *arthur* |
| awning | *orning* |
| Baltimore | *Bawlamer, Bawlmer* |
| baseball | *boisbol* |
| bathroom | *baffroom* |
| beautiful | *bootiful* |
| been | *bean* |
| bet you | *betcha* |
| Betterton | *Betterin* |
| blue | *ba-lue* |
| bobbed-wire | *bob-wire* |
| born | *burn* |
| bourbon | *boybin* |
| bread | *bray-edd* |
| buoy | *boe-way* |
| bureau | *beero* |
| Belair | *Blair* |
| Bethlehem Steel | *Bethum Steel* |
| careful | *keerful* |

| Charlie | *Cha-lee* |
|---------|-----------|
| Chesapeake | *Chesspeake* |
| choir | *quarr* |
| Columbia | *Clumya* |
| complexioned | *complected* |
| coroner | *cornner* |
| corrupt | *curup* |
| curious | *curyus* |
| curiosity | *curiusty* |
| Curtis Bay | *Curt's Bay* |
| dial | *doll* |
| dismissed | *de-smissed* |
| Druid Hill | *Droodle Hill* |
| Dundalk | *Dundock* |
| eager | *igger* |
| eagle | *iggle* |
| eat | *eht* |
| elite | *e-light* |
| escape | *excape* |
| estuary | *es-choo-air-ee* |
| Europe | *Yurp* |
| exactly | *zackly* |
| excellent | *exalent* |
| explain | *splain* |
| February | *Febrairy* |
| film | *fillum* |
| fire | *far* |
| fireaway | *farway* |
| flu | *falue* |
| Ford | *furd* |

| for | *fer* |
| Fort McHenry | *Fert McKenny* |
| forty | *furty* |
| garbage | *gabage* |
| garden | *gaden* |
| geography | *jogafee* |
| golf | *goff* |
| Glyndon | *Glenin* |
| goalie | *goldie* |
| Gough Street | *Guff Street* |
| governor | *guvner* |
| Greenmount | *Greenmont* |
| harbor | *harber* |
| have to | *hafta* |
| heard | *hoyd* |
| hell of a | *hellava* |
| Hippodrome | *Hippdrum* |
| hire | *har* |
| hired | *hi-red* |
| horse | *hoss* |
| horrible | *harble* |
| hospital | *hosbiddle* |
| Howard | *Harrid* |
| incubate | *incabate* |
| Inner Harbor | *Inna Harber* |
| interested | *inner-rested* |
| interesting | *inner-restin* |
| iron | *arn* |
| jagged | *jaggered* |
| jewels | *jools* |

| | |
|---|---|
| karate | *kroddy* |
| kindergarten | *kidneygaden* |
| league | *lig* |
| library | *lie-berry* |
| Little Italy | *Liddle Eitly* |
| Locust Point | *Luck's Point* |
| Lombard Street | *Lumbered Street* |
| marvelous | *mavalus* |
| Maryland | *Murlin* |
| mayor | *mare* |
| meringue pie | *moran pie* |
| mezzanine | *mezz-aline* |
| next door | *neck store* |
| no | *na* |
| nothing | *natink* |
| odyssey | *odd-a-see* |
| Orioles | *Oryuls* |
| oyster | *arster, urshter* |
| Patapsco | *Patapsico* |
| Patomac | *Potomic* |
| pavement | *payment* |
| please | *pa-lease* |
| police | *po-leece* |
| pollution | *plooshin* |
| portrait | *pawtrit* |
| postcard | *postcad* |
| psoriasis | *sore-asses* |
| Pulaski | *Plaski* |
| quarter | *corter* |
| Reisterstown | *Ricerstown* |

| remember | *rember* |
| rinse | *wrench* |
| roller-skates | *rower-skates* |
| royalty | *roolty* |
| Sagamore | *Sagmor* |
| secretary | *secertery* |
| sewer | *sore* |
| Sinai | *Sigh-a-neye* |
| sink | *zink* |
| smart | *smat* |
| soliloquy | *sil-lo-kwee* |
| something | *sumtink* |
| spigot | *spicket* |
| Sparrow Point | *Sparris Point* |
| Tallulah | *Tulla* |
| tarpaulin | *tarpoleon* |
| there | *dare* |
| thing | *ting* |
| think | *tink* |
| tomorrow | *tuhmar* |
| Towson | *Talzin* |
| twenty | *twunny* |
| umpire | *umper* |
| up there | *upair* |
| Vanderbilt | *Vandabill* |
| viaduct | *vydock* |
| violence | *vilence* |
| W | *dubya* |
| war | *wah* |
| Washington | *Warshtin* |

| water | *warder* |
|---|---|
| Westminster | *Wesminister* |
| What do you | *Whataya* |
| window | *winder* |
| with | *wit* |
| Wolfe Street | *Wuff Street* |
| world | *whirl* |
| worse | *wurst* |
| x-rated | *x-raided* |
| yellow | *yella* |
| yesterday | *yeserdy* |
| you | *ya* |
| you are | *yur* |
| yourself | *yursell* |

# APPENDIX

For readers who have enjoyed *ABERDEEN,* the benevolent author hereby gives a *Preview of Coming Attractions* of his next book. It may be a collection of real short stories, -- correction -- short, real stories about celebrities he's met during his 33 years in the art business in Los Angeles.

# I Remember Don Meredith

It was December 6, 2010 and I was glancing through the Obituary section of the Baltimore *Sun* and stopped to read their subsection, in bold typeface, **"NOTABLE DEATHS ELSEWHERE."** The sub-headline: "DON MEREDITH, 72, *Ex-Cowboys quarterback, broadcaster.*"

A smile immediately crossed my face as I recalled an incident around 1975, inside Security Pacific National Bank (now Bank of America). This was their Beverly Hills branch, located at the corner of Wilshire Boulevard and Camden Avenue, and I was making a deposit, a rarity for me since my art business wasn't exactly booming.

All of a sudden I heard at the teller station to my left, only two feet away, a commotion between the teller, an attractive young lady in her twenties, and the customer, a dapper, handsome Don Meredith.

Anyone who's ever read the sports section of a newspaper or watched Monday Night Football would recognize that beaming boyish face, perpetual smile and southern draw in his voice. Even women adored his crooning of Willie Nelson's "Turn Out the Lights, the Party's Over" near the end of a broadcast when the outcome of the game was obvious.

"But I need confirmation, before I can cash your check," the frustrated teller shouted back at him.

"Here's my driver's license. Isn't that enough proof?" he asked her calmly, nodding his head from side to side and laughing simultaneously at the weird and unexpected nature of the situation.

"But it's out of state," she responded. "How do I know it's yours?"

That was the gist of their conversation. After all, it was 35 years ago. At this point in the story, I suspect that the driver's license in 1975 probably didn't have a good picture of the driver on the license.

I barged in, looked the teller directly in her eyes and said, "Don't you know who this is? This is Don Meredith, famous football player and TV star!"

"I don't care if he's King Farouk," she answered. "I need confirmation."

"Well, would you take my word for it? I'm a customer of Security Pacific for over 20 years," I told her and showed her the receipt for the deposit made a minute ago.

"If you vouch for him, I'll have to put your account number on his check," she told me.

A few seconds later, she then turned to Don, still with a serious look on her face, and said, "In that case, I'll cash your check, Mr. Meredith."

I turned away and headed out of the lobby, stopping near the exit to catch one last glimpse of Don Meredith, still engaged with a stranger who held the upper hand as he repeated in a loud voice, "But I am *really* Don Meredith!"

As I walked two blocks to my gallery next to Tiffany's at the Beverly Wilshire Hotel (now the Regent Beverly Wilshire) in Beverly Hills, I began laughing again and thinking about this wonderful football star who faced many challenges on the gridiron during his playing days with SMU and the Dallas Cowboys, but who was now facing a *doozy* at the bank. I also realized that he never introduced himself to me nor thanked me. He was too busy trying to convince the teller he was who he said he was, namely Don Meredith.

This experience happened 35 years ago but it seems like yesterday, and I can still hear that bank teller shouting, "I don't care if he's King Farouk. I need confirmation!"

I've never told anyone, including my wife, about the incident at the bank, probably because no one would ever believe it. But now it seems appropriate to share this story and hope people will get a kick out of it, like I do, every time I think about someone special who died on December 5th. His name: Don Meredith.

# I REMEMBER MILTON BERLE

It was October 17, 1996 when I walked into Butterfields Auction House (now known as Bonhams Butterfield) on Sunset Boulevard in Hollywood, with no purpose other than to browse through catalogues of upcoming sales, not just in America but from all over the world.

These publications were easily accessible to prospective buyers like myself and scattered all over the lobby. It didn't take long to skim through a few catalogues of sales of fine paintings, my primary interest since moving my gallery, in 1980, from its prestigious location next to Tiffany's at the Beverly Wilshire Hotel (now known as the Regent Beverly Wilshire) in Beverly Hills to a 4,000 square-foot home in Pasadena that overlooked the Rose Bowl.

As I was about to leave the lobby, I noticed Milton Berle (1908-2002) sitting alone on a wooden bench near the front door. This was not the first time I saw him up close. Several times in the 1970's I watched him having lunch or hosting a roast at the Friars Club in Beverly Hills, of which he was a co-founder along with Jimmy Durante, Robert Taylor, George Jessel and Bing Crosby.

Being a former nuclear physicist with a penchant for trivia, I also remembered reading somewhere that he had changed his name from Mendels Berlinger when he was 16. As I continued to study him, another piece of data crossed my mind.

Yes, I knew there was something else that made me admire him, and it was nothing he said or did to make me laugh. Not many people know that he was among the first to insist on using the Four Step Brothers for an appearance on his show, over the objection of his sponsor and ad agencies who refused to hire black performers. His battle could have cost him a cancellation of his show, but won him a special place in my heart."

As I continued to study his posture, he looked to be in a hypnotic trance, his face frozen and eyes glassy, reminiscent of Rodin's famous bronze, *The Thinker*.

I sat down next to him and hesitated for a few seconds to decide how to interrupt his meditation and begin a conversation.

"Mr. Berle," I said with butterflies stirring around in my stomach, "I've been a fan of yours ever since our family in Baltimore watched you, beginning in 1948, on NBC's *Texaco Star Theatre,* on a small Dumont television, with a screen about the size of a postage stamp."

Berle continued to stare straight ahead, without even a blink in his eyes.

"My mother and father would never believe me if I told them that I'm sitting next to you today," I told him, with some apprehension in my voice.

His entire body was fixed so rigidly I wondered if he had gone into shock. After all, he was now 88 and his gaunt face showed some signs of wear and tear after a long career in the world of entertainment.

I decided to give it one last try, took a deep breath and slid my body slightly forward, away from the back side of the bench, so that I could look directly into his eyes.

"You know, Mr. Berle," I told him, "last week, I went to Sotheby's auction in Beverly Hills to see property from the estate of your friend, George Burns (1896-1996), and bought an Atmos clock."

Again, absolutely no response, however, I thought he might not be familiar with an Atmos clock and how it works.

"You know, Mr. Berle," I began to explain, "that's a clock where changes of atmospheric pressure make it run properly."

For the first time in one minute, he turned his head and looked quizzically at me with his eyebrows lowered as if I had said something that would start a fight between us.

"I have a wife just like that," he uttered, never breaking into a smile.

I laughed so much that my body almost slipped off the wooden bench. At 88 Milton Berle still had that magic touch and instincts that made you laugh at life. After he went back into his trance, I took a few steps towards the front door and gazed back at a legend who was still transfixed like Rodin's *The Thinker*, and couldn't help admiring the God-given talents of Milton Berle.

# I REMEMBER MUHAMMAD ALI

It was on a Wednesday in the last week of June 1977 when I walked in the rear door of my gallery, located next to Tiffany's on Wilshire Boulevard in the Beverly Wilshire Hotel (now the Regent Beverly Wilshire), Beverly Hills, California.

"Oh, I'm glad you're back from your lunch," my wife, Renate, said to me, then turned to a handsome gentleman standing nearby and said, "Mr. Ali, I'd like you to meet my husband."

Renate was 28 and had spent the first 23 years of her life in Munich before I married her in 1971. She surprised me by recognizing Muhammad Ali because sports was not in her line of interests, which included music, art and literature.

Before I could get a word out, Muhammad Ali turned to me with a menacing and suspicious expression on his face and gave me a quick examination from head to foot.

"You mean *this* is your husband?" he asked with lips tightened, in a voice loud enough to stir the dead in a cemetery, and pointing a finger at me. "He's so ugly!"

I burst out laughing, suspecting that he was just toying with me like he did in the ring. What else was I supposed to think at this moment?

As he raised his hands and clenched them into fists, I began to feel an incredible fear for my life.

"Come on. Show me what *ya* got!" he said, motioning and urging me to come forward and take a swing at him.

"Am I crazy?" I asked myself as he began dancing around in a short circle with his feet moving in his signature quick-stutter step. "He wants *me* to take a swing at him?"

It was a surreal incidence for me, facing someone very elegant, dressed in a gray suit, probably hand-made by one of the best tailors on Savile Row in London. Then, almost instantaneously, he dropped his hands, walked towards me with a broad smile and held out his hand to shake mine, thank God. Here was a handsome young man of great confidence and distinction, and he knew it. Boy, did he know it!

When things settled down, Renate walked over to a painting hanging on the wall of the gallery and motioned me to follow her.

"I've been showing this painting to Mr. Ali, who seems to like it but doesn't believe it's a real painting," she told me somewhat apologetically.

She then turned her attention to Mr. Ali and looked directly into his eyes.

"Mr. Ali, my husband's an expert in paintings and a senior member of the American Society of Appraisers," she told him. "Perhaps, he can explain that this painting is one of a kind, an original oil on canvas, in mint condition."

"My name is Joseph C. Szymanski," I said.

"What's the 'C' stand for?" he asked to my surprise.

"Cissors, which is my middle name," I answered facetiously. "We omit the 's' and pronounce it 'schizzors' in the old Polish way. I changed my middle name when I was 14."

"What was it before you changed it to Cissors?" he asked quickly.

"Joseph K. Szymanski," I responded, and before he could ask another question, said that the 'K' is for *Koincidence*, a middle name given to me by my mother and father who weren't sure that I was their baby.

"Hmmm," he muttered.

"My mother and father said that I didn't look like either of them and gave me the middle name, *Koincidence*. Many years later they told me that they were also considering *Kontradiction,* but never explained why they were stuck on the letter 'K'. Does that make any sense to you? If it does, it sure doesn't to me."

Realizing that none of this repartee had an impact on Mr. Ali. I asked him to have a seat beside my nineteenth-century, Louis XV-style, French Boulle-inlay bureau plat. This writing desk was an exceptional antique piece that always gave customers an impression of class. It was located directly below a ceiling light that illuminated the area. A minute later, I transferred the painting from the gallery wall to his lap and held the sides of the painting while he could view it under a bright light. To keep it in position and as vertical as possible, I stood in front of him, with the picture between us, and held the sides of the frame with my hands.

As he turned his attention to the painting, I couldn't help thinking that the idea or notion that anyone would question the authenticity or think one of my fine paintings could be a print was absurd. Anyone with an ounce of intelligence could see that the painting was museum quality, which is why it was priced at $35,000.

I pondered how to begin an explanation and hesitated a few seconds while he continued to study the composition. Another thought passed my mind quickly as I wondered how Tiffany's would handle a situation in which a customer would question whether or not their diamond ring was real.

I reached into a small drawer of the writing desk, retrieved a large magnifying glass and handed it to him.

"Have a look at the single long hair on the head of an old man about to have his head shaved by a young barber," I advised him. "This is a remarkable scene, executed in the academic technique by an American-artist, Edwin Lord Weeks, probably around 1880. He, no doubt, painted it over a period of several months while on location in a middle eastern country, possibly Morocco, Algiers or Afghanistan. You can tell the location by studying the precise details of the architecture and clothing of the people watching a barber cut hair in the passageway of an outdoor bazaar."

I paused for a few seconds, then asked him, "Don't you find that fascinating?"

When he failed to react to my question, I said to myself, "Wow. I wonder if he digested any of that."

"You're not sure of the exact location?" he asked me eventually, turning slowly his head clockwise to examine all four corners of the painting.

"I bought it a few days ago from a doctor in Chicago and haven't had time to do any research, but over the weekend, I'll read everything I can get my hands on to find out what countries the artist visited and if he produced any paintings there."

Mr. Ali studied the painting for a few minutes more while I held it upright with the bottom of the frame resting on his thighs. Since there was no reaction or emotional feedback from him, I thought it best to let him take his time to see the details of the painting, with the hope that its beauty would speak to him and entice him into buying it.

"A painting worthy of a discriminating collector like yourself," I said confidently.

"Who said I'm discriminating?" he asked me. "Every person is equal in Islam and, as for being a collector, I like a Rolls Royce and have two in my garage. Perhaps you could call me a collector, but it means nothing to me."

"Oh, Mr. Ali, please don't touch the painting with your fingers," I told him as he tapped gently the front of the canvas with the fingers of his right hand. "Your fingernails might scratch it."

"I've seen enough," he told me finally, "and have to go."

After returning the painting to the gallery wall, I shook his hand and thanked him for paying a visit to our gallery.

"Would you like me to call you a cab?" I asked him.

"Yes, I would," he answered.

"In that case, you're a cab!" I exclaimed, in the same loud voice he used to greet me, laughing that at least I had the last word.

After he walked out the rear door of the gallery and headed in the direction of the hotel lobby, my wife and I were looking at each other and shaking our heads.

"He got me, Renate," I told her. "He really got me. I honestly didn't know what else to do or say to him."

"You win some, you lose some," she answered. "It was not meant to be our day."

"Our time will come," I said, putting my arm around her waist.

The next morning, we were still beating ourselves over the head with a mental mallet, trying to reconcile what we might have done differently. Then, to make matters worse, a bell boy poked his head in the rear doorway and told us, "Did you know that Muhammad Ali, immediately after he walked out of your gallery at 3 p.m., took a cab to the Rolls Royce dealer down the street and bought a Rolls for $150,000? The salesman told us he was mumbling something about a painting in your gallery that didn't seem as real as the Rolls he bought!"

Later that day, while walking through the hotel lobby, I bumped into the hotel bell captain, who told me that Muhammad Ali was going to be married to his third wife, Veronica Porche, in two days, on the first of July, in the ballroom of the hotel.

"Perhaps that's why his mind wasn't on art," I said to myself after returning to my gallery. "I presume that he bought the Rolls as a wedding present for his intended bride."

As I adjusted my tie and began to feel rejuvenated, my wife handed me a fortune cookie that someone left on top of our bureau plat. After opening it, I read the fortune inscribed on a small strip of paper inside: "Always remember what your teachers taught, so life would not have been for naught. UR2GOOD2BCN."